THE WITCH OF BRENTWOOD

THE WITCH OF BRENTWOOD

A novel by

Réal Carpentier

Published 2022

THE WITCH OF BRENTWOOD

Copyright Year: 2022
Copyright Notice: by Réal Carpentier. All rights reserved.
The above information forms this copyright notice: © *2022 by Réal Carpentier.*
All rights reserved.

This book or any portion thereof may not be reproduced or used in any manner whatsoever without the express written permission of the author except for the use of brief quotations in a book review or scholarly journal.

This is a work of fiction. All of the characters, names, incidents, organizations, and dialogue in this novel are either the products of the author's imagination or are used fictitiously.

Published by Réal Carpentier

First Printing 2022

ISBN: **9798415184002**

This book may be ordered through booksellers,
www.barnesandnoble.com, www.amazon.com, or local bookstores

Cover art by Kiselev Andrey Valerevich, Nejron Photo, and
Ozz Design/Shutterstock
Cover design by Réal Carpentier

For my wife and children

The Witch of Brentwood

If vengeance must be served, it must be served swiftly and with permanent results. So, the crowd cheered; not for the prospect of ridding the town of another devil's child but rather for the sake of violence itself, which was forever lusted after.

Réal Carpentier

Prologue

From 1500 to 1600 A.D., 50 to 80 thousand suspected witches in Europe were executed. 80% were women. King James, who ruled at the time, declared that a woman is frailer than man is, so it is easier to be entrapped by the cross snares of the devil. The king also wrote the reference for the hunting and persecution of witches in his book entitled Daemonologie in 1597, which was very influential. It became the manual that many would follow to instruct them on how to proceed with the elimination of witches.

The years of the 17th century were also turbulent times in the new colonies of America, especially in Salem Massachusetts. Many were accused of witchcraft or being allies of Satan, mostly women. This was brought about mainly because of the puritan church. The puritans prided themselves as being the 'saved' ones who were brought together for the purpose of purifying the catholic church, which at the time was too powerful to be humble and extended their authority beyond the teachings of Christ.

Witches were mainly burned in Europe, while in the new colonies of America, they were usually hanged. Either way, physical evidence was crucial. If someone had a birthmark, a scar, or blemish on their body, it could be construed as the 'devil's teat';

a means by which the devil could make his pact with the person he wanted to possess. The theory was that the devil would suckle on the teat much like infants would nurse on their mothers' breasts. This provided a way for Satan to win the victim over to do his evil deeds among the people of the land, bringing harm to others through witchcraft, magic, and other supernatural methods.

Adding to the confusion of the time, were the 'cunning folk'. These were folk magicians who used charms, herbs, and spells to heal or even influence the weather. They were considered modern-day doctors since they were believed to heal diseases and wounds. They were also considered much more, since their powers were deemed supernatural. Herbal remedies, love charms, black toads, oyster shells, and linen cloth were some of their tools and some village folk entrusted them for whatever ailed them. These cunning folk walked a fine line, however. If they had such supernatural healing powers, it wasn't out of the realm of possibility for them to use these powers to bring pain and suffering to others as well. They could conceivably steal articles of clothing from someone to perform spells and bring them harm, or perhaps even use sympathetic magic like sticking pins in an onion representing the heart of someone to make that victim fall in love with them.

It was up to the magistrate of the villages to investigate witch accusations. These accusations could come from anyone; a disgruntled neighbor, a business partner, or an angry child. Whoever the accuser was, the accusation was deemed credible, and the accused was locked and many times shackled in a prison cell until a tribunal was held to determine the innocence or guilt.

Ironically, those denying the charges were found guilty and executed immediately but those who admitted to the charges because of being pressured to do so, were held in a cell to await their sentence. Many who confessed to the charges brought against them died in their prison cells because of the torturous conditions they had to endure.

The major culprit in all the hysteria at the time was surprisingly a fungus called ergot. Ergot can grow on rye and to a lesser extent, on other forms of grain. In the Middle Ages as people ate bread and other foods made from rye, ergot was the cause of mass poisonings which lead to diseases in gangrenous forms, causing extremities like fingers and toes to literally fall off the victim, or convulsive forms which created contortions in the victim. We now refer to the ergot-caused diseases as ergotism. Convulsive ergotism causes a nervous dysfunction where the victim is twisting and contorting their body in pain, trembling and shaking, and experiencing involuntary twisting of the neck. In some cases, these manifestations are compounded by muscle spasms, confusion, delusions, and hallucinations, as well as a few other symptoms. Therefore, it should come as no surprise that the modern-day hallucinogen drug LSD, is made from a derivative of ergot. It also stands to reason that the people of the 17th century, having little knowledge of the effects of ergot, would assume this kind of involuntary behavior to be the work of the devil. Anyone experiencing such symptoms would be more than willing to blame someone else for bewitching them, lest they be considered witches themselves. It was better to be bewitched by someone than to be considered a child of the devil. And so, accusations became rampant, and the leaders of the puritan church felt a responsibility to do something about it.

Today, we look at that period of time and wonder how people allowed themselves to be influenced and manipulated in such a way as to destroy innocent lives. But when one considers the power and influence of dictators in the modern world and the execution of thousands of innocent people all over the world in the name of religion and the greater good, it's not hard to recognize parallel traits that make us just as barbaric and primitive as those living in the earlier centuries who thought sure their decision-making process was the logical thought pattern needed to solve the problems of the day. In fact, paranormal activity, Ouija boards, and superstitions of Friday the 13th and broken mirrors still have an element of intrigue and curiosity, if not an ability to instill fear in many.

The witch trials of the 17th century and of centuries before were very real and devastating. To have lived in that period of time would have instilled much justified anxiety and paranoia. Today we use the term witch-hunt to describe accusations with dubious or no substantial evidence, which describes that period in time very accurately. Fortunately, today's witch-hunts are not literal in the sense that individuals may be executed for crimes for which there is no evidence. Unfortunately, this wasn't always the case.

The Witch of Brentwood

Réal Carpentier

And he shall cause the woman to drink the bitter water that causeth the curse: and the water that causeth the curse shall enter into her, and become bitter. *(Numbers 5:24)*

Réal Carpentier

Chapter 1

The noose around her neck was tighter than she thought it would be when the two men made their intentions clear to her. The frayed filaments of the rope dug in and stung her skin. She pleaded with them. She tried to appeal to the compassion of the small crowd that had begun to gather, but none would hear of it. The sound of rustling leaves in the wind did nothing to relieve anguish, nor was the fragrance of the honeysuckle, as the realization of her impending death rose to a fever pitch and was torture in itself. The sun shining in her eyes made her squint when she looked up to the sky for guidance and prayed for courage. Still, she always loved blue skies with a few puffy clouds on beautiful sunny days in the summer. It made her feel young, vibrant, and full of life. But not *this* day. This day marked the end of her life at the hands of her accusers whose denunciation without a fair trial or even a fair tribunal found her guilt an accepted fact.

Then, came the chants; *witch! witch! witch!*... and then *die! die! die!*...

She could hardly believe the enthusiasm of the mob was actually a result of hatred for her; the young woman who was considered outspoken, and at times very bold and defiant. *Was this the reason for the hatred?* She thought perhaps it was, but her character and demeanor were not evil in her mind. It was her way of life. At times her thoughts and actions were contrary to how the modern woman should think and behave. Her ways were intimidating to some and seen as evil as though she were possessed or at the very least, guided by evil spirits. She even tried to suppress her defiant tendencies, but she found them too difficult to contain most of the time. She liked to indulge in drinking alcohol at times, which made her even more outspoken and distasteful in the eyes of her family and friends. She was a friend of promiscuity and adultery but tried hard to keep this behavior a secret; not that she minded what others thought of her, but rather to avoid the consequences of such actions. Her actions were her own and she considered herself a righteous woman; as righteous as any other. Still, the chanting continued.

People pressed together as if to show their solidarity against the evil one, or perhaps they needed close comfort from one another, or both. It didn't matter because there was safety in numbers regardless of the reason. Each of them hated equally but also feared retribution from a final witch's curse before they were able to complete the task of stringing her by her neck until she was good and dead. Some even feared what might befall them from her grave after all was said and done. But everyone was in agreement as to the guilt and what must be done to correct the guilty. A woman with such disregard for proper behavior and order must be a witch and dealt with promptly to cleanse the colony and eradicate any possible contamination. The work of the devil had to be crushed swiftly and in full measure.

The twenty-foot rope was draped over a very thick limb of an oak with two strong men holding the end opposite the noose wrapped around the woman's neck. They began to pull while the cheers of the small crowd gave them more incentive and purpose to accomplish the task. The creaking of the tree limb was mostly drowned out by the chants and cries of the crowd but could still be heard as the men pulled. The noose tightened more and more around the woman's neck as she heard one of the men say,

"Pull, Clement! Pull!"

She debated whether to use her last breath to plead her innocence, or to contract her neck muscles in order to fight the tightness of the noose. She chose the latter. She held her breath and tried to keep her head up straight and maintain the contraction of her neck muscles, as her feet began to lift off the ground which provided her only stability. Soon, her feet were well off the ground and her weight was too much of a disadvantage for her to keep fighting. Her breathing became impossible. She tried to scream but couldn't. She felt her neck being squeezed by the rope and couldn't imagine being able to maintain the fight against the tightness any longer. As she tried to breathe her last, she suddenly felt her neck crack and started kicking her feet as a last effort to free herself. This only caused more pain through her bones, but still she had to try. The breaking of her neck was never heard above the cheers and praise of the crowd. Soon, her pain and effort gave way to numbness and then blackness.

The woman was dead.

Before the crowd dispersed, one of the men who was pulling the rope, wrapped it around the tree to leave the witch hanging. He then pinned a sign to the woman's thigh with a hunter's knife for all to see and believe. The sign read, *WITCH*!

The Witch of Brentwood

*****

The year was 1684. Amelia Whitlock lived in the Colony of Massachusetts in the town of Salem in a quaint little cabin which stood at the crest of a small hill covered with oaks and grass near a beautiful little stream. Her ten-year-old twin children, Isabell and Alexander, were beautiful children and everyone envied Amelia for having been so blessed. Although the word envy was never used by anyone complimenting her good fortune, since that vice was one of the seven deadly sins according to Catholicism. Even though the Puritans were distancing themselves from such doctrine, they didn't want to take any chances and the word had to be avoided at all cost. But secretly, every one of her peers were guilty of committing such a sin.

At the change of every season, the landscape would change with it; producing flowers in the spring, bountiful branches full of leaves in the summer, a colorful landscape with scattered acorns in the latter months of the year, and a wonderland of snow in the winter. Isabell and Alexander would play in the fields throughout the year, enjoying the fruits of nature God provided. Both children were healthy but of the two twins, Isabell was the fragile one, having respiratory problems as an infant and almost dying at two months old because of it. She also had a tendency to complain of aches and pains in her bones at different times of the year, depending on the climate. Still, she was healthy enough to enjoy life.

Both Isabell and Alexander grew into well-behaved, respectful children and were themselves aware of how fortunate they were and how fate had dealt them the best hand anyone could ask for. They loved their mother who was not rich by any means, but they could get by with what they had. Isabell not only loved her mother, but also admired her for many reasons including her fair features and her long black hair and blue eyes which were the right combination that accented her high cheekbones and smooth skin. She also cherished her attire which was mostly of very dark reds or blues with plenty of lace, ribbons, and flowers which she added herself to make her clothing more personalized. Some of her clothing was a surplus of garments given away by the church. But fashion statements were not important in the latter years of the seventeenth century, so most of what she wore was what she made with the fabric she had bought or was given. Isabell always wanted to be like her mother, so Amelia obliged to dress her daughter in the same fashion as best she could.

Isabell noticed how her mother had a fascination with animals; especially birds, which she could watch all day long and never get tired of. She once asked her mother about her love of birds and never really got a straight answer except that they were gentle and the personification of God's love. But even at a young age, Isabell knew that witches sometimes saw visions of birds coming into their bedrooms and such stories. So, she feared others would notice it as well and use the information against her mother and accuse her of being evil.

Isabell was easy to get along with and had very few friends who lived nearby. But she was always agitated when some of her friends teased her about her mother's nose and called her a witch because of it. Also, her mother often loved to visit *her* mother's grave at the cemetery with the twins, which fueled the 'witch' fire considerably. Witch was a dangerous word. The word was used so carelessly that when Isabell thought of her friends calling her mother such a name, she was ashamed of them, friends or not. Afterall, her mother's slightly crooked nose was not her fault. She had taken a fall as a child and broke her nose, which never healed correctly. The hook of her nose was just an inconvenience but her deviated septum was more of a problem, especially in those summer days when her allergies caused more breathing difficulties. Isabell often wondered if this was the reason for *her* respiratory problems as an infant but thanked God every day for providing the miracle needed for her to survive and get stronger with age. As far as the trips to the cemetery, Isabell was happy her mother brought her and her brother to visit a deceased loved one, even if the cemetery frightened her a great deal.

Although Isabell admired her mother, the truth was that Amelia was a 36-year-old, plain-looking woman who had lost her faith in humanity. Trust was not part of her vocabulary and there was a good reason for such an uncommon attitude among women her age. At least that's what both children were told continually, and she was sure to tell them to be wary of everyone, since no one in this world could be trusted; not for the slightest. Their mother was the only one Alexander and Isabell could trust, and trust in anyone else was not tolerated in the Whitlock home. Any such deviation would immediately be met with reprimand at the very least. The innocent twins had asked her why the world was so bad that any form of confidence in people would be a naive expectation. Amelia explained as best she could so they could understand that there was evil in the world and most people allowed themselves to fall into that temptation. There were mediums and spiritists who liked to engage in the rituals of black magic and witchcraft and other evil practices. This was reason enough.

There were other reasons, however, and Amelia refused to share those reasons with the children until they were old enough to understand. Afterall, the twins were only ten years old and were still too young to process the concept of rape, much less cope with the reality of it. The twins knew their father left them when they were babies. At least that's what Amelia had told them. But the truth was their father was some stranger who had raped her when she was naive, trusting, and carefree. Life had never been the same since. She detested the man for the abuse he perpetrated on her but loved her children. There was a time when she was unsure of how she would be able to love her children or love *anyone* again, for that matter. Fortunately, the sight of her babies coming into the world overshadowed her resentment and she loved them both with all the love a mother could give. But regardless of the way they were conceived, Amelia promised herself throughout her pregnancy that she would never treat her children as she was treated as a child. This was something else she would withhold from her children until they were old enough to process the evils people were capable of. She still had scars from her past, both emotional and physical, and those reasons were good enough to justify a cold heart for the world.

*****

The children didn't share any noticeable physical attributes that would indicate they were twins except for their blue eyes. Alexander was a hard worker whose eyes were always wide open and full of wonder as though he had yet to make new discoveries of the world. He had grown taller over the last few months before his tenth birthday, but his dark hair was devoid of any curls his mother had wished for. His posture was very straight and proper as though he'd had training to be a British Battalion Elite Grenadier, or at the very least, one of light infantry. The reds and blues of his garments his mother was so proud of, fit him well and made him look like a proper young gentleman. He spoke with clarity and always made sure to be accurate in what he was saying, lest he be ridiculed for not being well-raised.

Isabell was different. Her long brown-reddish hair was curly, and her skin was pale. The light freckles on her face were only visible from close, but they contributed to her beauty. She was skinnier than most her age and her frailty was apparent. The slightest motion of getting up from a sitting position too quickly made her light-headed and she often had to pause until the wariness gradually wore off. Isabell hardly ever smiled. Some thought it was probably something she'd learned from her mother. Regardless of that, she was a happy child; happy to have a mother who loved her, a brother she loved to play with, and an appreciation for beauty in nature. She also wore clothes customized by her mother but always included little trinkets she found or received as gifts on special occasions. These, she wore on her attire or around her neck and wrists. She always loved to wear a little pouch wrapped around her wrist for carrying little shells or other little things she'd find while playing outside. She appreciated her mother telling her she was the essence of physical beauty in the world but didn't really believe it. Her physical flaws were an affirmation of her disbelief. She had skinny arms and legs, crooked toes, and a birthmark on her neck. She convinced herself the arms and legs would fill out over time, and her toes were hidden by her shoes, but the birthmark was forever there for everyone to see. It had an oblong shape and a rather dark brownish tint. She considered it to be the very first thing everyone noticed about her even from a far enough distance. She despised it, but it was part of her and if she could cut it off without leaving a scar, she liked to think she would do just that.

Much like any other young girl, Isabell loved to run and play, especially in the play fields with Alexander where he could make believe he was a soldier; one of the good guys, not some treasonous traitor giving military secrets to the enemy for monetary gain. Isabell was always the enemy.

"You shall die from the bullet of this flintlock for your invasion of our territory!" shouted Alexander as he held a lead pipe horizontally, pointing it at Isabell who was about ten feet away.

"This is *our* land; the land of our fathers and their fathers before them." she returned, with great patriotic conviction.

"Take *that*!" he said, making a gunshot pop with his mouth.

Isabell held her heart as she fell slowly to her knees and then to her side. "I shall avenge my people." she said gingerly while taking her last breath.

Alexander looked at her for a moment in disbelief and said, "Isabell, you were to run. Why didn't you run? Now the game is finished."

"I don't want to play this game today." she said, looking up at him from where she lay.

"What then?"

"Let's collect flowers." she replied, getting back on her feet.

"Flowers?"

"Yes, I'd like to gather flowers and arrange a bouquet for mother."

"Flowers? Leisure activity of peasant girls." he said, waving his hand as if to discard the very notion. "I have territories to conquer."

"Alright then, King Louis the Fourteenth. Have it your way. I'm gathering flowers." Isabell said as she went about her business of gathering flowers for her mother.

Alexander returned to his make-believe play of soldiering with pretend enemies which he was able to kill off one by one with great accuracy.

"Don't stray too far, Alexander." Isabell added.

"DEATH TO YOU, PEASANT GIRL!" he shouted back.

"Alexander Whitlock, you evil indulgent boy, I should tell mother on you!" she returned in a playful voice as she continued with her collection of flowers, anticipating the look on her mother's face when she saw them.

The children continued to go their separate ways until they were far enough apart to not see each other through the large bushes and trees. This was usually how their game playing ended. They would start playing together and one of them would get tired or bored with a particular game and suddenly they were alone until they returned home.

Isabell collected a variety of flowers as she walked through the field, making sure there wasn't too much contrast between their colors. *Mother will be so happy.* The abundance of wildflowers never seemed to end from where she was and all the way into a sparse section of trees which was no more than a quarter of a mile away from the play field. She followed their trail while enjoying the fragrance of each. The wind had begun to pick up a bit since they had arrived at the play field, but it was all the more enjoyable to feel the cool breeze through her hair. It's a shame Alexander didn't enjoy the finer things of nature, she thought. *He'd be more inclined to welcome the wind if it proved to be an advantage to his side of his make-believe war.*

As she drew nearer to the group of trees, Isabell began to feel strangely; like there was something wrong. She could feel it. She could smell it. She suddenly felt alone, and an anxiety that made her heart race a little and her breathing labored. She tried to think logically and attributed the feeling to being winded from the walk. Still, the disquieting feeling of uncertainty and apprehension didn't abate, but rather became more intense with each step she took towards the trees. Determined as she was, she continued on to explore what other types of flowers her path would lead to.

Next to a big oak, she happened upon the most beautiful flowers yet and vowed to return home after gathering *those*, which would complete the most colorful and fragrant bouquet she had ever assembled for her mother. She hurried and approached the flowers in haste, revealing more and more of what was behind that big oak tree. At first, she hardly noticed but as the vision became more exposed from behind the tree, she could plainly see something she had never seen before; something she'd only heard or read from make-believe stories.

She stopped dead in her tracks and stood looking at the woman hanging from another tree not twenty feet away. At first it felt surreal, as though she were in a dream. Her imagination took over and recalled a story she'd heard long ago. But as she kept looking, the reality of the vision soon became undeniable.

Her eyes were drawn to the rope the woman was hanging from. One end was tied to the trunk of the tree and continued up to its first branch which was thick, full of leaves, and appeared to be very sturdy. The rope, then, made its way around the top of the branch and came back down with its noose tight around the woman's neck. The woman's eyes were still open and bulging. They were lifeless but seemed to look at Isabell where she stood. It was as though the hanging woman was looking but couldn't see, which gave her the same eerie look of a doll with fake eyes. Her face was a bluish tint. Her swollen tongue was hanging and resting on the lower lip of her gaped-open mouth. Isabell wondered if the woman's mouth was an indication that she tried screaming out her last breath. The woman's arms were dead limbs resting on each side of her in apparent surrender of her fate, and her body was swinging back and forth a little because of the wind that had picked up since Isabell's departure from her brother. With each swing, the rope made a creaking noise coming from its contact with the tree branch. There was a square piece of cardboard attached to her left thigh with a note on it. The note read, *WITCH!* It was held in place with a knife going through the cardboard and deep into the woman's thigh. She had one shoe on her left foot, which was dripping with blood from the knife wound, but the other foot was bare. Isabell's eyes reactively roamed and searched the ground for the other shoe, but soon came to her senses and wondered why in the world the location of her shoe even mattered. Nevertheless, she found it about six feet away from the hanging woman, who had apparently kicked it off when she tried a final feeble attempt at kicking herself free.

After enough inspection of the dead woman, Isabell's frailty got the best of her. She became weak and started trembling. Her knees were becoming too wobbly to support her weight and she was sure she would not be standing much longer. She dropped to her knees, still looking at the hanging woman, and began to scream out Alexander's name in a shriek as loud as she'd ever screamed before. She screamed several times and hoped Alexander was not too far away so that he wouldn't hear her cry. Soon, Isabell could withstand no more of the awful reality. It was at that moment she looked at the dead woman's eyes one last time before dropping to the ground and losing consciousness.

*****

The room was dark and damp even though it was still daylight outside. There were candles in their holders affixed to three of the four walls to be spared and used only at night. The one bed was hand-made and stuffed with straw, but as comfortable as any other. The chair near the bed served as a place of reflection and bible reading as the day drew to an end, making way for the sounds of coyotes and other night creatures that normally prowl for food at night.

When Isabell opened her eyes, everything was blurry. It appeared her mother was sitting next to her on the side of her bed wiping down her forehead with a cool damp cloth. She also thought she saw Alexander standing close by. The cloth felt like a breath of fresh air, and she never imagined something as simple as a cool cloth on her face could feel so wonderful. But she was very confused as though she had woken up from a very deep sleep. She looked up to see the peach-colored bed curtains hanging about her bed posts and canopy, which were slowly coming into focus and beginning to look familiar. On the wall to her right was a half-open window next to the framed portrait of her and her mother and brother. Seeing this, brought her back to reality and she suddenly became aware of her surroundings. She was safe in her bedroom with her mother and Alexander by her side.

"Are you alright, child?" her mother asked.

Hearing her mother's voice was as soothing as the wet cloth on her skin. She suddenly felt safe and secure as she began to speak. "Oh mother, it was dreadful. I saw a woman hanging by the neck from a tree. She had…"

"Easy...easy. Don't excite yourself, Isabell. I'm right here by your side. Everything is alright." said her mother.

"But everything is *not* alright, mother. Someone was killed. She had a knife in her as well, and she had the fear of all terror in her face."

Isabell suddenly felt the pain on the side of her head for the first time since waking. She brought her right hand to the sore area and winced in pain.

"You had a fall, dear. Your head hit a rock and caused quite a bump and a cut." her mother said. "Alexander heard you screaming and ran to meet you."

"When I got there," Alexander began, "I saw the woman hanging and was startled to death. Then I noticed you were on the ground not moving and your hair all bloodied. I lifted you and ran home all the way carrying you."

"Thank you, Alexander." Isabell said, looking concerned for *his* well-being.

Alexander resumed, "They hanged a witch, mother. That's what the sign said. It read, *witch*."

Amelia quickly quoted from the King James Bible, "Thou shalt not suffer a witch to live. This, the bible tells us in Exodus." Then looking up at Alexander with concern, she said, "Alexander, you need to sit. You must be as shaken as poor Isabell."

"I'm alright, mother. But I don't think Isabell is fine. After all, she's the fragile one with a head wound."

"I'll be alright now." Isabell replied, as she began to shake again from the renewed reality of what she had seen.

"Are you sure, dear?" inquired her mother. "Let me take care to make you well. You're shaking, you poor dear."

"Mother, how do you suppose she became a witch?" asked Isabell.

"I don't know, and it isn't something we should entertain in conversation. Talking about such things could very well allow evil to come into our home."

"Will she stay there for very long? I don't want to go to the play field anymore."

"Now Isabell, they shall take care of her body in short order. In the meantime, you and Alexander can stay close to home and not venture out too far."

"Are we sure she was a witch?" asked Alexander.

"Enough of this! I'll hear no more talk of witches!" Amelia said sternly. There was a moment of silence before she turned to Isabell and spoke more softly. "Now you just rest in bed until you're strong enough to go about. If you need anything, I'll be in the next room to pray. You children, do the same."

Isabell acknowledged her, knowing she was right about such talk being an invitation for evil to creep in when they least expected it. But she was also sure part of the reason her mother wanted to end the conversation of witches was that she was terrified to death, as she and Alexander were.

"Mother, may I stay with her a while?" asked Alexander.

Amelia thought for a moment before answering, "Yes, but do not make her more unsettled than she is, the poor child."

"I'll be alright. Thank you, mother" Isabell replied.

Amelia kissed Isabell on the forehead, making sure to avoid the bruised area, then picked up the tray of bandages and ointment she had brought in to tend to her. She quietly left the room as Alexander followed to shut the door behind her. With his hand still clutching the doorknob, he looked back at Isabell for a moment and then walked to sit next to her.

Isabell looked pale, which was understandable even to the ten-year-old Alexander. As he walked over to her, he glanced at the mirror on the ebony dresser to see his own reflection showing a young face just as pale as his sister's. He wondered if they could ever get over the shock of what they saw while at the same time, knowing full well they would never forget the sight that would stay with them for the rest of their lives. It would haunt them as a permanent image forever engraved in their minds.

He sat as they looked at each other, not saying a word. Finally, Isabell began.

"You've seen her, haven't you Alexander?"

"Who?"

"You know very well who. The woman they killed."

"Yes, I saw her."

"That isn't what I mean. You've seen her before."

Alexander was reluctant to answer, but finally admitted, "Yes, I have. I've seen her and you've seen her as well; in the play field. What of it?"

"I don't believe she was a witch."

"How can you say that Isabell? They hanged her, didn't they?"

Isabell put her finger to her lips to indicate his voice should be lowered lest their mother overheard such discussion.

"How could they hang someone who wasn't deserving?" she whispered. "Perhaps a mistake, or someone might have accused her."

"But how do we know she wasn't deserving? We only saw her in the play field walking among the grass and the flowers on fair days. We didn't really know her."

"She was a fine woman, Alexander. Sometimes when you were playing on your own and left me, I would see her and wave from a distance. She would wave back and smile. I remember thinking she was so lovely the way she carried herself and the fine garments she wore and the way her hair blew in the wind."

"Stop it! Mother said to not talk of such things. It's evil."

"She wasn't evil."

"How do you know? You can't be sure."

"Evil is ugly, not lovely as she was."

Alexander knew he could never change Isabell's mind when she was sure of something. He also wanted to end the conversation as soon as possible.

"Isabell, if she was a witch or not, it would be best to distance ourselves from ever knowing her or seeing her. We don't know who people will accuse next. We don't want people to start wondering about us or mother, do we?"

"No, we don't."

"Then stop. Let's try to forget and never mention it again."

"I'll never forget, Alexander."

"Well, don't mention it then; never again."

Isabell nodded in obedience and held out her arms for him. The twins embraced tightly, as the sounds of nature coming through the half open window filled the room; sounds that normally would bring inner peace to the soul. But from the moment of discovering the hanging woman, the existence of peace was overshadowed by the realization of the scary and unnatural ways of the world.

Réal Carpentier

Chapter 2
Eight years later

The rustling of the leaves and crackling of the twigs under her feet were a pleasant sound while she walked along on this beautiful Sunday afternoon just admiring the view of nature. The sun shone through the leaves and provided warmth; enough to be able to discard the extra layer of clothing her mother insisted on before she left the cabin. The eighteen-year-old Isabell was happy to be alive in such a world that could touch her senses and make her feel like she was one with the earth and sky. A rabbit scurried across her path as if to say good afternoon, which made her stop in her tracks and admire the picture-perfect scene. She wasn't much of an artist but if she had had a canvas and brushes in her midst, the inspiration of this scene alone would have been enough to produce a painting that could otherwise never have been created. She didn't take for granted the slightest moment of what life had to offer on this wonderful day.

Her thoughts were suddenly interrupted by the sound of people approaching. They sounded angry as far as she could tell. She heard things like '*there she is*', and '*hurry 'fore she gets away*'. It's unclear why she didn't run away when she had the chance. She may not have had the time to process what was taking place, or perhaps she was too much in shock from what was happening. At any rate, she couldn't move before they reached her.

There were about a dozen angry men and women. Some were carrying clubs and rope, while others had shovels and instruments of torture like very thin nails and clamps. She felt that familiar discomfort in the pit of her stomach all the way down to her intestines as though she were stricken with some kind of stomach virus. Although she felt like she had to use the outhouse in a hurried urgency, she knew she had to hold it in lest someone in the crowd got offended by her filth.

They surrounded her. She began to speak but they grabbed her before she had a chance to utter the first syllable and carried her to a nearby tree; the one she admired so much with the sunshine peeking through its leaves. There, they began their attack.

"There be the devil's teat we heard talk about!" one of the men remarked, pointing to Isabell's birthmark on her neck.

"That's the mark! She's a witch!" another shouted.

"Hang her by the neck!" the crowd began, "Kill the witch!" they repeated after one another.

Isabell tried to speak again to explain the birthmark was not the devil's teat; that it wasn't a means by which the devil made a pact with her. But a long-haired bearded man holding wrought iron tongs rushed her before she could say much, grabbed a hold of her birthmark with the forged tool, and began to pull on it with all his might in order to remove the vile thing from her neck before she could summon her evil spirits. The iron pliers dug in, producing a flow of blood down to her shoulders. Her neck was on fire and it felt as if the entire side of her face was being pulled apart. She felt her flesh tear from the side of her neck when the birthmark was ripped out and began to scream in pain as the crowd cheered. Next, two men approached and grabbed her by the hair that was so admired by her mother because of her beautiful curls. They pulled, dragged her down to the ground, and stepped on her hands so she couldn't move while another pulled off her shoes and began sticking needles in the bottom of her feet. She screamed with every prick, but her screams just blended with the cheers of the crowd. Next, someone tied a rope around her neck and pulled on the other end with all his might while she lay on the ground defenseless and in pain. The rope dug into the wound from the torn flesh on the side of her neck and she could hardly breathe. At that moment, she wished death would be swift and silently prayed.

She was on the brink of death when she looked up and saw the hanging woman she had seen eight years before. The dead woman's eyes were bulging and staring at her with what appeared to be a smile on her face. The woman seemed to mock her as Isabell took one last breath to scream out a final scream of fright.

Isabell was suddenly awakened by her frantic mother who heard the screams of her daughter in the middle of the night.

"Isabell, are you alright child?" Amelia nervously asked her daughter, while shaking her out of her nightmare.

It took a little while before Isabell was able to recognize her mother and realize she was in her bed and had dreamt an awful dream. Tears streamed down her face as she tried to catch her breath from the horror of this indescribable night terror, while her mother embraced and held her tight.

"Oh mother!" Isabell cried.

"It's alright, child. It was only a dream. It was only a dream."

"Oh mother, it was terrible. They accused me…" she tried hard to catch her breath as she cried, "They accused me of being a witch!"

"It was a dream, Isabell. Try to be calm."

"I saw the hanging woman from years ago. She looked at me…"

Isabell could no longer speak amidst her trembling and crying. Amelia held her daughter tightly and swayed back and forth in order to provide some comfort. But Amelia knew her daughter would forever be haunted by the awful sight she saw as a child.

The eighteen-year-old Isabell still had recurring dreams that had started with the discovery of the hanging woman. There were many times Amelia would come running in the middle of the night just to hold Isabell in her arms to calm her and assure her it was only a dream; that the woman with the bulging eyes was not real and only lived long ago and in her memory. Isabell knew this and the reassurance of hearing her mother say it, gave her the confidence to realize it. It didn't make the dreams go away, but it was still comforting.

Alexander had dreams also but didn't wake up screaming. He was able to contain his emotions much more than the cold sweats, racing heartbeat, and labored breathing. Still, his mother was aware Alexander had the same dreams as Isabell. She didn't let on to the fears of his memories because of his pride, but she knew.

The Witch of Brentwood

*****

At eighteen years of age the children no longer played in the fields like they had growing up. Indeed, they were no longer children, but had grown into fine young adults who were well educated and customarily busy working around the home. Alexander usually tended to chopping firewood and making sure there was enough to last most of the winter months. One never knew how harsh the winters would be, or even if some pilferers would come around in the middle of the night and help themselves to a good portion of the coveted fuel. In his younger teenage years, he'd also learned how to mix his own paint in case something needed a different look; perhaps the fence that contained the cattle or the firewood. Most surfaces in town were not painted because mixing paint was such a grueling process. This made him want to learn and be successful at the process even more. Grinding the pigment and mixing it with linseed oil was quite a chore but once that was done, he had a great sense of accomplishment. He felt good about having developed a skill most didn't have. He was also very good at grooming and taking care of the horses that were so important to provide leisure riding in the open fields, or transportation into town and beyond to get needed supplies. He didn't mind running errands. He considered it a break from chopping wood and other physical chores.

Isabell was also busy inside the home, helping her mother since they were too poor to afford a servant. She didn't mind in the least. Afterall, she was doing chores a young lady was expected to do; spin wool and linen, learn how to make her own soap and candles, and help with food preparations. She didn't care for washing and cleaning, but that was also a necessary skill.

Her weak frame sometimes got the better of her, as well as a persistent cough she had developed over the previous days. But she would rest a while in between chores which gave her a chance to daydream a little without being too conspicuous and risk getting her mother angry. Daydreaming was a waste of time at the very least, but mostly the devil's work. Still, she couldn't help daydreaming.

As her coughing became almost incessant and her weak frame seemed to require rest more and more often, resting and daydreaming became a regular occurrence; especially daydreaming.

"May I have this dance, my lady?" asked the fair gentleman with the broad shoulders, strong chin, and dark mysterious eyes.

"You may." replied a smiling Isabell, who was wearing a garment made for a queen and several rings on her fingers.

The young lady rose from her seat, taking the gentleman's hand, and approached the dance floor as the music played a soft waltz. He bowed to her, she curtsied, and they danced to the music. Their bodies swayed as a feather floating in a soft breeze. Her happiness for the moment made her want to jump for joy even though she knew such a reaction would disrupt their dance. But the aching in her body for him to kiss her was almost too much to bear and she would directly burst from the suppression of her feelings. Soon, the gentleman got closer; close enough to whisper in her ear. She could hardly discern what he was saying because the music filled the room with such plenitude, but she knew it wasn't all that innocent by his tone. She couldn't help but look at him pleasingly and giggled at his brazen courage for daring to speak so to a young lady. They both smiled as they felt a sudden love. Never would her mother agree to such a relationship.

She looked deeply into his eyes for danger. She saw none; just the beauty of a deep soul who finally appeared out of nowhere to make her the happiest woman on earth. A sudden fear overtook her when he moved to kiss her, but it dissipated just as quickly when he pressed his strong lips to hers. She closed her eyes and surrendered herself to him with her whole heart, her whole soul, and her whole being. How wonderful life would be to marry such a brave and handsome man; to be together and raise strong children, and…

"Isabell!" her mother exclaimed, as Isabell's fantasy suddenly came to a halt. "What in heaven's name are you doing, child? Are you daydreaming? Don't you know this idleness is a trap set by Satan himself?"

"No mother, I wasn't…"

"Lying is another tool he uses to entrap the liar and their victims! Now get to work!"

"Yes, mother."

"And pray you won't fall prey to this sin again."

"Yes, I will, mother."

Anticipating no other forthcoming punishment from her mother, Isabell got back on her feet to help and silently vowed to herself to avoid further temptations of fantasizing about such evil. Staying busy curing bacon and salting meat was the best way for both women to not get distracted by other less important activities like daydreaming.

"We shall be visiting my mother's grave again today, Isabell." her mother said.

Isabell didn't respond. It seemed to her that her mother knew about the fear she had of cemeteries; more accurately, her fear of the dead. She had that deep fear even before the nightmares began after seeing the hanging woman on the tree that fateful day. She wished mostly that the nightmares would go away. Her fear of the dead could be kept under control if she didn't visit cemeteries. Unfortunately, that day would be a cemetery day and she would have to cope with it as best she could.

It was on that particular day Amelia noticed that her daughter's cough was not getting any better. In fact, it seemed to her it was getting worse. Isabell also seemed to look more drawn and thinner than she looked days before, and her recent lack of energy to the extent that she would take frequent naps during the day, was also alarming. It was then Amelia started to suspect that her daughter was afflicted with consumption; the dreaded disease that attacked the entire body, but mainly the lungs. (The disease was known by many names including 'the king's evil', 'scrofula', 'phthisis', and soon to become known as 'the white plague'. But about one hundred and fifty years later, it would become known by its current name of tuberculosis.) She knew full well what consumption was capable of doing to the human body; everything from weight loss to coughing up blood to even death, as she had witnessed as a little girl. As far as she knew, there was no cure. All a person could do was drink the remedies of the time made with herbs, get plenty of rest, and pray. She also knew that Isabell would most likely be bed-ridden soon and it broke her heart to think her still-very-young daughter had fallen victim to such a debilitating disease that would most likely take her life. The pain she felt in her gut to think of such things, made it hard for her to pray but she didn't dare question her faith. Such a notion would, without question, invite more evil.

*****

Isabell and her mother walked hand-in-hand. It was Isabell's idea. As they walked to Amelia's mother's grave, they saw some gravestones that stood erect, but most were leaning to one side or the other; undoubtedly from the ravages of time and the elements. Some were vandalized as well with unpleasant words like *witch* or *good riddance*. To Isabell it was a very somber place in which to be, on such a beautiful day and yet she understood the need for her mother to be there. She guessed that her mother thought Isabell had the same need, but nothing could be further from the truth. She hated it. Even if she didn't have a deathly fear of the dead, she could think of so many other places she could be.

The stroll among the gravestones made her think of the hanging woman whom she was sure was the reason for her recurring nightmares. It was likely that the woman was buried under the very ground she walked on. She never knew the woman's name but could never forget her face with the noose wrapped around her neck. As she thought of her, Isabell brought her hand up to her own neck to try to soothe the pain the hanging woman must have felt before she died.

She looked at each name on the stones very carefully, making sure she didn't recognize any of them. It was always better, she thought, if she didn't know anyone in the cemetery. Her grandmother was not someone she had ever known, so visiting her grave was no worse than visiting some other faceless dead person.

Regardless of the vandalism and the crooked stones, at least the grounds were well maintained. She was happy with the fact that her grandmother's grave and stone were not damaged in any way. Amelia made sure of that. Any sign of overgrown grass and litter was taken care of immediately, which was another thing Isabell admired about her mother. She was so diligent when it mattered.

They finally reached the grave where the body of Amelia's mother rested in peace. Amelia had brought some flowers to replace the ones she had brought last time they had visited. She placed them on the stone and closed her eyes for a moment to reflect. Isabel saw a tear rolling down her mother's cheek while she waited in silence. After a moment, they remained holding hands as both got on their knees to pray, but all the while, Isabell remained vigilant to her surroundings. Not that she really believed some dead bodies would rise from the ground or a ghost would suddenly appear out of nowhere, but terrible fear usually makes one react irrationally; especially when in a cemetery and dead people are among one's biggest fears.

There were alarming sounds at times which made it hard for Isabell to not show any signs of being terrified. Dogs barked and howled, crows called out to one another and made loud raspy 'caw' sounds, and the wind made a howling noise as it whipped through the wind tunnel, she and her mother seemed to be in. These things didn't bother her mother, apparently, perhaps because she was occupied with prayer and concentrating on the important things of the moment, unlike Isabell.

Finally, Amelia wiped her eyes with her handkerchief and stood up with Isabell. She touched the stone one last time in reverence before she and Isabell turned to make their way back home. They didn't speak on the way back much like when they were walking to the cemetery. Their walk home was still a solemn moment out of respect for the dead, and quite silent which Isabell was more than happy with. The last thing she wanted was for her mother to hear the trembling and quivering in her voice from fear. It was somehow disrespectful to the dearly departed. This, she knew.

Once out of the cemetery, Isabell sighed a big sigh of relief which made her cough even more than she was used to doing of late. Amelia looked at her with concern because it sounded worse than usual.

After her coughing spell, Isabell turned to her mother and said, "Don't worry, mother, it's only a nasty virus. I only wish I don't fall very ill with it and hope you or Alexander don't succumb to it as well."

At that, Amelia wiped the concerned look from her face but knew enough to still remain concerned. Isabell was correct in calling it a nasty virus but after all, had no idea of how devastating it could actually be; not only for the one inflicted but also for the loved ones at home taking care of the ill child.

Their cabin soon came into view and Isabell started feeling much better about the day even though she was feeling herself get progressively worse physically. She had gone to the cemetery with her mother and didn't break down in fear, but more importantly, they weren't there anymore. They were home and she thanked God for the solace of home.

All while walking, Isabell fantasized again about the young man of her dreams. She did this silently and without expression in her face lest her mother whom she was still holding hands with, became wise and asked what she was thinking. *Some things must remain private.*

The joy of her silent fantasy at times gave way to coughing fits and her mother's frequent concerned looks, but she didn't care. This was her own little secret world where disease doesn't exist, where there are no bad people to hurt you, and where there are no dead people to visit in scary cemeteries with evil noises from nearby creepy animals.

In the back of her mind, however, she knew it was only fantasy and the real world has a way of coming back to life to overshadow your life. Tried as she might to prevent it, her fantasy soon evaporated into a mere previous thought to be ignored. Still, this dream was preferable to the recurring nightmares which were becoming more intense with every passing night.

The Witch of Brentwood

*****

The sound of hooves against the ground was veritably satisfying to Alexander, as he galloped on his favorite horse into the north end of town. Although he was no longer a child, he allowed himself to fantasize about being a soldier without the dangers of actually being one. *Piercing someone's heart with the end of a sword is so much easier when riding at full speed.* The wind sometimes stung his eyes but that made the fantasy seem that much more real, since danger is imminent when fighting the good fight in a war against insurrectionists.

It was a small section of town he rode into; perhaps about a dozen homes and a few businesses to supply provisions. Some of the homes were solidly built, while others seemed more like straw huts that could easily be destroyed with one good windstorm. Alexander thanked God often for having been born into a home that could withstand a good beating, as poor as they were. He was thankful he and his family were able to maintain their home by doing work for folks who needed assistance. Alexander was a good handyman, whereas Amelia and Isabell were both good at sewing garments for those willing to pay or trade to have someone make them. Many times, those chores were done for charity, since Amelia was not one to measure riches by how much material possessions they had, but by how much they could help their neighbors. Amelia always reminded her children there were others not as fortunate as they were, which was made evident by some of the homes he saw.

Alexander arrived and stopped at a general store. The owner, Mr. Gooderidge, used to be a roving peddler before he accumulated enough capital and inventory to establish a permanent location. He was a short, stubby man with only gray hair around the side of his head. Alexander guessed him to be at least in his seventies. His wild bushy eyebrows which he could move at will, were the main focal point of his facial expressions. And when he blinked, only one eye seemed to shut and the other remained slightly opened. This was something Alexander always marveled at. Mr. Gooderidge always wore the same black pants and brown shirt with a white apron around his waist and spoke with a high voice through a few missing teeth in the back and a few rotten ones in the front.

Alexander liked Mr. Gooderidge, though, and enjoyed his conversations. He usually learned something new from him every time they talked.

"Good day, Mr. Gooderidge. God be with you." Alexander said, upon entering.

"Aahh, good day to you as well, young man." replied Mr. Gooderidge, "Always nice to see you; makes my day much easier to cope with. What brings you in town on this day? Not that I mind you."

"Sugar and flour, please."

"Let me guess...pound cake?"

"You have an uncanny way of reading minds, Mr. Gooderidge." Alexander returned with a smile.

"I also fancy that the taskwork might be the effort of Miss Whitlock *and* Isabell?"

"Right again."

"What wonderful kinfolk you have, boy. You know, it's not everyone who appreciates family as yours. There are some who accuse their own of this and that, and then dare to denounce them in the presence of the court."

"I know. It's shameful."

As the conversation went on, Mr. Gooderidge took the opportunity and began telling the story of someone he knew when he was much younger. This was his usual routine when he had the occasion to educate young Alexander in the lessons of the world and what malice the human heart is capable of. As he spoke, he flailed his arms with great enthusiasm and looked about the room with eyebrows moving wildly to exaggerate every emotion he wanted to convey. This was another reason Alexander enjoyed conversations so much with Gooderidge. Not only did he learn new things but was also entertained by the animated way the stories were told.

As Alexander listened, he heard someone walk into the store. He turned in the direction of the new patron to see the most beautiful girl he had ever seen. She was accompanied by a much older man, whom he guessed to be the young girl's father. Now Alexander was not one to be disrespectful. Indeed, he always extended the utmost courtesy to anyone he conversed with, but this time he couldn't help but totally ignore what Gooderidge was saying. He was mesmerized by the girl's beauty.

Myrna Arington was her name. Her red velvet hair reached her shoulders and was adorned with a perfectly fitting flowery hat slightly tilted to one side. She had shapely eyebrows with long eyelashes that fully complemented her green eyes. The freckles of her face reached down to her neck, which was slender as it should be for such beauty. Dressed in colorful attire, the rest of her body suited Alexander just fine as he kept looking at her, not noticing that Gooderidge had stopped telling his story.

What was the use of continuing the story when it was obvious his young friend was abruptly afflicted with newly found deafness? Alexander was not aware of his smiling from ear to ear as he inspected Myrna from head to toe. It would have embarrassed him had he been aware of how foolish he looked, but it made Myrna smile back at him with a gleam in her eyes.

Seeing there was no sense in continuing his story with Alexander, Mr. Gooderidge gave him a forgiving smile and walked over to the man who had walked in with the young girl to see if he could be of assistance.

The young girl's father, Clement Arington, was no stranger to Gooderidge. He was a frequent customer who lived nearby with his daughter. Arington was a widower in his mid-forties with a stern face that spoke of hardship both past and present. This tall and intimidating man hardly smiled, since there was nothing to smile about. One could tell by his build that he was used to hard labor, but perhaps a very handsome and formidable young man in his prime. However, if that were the case, the years had caught up to him; perhaps imparting emotional scars, one too often gets after a lifetime of hardship.

As the two older men engaged in small talk about the weather, family well-being, and needed items, Alexander thought it was the proper moment to approach the young lady who was at some distance from her father.

"Good day." Alexander said with the most soft-spoken voice he could muster. Holding out his hand to her, he continued, "My name is Alexander, Alexander Whitlock...and who might you be?"

"I might be Myrna."

"Pleased to meet you, Myrna. You have a lovely name."

"Thank you. I don't recall seeing you in this part of town."

"No, I'm from the southern section. I buy from Mr. Gooderidge often, however." replied Alexander.

"As do we; my father and I, that is." she said, looking in the direction of the two older men. "Our paths have never crossed until now, I suppose."

"I suppose you're correct. I'm happy they finally have." Myrna could only smile and blush, which was the perfect response Alexander was anticipating. "I hope they cross again soon," he said.

"Yes, that would be very nice."

"What is your surname?"

"Arington, Myrna Arington."

"Hmm, Arington...Arington. The name is familiar to me."

"My father is a handyman. He goes about doing chores for those who pay him. Perhaps you've heard of him from neighbors."

"Yes, perhaps." he replied, and thought for a moment, "If I were to need his services, do you think he would be willing to travel to the south end of town?"

"I'm sure."

"Do you think he'd be accompanied by his beautiful daughter, Myrna?"

She giggled and shook her head. "I don't usually go where my father works."

"What if my mother needed outside help; a helping hand from some beautiful young lady, perhaps? It would be a great way to earn more for your father."

"I would have to ask if indeed you were in need of extra help, that is. Or are you only making conversation for the sake of passing the time?" she said with a dubious look.

"It would never occur to me to fabricate such stories," he replied.

During their conversation, Myrna's father who had completed the purchase he'd come for, was waiting at the counter and losing his patients with Mr. Gooderidge's rambling. Finally, he'd had enough.

"Myrna!" exclaimed Clement.

The youngsters' gaze was broken instantly at her father's call. She rushed to him immediately.

"Yes father?"

"Let's make haste. It's time to go, not dally with strangers." he said sternly.

"Yes father."

"And it's almost time for you to prepare the meal before I lie famished. So, off with us."

"Yes sir." she replied humbly.

It was then that Alexander saw her father for what he was; an unpleasant soul who likes to order people around at the very least, even his own daughter. As a devout Puritan, he tried not to judge anyone. But as for her father, things were different. It may have been due to Alexander's infatuation with Myrna's beauty (which would have been regarded as disgraceful by his mother, had she been there). But regardless of the reason, Clement was easy to despise.

The two older men bade their well wishes and then the Aringtons proceeded towards the exit. On their way, there was a quick smile and a glance between Alexander and Myrna, to be sure.

Soon, Alexander stood silently in a daze while Mr. Gooderidge resumed his previous story that continued to fall on deaf ears since Myrna had made her entrance.

Réal Carpentier

Chapter 3

Amelia never really concerned herself with rumors of children catching certain viruses that were very dangerous. She was not to be taken into the temptation of believing such a fate would befall her beloved family. She and her twins prayed every night and read their favorite bible verses. This was a ritual Amelia encouraged to not only find favor with the Almighty Creator but also to make known that her family was a God-fearing family and perhaps influence others to be the same.

In this particular late spring of 1692, however, Isabell's condition deteriorated to where she spent many days and nights in bed. Her cough got worse still, and she began to lose more weight. She was getting too thin as far as her mother was concerned. Isabell was always such a happy child but since she had taken ill, the situation was not only unbearable for Amelia, but also very dangerous lest someone take notice and become suspicious of evil existing in their home. Afterall, there was anxiety in the air. Things like a change in behavior or even a severe unexpected illness was reason enough to raise suspicions about falling victim to the devil's work. Everyone feared everyone else and accusations of witchcraft were plentiful within the immediate region. It was also widespread, as there were accusations as far away as London. Amelia cared about *those* people too, but honestly, *that was their problem.* The immediate concern was for her daughter, not some folks in a faraway place.

Isabell's worsening condition was devastating, but the silver lining was it gave an opportunity for her and her mother to spend time together as she was being fed and taken care of.

It was on a clear spring day that Isabell's mother was with her as she lay in bed ingesting the mixture her mother was used to making for such viruses; a mixture of various kinds of parsley, honey, and a little wine. This was the perfect mixture for 'coughs of the lungs', which was one of the recommended remedies for this type of cough. There were others, but to Amelia it was the best one and the one handed down to her by her father.

"It's quite sweet." Isabell stated, after gulping down her mother's homemade concoction.

Amelia replied, "Yes but more importantly, it's very effective for your cough and other symptoms. Take heart, girl, you shall be better soon."

"I've heard tell of consumption." Isabell said and then paused to take a breath and look in her mother's eyes, "I'm afraid."

"Have faith, child. God Almighty will not allow evil to ravage his people. This is a test of faith. Be strong and be thankful we have remedies that cure, unlike years ago." Isabell simply nodded and trusted in her mother's confidence. "Are you feeling better?"

Isabell's voice was weak, "My cough is terrible, and it hurts to breathe. I'm also a little light-headed."

The Witch of Brentwood

She would have liked to say she felt better but couldn't lie even if it meant that her response made her mother feel bad. Even at the innocent age of eighteen, she knew that parents of any child would rather endure whatever ailment there was than have their children suffering it. Amelia just nodded and ran her hand through her daughter's hair. She could feel the heat of her fever. She knew her daughter was sick of being tired and tired of being sick, but nothing could be done except follow the medicinal protocol of the time which didn't seem to help very quickly, if at all. Her face was covered with red blotches, her head ached, and it pained Amelia to see her daughter trembling from chills and fear.

Whenever Isabell coughed, she made sure to cough in a towel away from her mother, even though Amelia tried to keep her distance. Also, every precaution was taken to make sure the disease didn't spread to Alexander. Amelia made sure to keep him busy with errands and chores so he could remain outside and out of the way of her disease.

"I should leave and let you get rest." Amelia said.

"No." replied Isabell, "Please don't leave. Sit with me."

"You really need your rest."

"Please, I don't want to be alone right now. Please, sit with me."

After some thought, Amelia moved the bedside chair a little closer and sat.

"Would you like me to read from the Bible?" her mother asked.

"Not right now. I'd like to talk, if that's alright." Her mother looked at her sadly and nodded that it was okay. After a moment,

Isabell let out a sigh of relief from not being alone and began to speak. "Tell me about you as a child."

"Whatever do you mean?"

"We never talked about your childhood."

Isabell knew her mother well but never knew of her childhood. She didn't dare ask about it because her mother never shared such stories. Isabell figured there must have been a good reason she stayed away from the subject, but it seemed the opportune time to be open; perhaps even to relieve some of her mother's repressed emotions.

"Some things are better left alone, child. Those are things of the past."

"Still, I'd like to know." After a moment, she added, "What was grandfather like?"

Amelia hesitated. Finally, she replied, "He was in no small way a hard man."

"How do you mean?"

Amelia just looked down as though she were reflecting on her past. After a while, she gave Isabell a serious look and said, "You must never repeat any of this to anyone."

She waited for her daughter's acknowledgement. When Isabell nodded in agreement, Amelia finally shared a story that had been bottled up inside her for decades.

The Witch of Brentwood

*****

Amelia's father was a big man from what she remembered of him; tall and muscular. As a blacksmith by profession, he was well respected in the community, and everyone knew he was good at his craft. His work attire was what he wore at home, church, and anywhere else he went. All he had to do to change out of his work clothes was remove his apron he wore only for work. That was sufficient as far as he was concerned. He had brown eyes and hair to match, just above shoulder length to hide the scar on his left ear he received from a drunken neighbor not quite happy with the advances the beloved blacksmith had made towards this man's wife. Had the neighbor not been drunk, he would have known better, since he got the worse of the confrontation.

Young Amelia Whitlock was only four years old when she was first locked in that small closet in her room. At least, that's as far back as she could remember when it first happened. The closet was quite darker than she had imagined. She had no recollection of why her father locked her in there, but there must have been a reason and a good one at that. Why else would he lock her in for most of the day? Still, it was better than the other punishments.

Her mother had died of consumption, but Amelia knew if she were alive, her mother would have convinced her father to let her out early if she didn't cry too much. But she wasn't alive, and trying to convince her father herself was usually a vain attempt. So, all Amelia could do was cry and sometimes scream, which didn't help her cause. Those cries were not from want of being freed, necessarily. They were mainly from fear of the dark and closed spaces. At times she couldn't breathe because of the claustrophobia, which made her think she also had the evil disease that took her mother and would soon die from it. She feared the little noises she heard from within the closet; imagining there were rats or other critters locked up with her. It was too dark to see, and she was too young to realize how powerful a young girl's imagination could be. What she feared most, however, was having the urge to pee, or God forbid the urge for the other thing. Not having access to the outhouse meant making a wet mess or brown mess in her under garments and the floor, which she would have to endure during her entire stay in her dark little penitentiary. Either one of those messes would unleash her father's fury to the point of being whipped when he finally let her out. As much as she remembered the closet, the feel of her father's snake belt was most vivid in her mind; the one he wore when it wasn't hitting her skin. But no one knew of his punishments toward his only child, and she was happy about that. She didn't want anyone to know of her behavior that gave her father frequent reasons for such discipline.

When her father was angry at something Amelia did and the closet punishment was not his discipline of choice, she sometimes went without eating for hours; sometimes an entire day. Fasting, after all, was good for the soul. So in effect, a means of sacrificing to God was achieved in no small measure. It really didn't matter if her stomach hurt from hunger pains or felt lightheaded once in a while from not eating. A severe punishment was usually well deserved, and if it addressed a worthy cause in like manner, all the better.

Amelia's relationship with her father was not all bad, however. There were times when they would play a game together to pass the time after all her chores were done and he was nice and drunk. One of her favorite games was hiding an object from him without his seeing. It had to be an object of his choice, which changed from time to time. But mostly, his choice was a brooch Amelia's mother owned and wore before she died; the one she loved so much. It was blue and shaped like a star with a white pearl in the middle, surrounded by five diamond chips. He kept it in her mother's little trinket box in his bedroom. Her wishes were to be buried with it which he agreed to, but he had secretly planned otherwise. He didn't know exactly what the value of the brooch was, but he knew it was valuable. If his financial situation ever had a turn for the worse for whatever reason, it would prove to be a profitable trade.

Amelia's father was brilliant at their hide-the-object game. Much to her amazement, he always found the hiding place she was so careful to select. There was no possible way he could ever discover the object where it was hidden, especially when she was sure he hadn't seen her hide it. But he did find it; always. She was amazed and sometimes a little scared because of it. Before the start of every search, she would hear him silently recite something under his breath; something that was incomprehensible to her; words she had never heard; words with apparently no meaning; words which seemed to be in another language. At first, it made her laugh. She thought it was part of the game and thought it funny when he told her he had supernatural powers and his silent oration helped him channel this mystical ability. But the real power, he told her, was in the brooch. After a while, she became afraid and refused to play; thinking it was indeed mystical and unnatural. He never questioned why she wouldn't play anymore, and she was happy about that. Admitting her fear of him would be embarrassing, but mostly disrespectful; a disrespect that would undoubtedly unleash a well-deserved punishment.

Still, her father was a respected man in the community and Amelia could only wish she would someday command that kind of respect from anyone. Indeed, she never did until she bore her own children who gave her the respect she longed for, and she loved them with all her heart because of it.

"He sounds evil, mother." Isabell said, trying to suppress a cough.

Amelia just looked at her without replying for a moment. She saw her daughter lying in bed, suffering from the same disease that took her own mother and left young Amelia with the man she feared most of her life. After a while, she finally answered, "Perhaps he was."

"Thank you for confiding in me. Why didn't you speak of it sooner?"

"You were too young to understand. Your grandfather is deserving of the respect he is due, as all the deceased are. So, you must never tell anyone."

"I won't." Isabell waited a moment, then asked, "How old were you when he died?"

"I was your age, dear." Her response was interrupted by Isabell's cough. Amelia touched her face to feel how high her temperature might be. It was burning hot. She also noticed her trying to keep her eyes open in defiance of the inevitable sleep she was fighting. "Enough talk now, Isabell. You go to sleep, and I'll look after you directly."

Amelia stood up from her chair, placed it back in the corner of the room, and came back to the bedside to make sure Isabell was properly tucked in and comfortable. As she made her way towards the bedroom door, Isabell called for her.

"Mother?"

"Yes?" Amelia responded.

"What happened to the brooch? Was grandfather buried with it?"

Amelia didn't respond verbally but simply smiled, reached in the pocket of her apron, and pulled out a beautiful star-shaped brooch; complete with an array of diamonds surrounding a white pearl. Isabell smiled as her mother closed the door behind her.

Left alone, Isabell was able to reflect on the story her mother had just told her about her parents, and specifically about the

The Witch of Brentwood

brooch that was now in her mother's possession. She imagined herself wearing that fine piece of jewelry around her neck, being the envy of every girl who saw it, and the coveted prize for every boy she met. She imagined how well she would care for such a gem.

But those thoughts soon gave way to weariness partly because of her illness and partly because of the remedy her mother had given her. Soon, she was half asleep with images of the brooch, and her grandfather abusing her own mother. Her emotions of fascination and dread intertwined together until she was in a deep sleep only to be haunted by the continuous nightmare she'd had since being an innocent ten-years-old girl.

She didn't scream that night. Perhaps she was too tired or too sick to build up her strength, but she again lived through the same old nightmare. Only this nightmare didn't end with her waking but continued to reveal what it was like to die. Hell is no place for a young girl but in the dream, it was her new home. She saw many people there who might be considered the evil type including the hanging woman. She tried to reason with those she met and explained that she was a God-fearing girl but they only responded by calling her witch and telling her she'd better accept her fate lest the master gets angry and ties her up smeared in honey so the wild hungry dogs could feast on her.

Isabell woke up the next morning in a cold sweat with sheets and blankets drenched from the perspiration. She wasn't quite sure if it was the result of her fever breaking or the nightmare that lasted longer than it should have. It didn't matter. No matter what the reason, she would have been happy to just suddenly die and be relieved of her misery.

Réal Carpentier

*****

The pot of soup had been boiling over for a little while. The top of the wood stove was wet and steaming from the overflow with a sizzling sound that filled the room. Amelia rushed to the pot with a dry rag as soon as she could but there was quite a mess to clean up. She wanted to curse but was able to contain herself from doing so, knowing full well that wanting to was just as bad as the act itself. Not thinking, she picked up the pot with her bare hands to remove it from the hot burner and let out a soft moan because of the pain she received from the very hot handles. The pain was not only to her hands, but rather had gradually traveled throughout her entire body. Her wariness may have been the cause because she had gotten burned before and never felt pain as she did at this moment. Still, she tried hard to ignore it since there was much work to be done in haste. She hurried to clean the wetness, trying carefully to not get burned again. Then after the overflow was cleaned and the pot of soup was again under control, she sat down in the rocker, gently rubbing the burns on her hands, and began to cry silently.

If someone had seen what happened, they would undoubtedly think she was crying from the burns but that wasn't the only pain she felt. Having reminisced with Isabell about her own childhood and living with a father she feared, all the punishments she had to endure without knowing why, her frightening realization that her daughter had contracted the same disease that took her mother's life, as well as the everyday hardship she was going through now; these things all contributed to her own overflow of emotions with a boiling over of their own. She was relieved, however, that no one was there to ask her what's wrong.

The outside door suddenly opened, and Alexander walked in to see her crying.

"What's wrong mother?" he asked with great concern.

"Oh, it's nothing." she replied with a fake smile.

He rushed to her.

"Why do you cry, mother? Did something happen to Isabell?"

"She's sleeping now. I'm sure she'll be alright soon. Take care to not make too much noise, dear." She saw him staring at her to try to determine what could possibly be the cause of his mother's crying. She looked back at him and said, "Trust me, Alexander, there is nothing wrong except some burns I have from a boiling pot of soup."

"Are you sure?" he asked.

"Yes, I'm sure. Not to worry."

He gave a comforting smile of support and gently took her hands to kiss them. This simple act eradicated all of the hardships she was mulling over in her mind just minutes before.

Alexander was no fool. He knew life was hard for his mother and always felt something should be done to eliminate some of the burden. He thought perhaps getting the proper help with the chores would be a good idea and he knew just who to recommend. It was an opportune time to talk about maybe hiring the man he'd met at the general store; the one with the beautiful daughter, Myrna. It would be a wonderful idea to hire her to relieve some of his mother's chores as well, since Isabell was in no condition to help. In fact, he thought perhaps Myrna could help with cleaning Isabell's room and taking care of giving her the medicine at the proper time; not to mention helping with cooking, sewing, and such.

"Mother, I'd like to talk to you about maybe hiring some help," he said.

"What do you mean?"

"I mean hiring someone to help around the home; fixing the fence, building a bigger shed for the firewood, cleaning, mending; that sort of work."

"Alexander, we need not hire someone to do our work. We can take care of it ourselves, don't you think?"

"Not with Isabell as sick as she is. We're overburdened with work, mother."

"I'll admit it's been harder lately, but to hire someone…"

"I met someone who would be willing to come and help. A man I met at the general store makes a living doing this for surrounding neighbors, and he has a daughter who would be willing to come help you in the kitchen and take care of Isabell, and other such chores."

He knew he'd stretched the truth, if there was any truth to what he was saying. But he also knew that there was a time for everything; even stretching the truth if it was meant for the greater good. As far as he was concerned, this idea was for the greater good; notwithstanding his desire to get to know the beautiful Myrna a little better.

"Won't you think about it, mother?" She didn't respond, but just looked at him pensively. "It would be such a help and make life so much better," he added.

"I shall sleep on it, Alexander."

"Thank you. You shall see. Life will be a lot easier."

He gave her a smile and then quietly went to his room so as to not wake Isabell.

The Witch of Brentwood

Amelia sat nursing her burns as she thought of the last thing Alexander had told her. *Life will be a lot easier.* It was exactly what she needed to hear. The idea of getting extra help around the home was beginning to appeal to her more and more. She sat in her rocker for another three quarters of an hour until the soup was ready. All the while, she thought about the proposition her son had made and it became a more sensible idea to her with the passing of each minute.

Seeing the soup was now ready, she set the table for three, hoping Isabell would be well enough to join them. As she worked preparing the table, she heard Isabell begin to cough again with a cough that had gotten worse since before she fell asleep. Amelia hurriedly went into Isabell's room and saw her poor daughter coughing blood and crying from pain and exasperation. It was then she decided to take Alexander up on his offer. Seeing her daughter suffering as she was, Amelia was now convinced of the idea of hiring help. Afterall, her previous reluctance to the offer was a matter of pride and she knew full well that pride was a sin. After supper, she would pray for forgiveness and her daughter's wellbeing.

Réal Carpentier

Chapter 4

The newly-hired hand was Clement Arington, much to Alexander's satisfaction. Clement was a good worker but what was more important was that Amelia had also hired Clement's daughter, Myrna, for household work as well. Not only did Alexander and Myrna develop a close relationship, which secretly developed into a love affair, but Amelia and Clement also became good friends. This was by no means a romantic relationship, but rather a relationship that involved a means of support and even time for laughter and slight deviation from hours of work.

Clement's hold on his daughter was evident and even reminded Amelia of her own childhood relationship with her father. There was no immediate evidence of punishment, but it was obvious that Myrna knew her place and was careful not to cross any lines that would merit such disciplinary action. Still, even with his stern look and apparent control over his daughter, Amelia liked him; not for romantic reasons but simply because in a way, he was a man in her life. She was also happy to have Myrna's help around the home. It gave her an opportunity to spend more time with Isabell and nurse her back to some form of normal health.

The hired help had been a constant for some time now and payment for the worker's help was not a problem at first, but it was soon obvious Amelia wouldn't be able to continue to afford the same arrangement. She didn't want to let the workers go because the help was needed, and the man-in-her-life situation made her feel more secure. That's when Amelia decided to negotiate a proposal of her own. Afterall, some sacrifices are worth making for the good of the family. So, one sunny afternoon when all was quiet, Isabell was asleep, and Alexander had taken Myrna into town for food, she implemented her plan.

Clement was quite busy fixing a portion of the fence that needed fixing for the longest time. The sky was blue, the birds were singing, and the time was right. She approached him.

"Beautiful afternoon, wouldn't you say?" she asked.

"Quite gorgeous, yes." replied Clement, never bothering to stop work to make eye contact.

"Myrna is quite a big help around here. It's given me the opportunity to be with Isabell and tend to her condition. I truly appreciate that."

"Good, I'm glad about that." he said, still working.

"It's also nice to have a man around to help Alexander, if I may say so. I'm sure he really appreciates it."

"Yes, he's a fine boy. A good worker too."

"Have you never had a son of your own?"

"No, I guess it wasn't meant to be. Myrna was born and my wife died soon after."

"I'm sorry."

He paused for a moment to concentrate on a stubborn fence post, then added, "It was years ago."

"You were never of the mind to remarry?"

"Never really thought about it. My wife, God rest her soul, was not well and I struggled in the last few years of her life. I reckon I didn't want to go through that again."

He sounded much too crude to Amelia's liking just then but, in her experience, the men in her life lacked proper emotional tact anyway. He was just another man.

"I'm sorry to hear that." she said. "What was wrong, if I might ask?"

"Well, it's a story we'll have to make time to discuss. Too long to tell it now."

She hesitated, then touched his arm and said, "I'd like to make the time, if you'd like."

This made him cease from working to look at her. It was the first time he'd noticed the color of her eyes. They stood looking at each other wondering what the other would say next. He waited for her to speak again. He knew she would. She didn't disappoint.

"Perhaps you'd like to break from work for a while and have tea with me." she said timidly.

He didn't answer but just kept looking at her trying to read her mind. Perhaps it was the hesitation in her voice or her delicate look that convinced him of her intentions. Either way he felt confident enough to get closer to her, while his facial expression remained stern. It was the same look he gave the stubborn fence post just moments before.

He delicately brushed her arm with his hand while looking for any change of intentions in her eyes and asked, "Why would you have me break from work?"

She took his brushing hand while her eyes returned clear intentions and replied, "How can a woman resist such strong hands as these?"

At that, he grabbed her shoulders and ran his eyes up and down, surveying the woman in his grasp. His facial expression suddenly changed to reflect his confidence, as he pulled her towards him and kissed her. He felt only the slightest reluctance, which dissipated almost immediately. He thought perhaps it wasn't hesitation at all, but rather some kind of innate defense reaction.

He moved from her lips to her neck in haste with no hint of further reluctance on her part. But then, she pulled away.

"Wait," she said, "not here."

She took his hand and led him to her bedroom, being careful not to wake up Isabell. All the while, he watched her walk and could only imagine the woman he would soon discover. Once inside her bedroom, she whispered, "You must hurry before the kids come home."

Nothing further needed to be spoken. Indeed, nothing *was* spoken. All one heard, if one could hear, were the sounds of the bed springs and mutual relief from years of frustration.

The noises were enough to rouse Isabell from a deep sleep. Until then, she always considered her mother to be just a mother; certainly not a woman with sexual desires. *Mothers don't have those needs. The desires of intimacy, sometimes evil, are for younger women wanting to procreate; not older women who have important work to tend to.* She covered her ears. The sounds still reverberated through the thin wall between her bedroom and her mother's, and there was not much more she could do but wait until the moment was over. She didn't want to admit to herself there was a part of her that wanted to hear; not out of curiosity, but out of a sheer desire of her own. She thought about how it would be to do the same with boys she'd met; boys who wanted to give her first experience of womanhood. Inside her, was a bad feeling she tried to suppress; a mixed feeling of want and fear. She wished the sounds would just be over with soon.

Finally, there was silence. She tried hard to suppress her cough so as to not let her mother know she was awake. The discovery of her eavesdropping would rightly be reason for discipline.

In the other room, Amelia and Clement hurried to get dressed lest anyone found out about their evil deed. But it was not so much a concern for Clement as it was for Amelia. Once dressed and sure the bed was tidy again, they proceeded outside where Clement went back to work, as Amelia waved to Alexander and Myrna who were a ways down the road arriving from their errand.

As normal as things seemed, Amelia was sure she would no longer have to worry about payment for the hired help or being without a man again.

*****

Alexander carried the ham and assorted vegetables in one hand and held Myrna's hand in the other as they walked back home from the local store. He saw his mother waving but ignored her. He was too busy as the lovers looked in each other's eyes more frequently than the ground they walked on. Even from a distance it was obvious they were becoming more than friends.

"I'm really glad you and your father decided to help our family; especially help for my mother." Alexander told Myrna.

"Is that the only reason?" she asked with a teasing smile.

"No." he replied. "From the moment you told me of your father being a handyman, I got the idea to hire him only to get to know you better."

"That's sweet."

"It was Isabell's illness that helped my mother's decision to have you. I consider myself blessed."

"Alexander, that's terrible."

"I'm glad you're with me, is all I meant, not her illness. I don't consider myself blessed for her illness."

"How did she get sick?" asked Myrna.

"Perhaps she contracted it from someone she came close to. We don't know. She's always been the one to be fragile; always complaining about this or that. Even when she was born; mother told us she came out looking gray. She didn't even cry at first. My mother and the midwife both thought she was dead."

"And you?"

"I was perfect." he said proudly with a smile.

"As you still are." she replied timidly.

"And as *you* are." he added with an honest look in his eyes.

Alexander stopped walking which made her stop in kind, and they looked at each other for the first time with a seriousness that was new. He held her closer and kissed her, feeling no resistance. Pressing hard against her, she pressed harder still with a clear indication that she was now his. He didn't dare go too far lest her willingness turned into reluctance, but she noticed this and in no uncertain way, showed him it was alright to go further. She trusted him and wanted to prove it.

Soon they were far from the road, lying in the thicket of the golden field where the wheat stalks were tall enough to provide complete privacy from anyone. There, they would avow their trust for one another and consummate a new-found love.

When they arrived home moments later, Clement was working on the fence post, and Amelia was tending to the chickens and horses. Alexander kissed Myrna before going to lend a hand with the fence, while Myrna proceeded inside and gently knocked on the door of Isabell's bedroom.

"Yes?" Isabell acknowledged.

"It's Myrna. May I come in?"

"Yes. Please do."

The door opened slowly, and Isabell was greeted with a smile.

"How are you feeling? Better I hope." Myrna began, as she tiptoed towards the chair beside the bed.

"Better, it seems."

"Good. Glad to hear it. Do you need anything?"

"If you don't mind, I would like a drink of water."

"How about something to eat; perhaps some of your mother's soup?"

"Perhaps later. Just water for now."

Myrna filled a glass on the table near the bed from a pitcher of iced water as she continued her conversation.

"I was at the store with Alexander. We brought home some ham and some vegetables. *That* should give you strength as you get better."

"I'm beginning to feel better now. Restful sleep is what I need."

"You still look drawn, though."

"I haven't been getting very much sleep lately."

"Why not? Your coughing?"

"That and other things too."

"Such as?"

"Too many dreams. I know it sounds crazy."

"Good things, I hope."

"No, I have dreams about scary things"

"What things?"

"Things that happened years ago. Things that are constantly on my mind and haunting me. I try to forget but I can't. Sometimes I'm not even sure if it happened at all or if I'm wishing it never happened. I don't know."

"What things?" Myrna asked again.

"Never mind."

"It may help if you talk about it."

"I shouldn't, really."

"Tell me, silly. Nothing bad will happen."

Isabell considered it in her mind. *What harm could it bring to talk about dreams?* She hesitated, but then began to speak.

"When I was younger, about ten years old, I happened upon a dead woman who was hanged on a tree." Myrna just listened intently as Isabell recounted her experiences, taking moments of coughing in between her story. "She had the fear of evil in her face, and I can't seem to get that picture out of my mind. I dream about it often. Sometimes mother comes in to wake me, so I know I scream loud enough to wake her."

She hesitated.

"Go on." Myrna insisted.

"The hanging woman's eyes were open, and she seemed to be staring right at me. Fortunately, Alexander was there to carry me home after I fainted and hit my head."

"Is that the mark I see there?" Myrna asked, pointing to the scar from the fall.

"Yes."

"Tell me more. What else?"

"She had kicked off one of her shoes and there was a knife deep in her thigh. It held a note that read witch!

Suddenly Myrna's facial expression changed completely and even her body became more rigid, which alarmed Isabell.

"Are you alright, Myrna? You've become pale." Myrna didn't answer but just stared at Isabell in fright, it seemed. "Myrna, what's wrong with you? I can stop talking about it if it upsets you."

"I have to go, Isabell." Myrna said quickly.

"What's wrong?"

"I have to leave!" she repeated with a sterner voice.

"Myrna, I don't know what's…"

Myrna didn't let her finish. She got up from the chair and proceeded swiftly to the door. Before she closed the door behind her, she said with a quivering voice, "Let me know if you're in need of anything." Then, the door closed, and Isabell was alone in her room again.

She wondered why Myrna behaved in such a manner just then but couldn't come up with an answer. She was also too weak and tired to even speculate.

The truth of the matter was that it was in fact a moment of reflection that created such strong emotions from Myrna; nothing else. From Isabell's description of the dead witch, memories of the past rushed through Myrna's mind, which made her run out of the cabin in haste after leaving Isabell's room and stopped for no one asking what the matter was. She kept running until she found herself alone in the wilderness with thoughts of buried secrets that could never be revealed for so many reasons.

The Witch of Brentwood

*****

A rapid knocking at Isabell's bedroom door sounded desperate and alarmed her greatly. She sprung up in a seated position in her bed wondering if someone had gotten badly hurt. Before she could respond to the knock and invite whomever the frantic person was, the door swung quickly open revealing her mother standing in the doorway with a look of terrible concern in her face.

"What is it, mother?" Isabell asked with great urgency.

Amelia's desperate expression suddenly changed to a look of relief as she exhaled a deep sigh and said, "Oh dear me! I thought something was surely wrong with you. The way Myrna ran out of your room made me think the worst of your condition. Are you alright, child? You seem no worse than you were."

"I'm alright, mother, just a little shaken up by your knocking so alarmingly."

Isabell rearranged herself back into a lying position in bed and tried with some success to contain herself from her elevated heart rate. Before Amelia approached her, she closed the door gently behind her in a way that was in direct contrast to the way she opened it. But this gentleness made Isabell feel a little better.

Amelia picked up the chair that was in the corner of the room and moved it closer to the bed where she sat next to Isabell, as the poor girl's cough had resumed to its full measure.

Once seated near her daughter's bed, she asked her, "Why did Myrna run out of your room? What happened that made her dart out of the cabin with such urgency; such fright?"

"I really don't know, mother."

"What did you talk about?"

Isabell hesitated, then finally said, "I know it's wrong and I know you'll be disappointed at the very least in me."

"What is it, child?"

"The subject of my night terrors arose. She wanted to know the details of my dreams and why I sometimes scream in my sleep."

Amelia tried to control a look that became grimmer, being careful to not upset Isabell any more than she was. "Isabell, you know no good can come from such discourse."

"Yes, I know and I'm sorry."

"What was said that made her escape in such fashion?"

"I only described what I see in my dreams; the eyes, the bare foot, the blood from the knife the note was attached to…"

"Perhaps all this talk of evil frightened her out of the poor girl's wits." her mother said.

"I don't know. I only know I shouldn't have revealed my dreams to such detail."

"Yes. Some things are better left inside ourselves and try to pretend they never happened. That's the best way to recover from trauma, I'm afraid. Also, I've told you in no uncertain terms that such evil should not be the topic of discussion in this home or anywhere else where evil may present its ugly face."

"I know. Will God forgive me, mother?"

"Of course he will, child. Think no more of it." Amelia replied as she cooled her daughter's forehead with a damp cloth.

"That feels wonderful, mother."

"Yes."

"I should have done this moments ago." Isabell said.

"But you were asleep, Isabell."

At that, Amelia and her daughter looked at each other for what seemed to be forever without saying a word. The mere thought that Isabell might have been awake during her lovemaking with Clement in the other room, destroyed her insides. Her face must have shown the guilt of her decision to have sex for personal gain, but she hoped to perhaps come up with an excuse for the moans and other noises if she had to. *Perhaps Isabell is still too young to fully understand what was taking place in the next room, if she indeed had not been sleeping.* Unfortunately, Isabell's facial expression had also changed with a characteristic of its own; a change that revealed the truth. There was no real doubt at that moment. The secret had been revealed and there was nothing left to do but discuss it openly, woman to woman.

"So...you *were* awake?" Amelia asked, hoping her daughter would be clueless as to what her mother was referring to.

"Yes I was." Isabell said quietly and with a level of trepidation.

"Isabell..."

"Mother, you don't have to explain."

"What did you hear?"

Isabell hesitated to answer but realized there were consequences for not being honest. Finally, she replied, "You and Clement were making love in your bedroom." This admission seemed to bring about a renewed coughing episode from Isabell.

As the coughs persisted for a time, Amelia had a chance to reflect on the reality of her situation. She now found herself in a situation where she had to admit her intentions where Clement was concerned. There had been no prior romantic interest from either of them towards one another. This Isabell knew well. It, therefore, appeared to be obvious there was another motive behind the sudden sexual interest. Amelia wondered if her daughter could possibly understand the dire situation they were in financially, and a means of rectifying that situation with only a small loss of a mother's dignity with her daughter.

Amelia gazed out the bedroom window for a while wishing she were miles away and years in the past as well; a time when the twins were young, innocent, and playing war in the fields. The sky was blue with only a hint of puffy clouds. The wind made the tree leaves move slightly so as to not disturb the tiniest of insects that might have been crawling or resting. The sound of farm animals and fowl gave an impression of the day being a perfectly normal day to any person without a care. But these sensations were only for *other* people to enjoy, not Amelia who was now daydreaming to escape the reality of embarrassment or fear of losing respect from a daughter who until then, looked up to her with the greatest of admiration.

The coughing passed temporarily which brought Amelia back to the present where life was not as simple as when her twins were young. She looked in her daughter's eyes and immediately began to cry; partly because of the guilt she felt, but also partly because her daughter should not have been exposed to such lewd behavior from anyone, much less her own mother.

Upon seeing her mother cry, Isabell repositioned herself in bed to be able to reach out and take her mother in her arms. Her shoulder became wet with her mother's tears as she felt her mother heave heavily and shudder with the realization of what she'd done. Finally, Amelia was able to contain herself to where she and Isabell could talk further.

The conversation was honest and open, which was something Isabell didn't expect from her mother. The surprise of her mother's candidness and womanly desires gave Isabell the motivation she needed to be as candid with her mother as well about her *own* desires. She was honest about how she felt when she'd heard them through the much-too-thin wall; not wanting to hear, but at the same time wanting to hear more as the sounds of lovemaking were enticing and aroused her curiosity. Amelia, for her part, didn't admit to any pleasure but emphasized a woman's need to do what has to be done in order to survive under difficult circumstances; be they financial or otherwise.

Much was said. Much was admitted. Much was revealed. It is fair to say that Amelia learned as much about Isabell as Isabell learned from Amelia. Both were truthful, and apart from little white lies here and there to protect the smallest sense of dignity, mother and daughter became closer as a result. Their honesty was contrary to the opinion that being too honest can be as harmful as a hungry wolf in a sheepfold. Mother and daughter, hence, became as friends.

The heart-to-heart was drawing to a close when both were in agreement that no mention of any of their personal conversation should ever leave Isabell's room. Amelia was the first to make the suggestion.

"I shall speak none of this to anyone. I hope you remain steadfast." Amelia said.

"I swear to never speak of it on a firm condition." Isabell returned with a smile.

"You willful child!" replied her mother, playfully. "Do you dare defy your own mother's wishes?" They laughed, but the laughter caused Isabell a good amount of chest pain, which was obvious to both women. "Oh, you poor, poor child."

"I'm earnest, mother. I'd like something if you're willing." Isabell said after she was able to compose herself from the pain.

"What is it, Isabell? Name it, and it shall be yours."

"I should like grandfather's brooch."

"Why should you want such an old thing as that?"

"Grandfather told you it possessed special powers."

"Why, you don't believe that for one moment, do you?"

"I would believe anything that can make this illness go away. I shall cherish it as *your* mother did and keep it always as a reminder of our bond."

Amelia smiled, reached in her apron pocket, and retrieved the brooch which had been so dear to her. The giving of the brooch to Isabell would become a symbol of their mutual trust from that moment on. She handed it to Isabell, who closed her fingers tightly around it to keep and cherish, as one would welcome a lost sheep that made its way back to the fold.

The Witch of Brentwood

*****

As Isabell and her mother were involved in their candid discussion, Myrna was walking alone in a nearby field to reflect on why she was compelled to run out of Isabell's room in such fashion.

Clement Arington loved his daughter, Myrna. She was always his little girl and whenever she had any problems, she could run to him to solve it. In fact, he was the only one she *could* come to for help or to confide in, since her mother wasn't able to give advice or guidance with any confidence. Her poor mother, Adella Arington, suffered from a condition that would come to be known as a dissociative disorder centuries later. There were some in the village who knew Adella was 'mad', but they kept their distance and spoke nothing of it. Some thought the 'madness' was the devil's work, including her husband, but Myrna loved her for who she was and not for her 'odd' behavior.

Adella was not able to maintain good hygiene and sometimes laughed or spoke to herself out loud, which gave her the appearance of being a wild animal. This embarrassed Clement. He was also afraid of the evil that lurked inside her. Beating the behavior out of her was a regular routine; sometimes striking her in the face or arms and legs with his open hand and fist. But mostly, he hit her anywhere in the torso, for that was most likely where the evil resided and caused the most harm. When this happened, Myrna would run and hide to avoid seeing and hearing the terrible beatings perpetrated on her mother. She felt bad for her but also realized that her father knew what was best. *If the evil spirits can be beaten out, so much the better.* Adella never went out into the village nor did anyone come by to visit, so her bruises were never incriminating proof of wrongdoing. In fact, even if her bruises were ever exposed to a reasonably rational individual, one would certainly understand the reasoning behind those beatings as being proactive against evil possession.

Something happened one day when the sky was covered with dark gray clouds and there was an eerie silence outside. The normal sounds of chickens clucking and of dogs barking were almost completely lacking, which gave a hollow feeling of dread to any sane person. One could hear the rustling of the leaves that swayed back and forth, totally enslaved by the wind that made Myrna shiver from cold and fear. On that day, Adella's 'madness' was so horrific that the town clergy was brought in for an exorcism. Myrna had heard of such a thing at church services, but always thought it was a practice best reserved for people who were on the brink of being damned for eternity. Never had she thought her own mother would be subject to such an existential condition. The ceremonial practice went on for what seemed like hours until all that could be done, was done. Adella was finally so exhausted from the ritual that lethargy overtook her, and a deep state of sleep soon followed.

After that, the men took their leave of her and went outside to discuss further strategies and a new hope for victory over evil. As the men were talking, Myrna walked towards them, keeping her distance to the point where she could overhear what they were saying. Approaching too closely was to be avoided at all cost lest the reverend saw evil in *her* and decided on performing an exorcism in kind for the benefit of her own salvation as well. She felt such fright when the reverend asked about Adella's bruises but felt even more fear when she heard her father lie;

making up stories about self-inflicted wounds and throwing herself against walls and fences. *Lying is a sin and there's already enough evil to contend with.* But soon the reverend was on his way, and both had renewed hope, so Myrna felt much better about the future of things and her mother.

However, Myrna remembered that day vividly for the rest of her life. As bad as it was to have her mother exposed to such an exorcism ritual and the torment that it brought not only to her mother but to herself as well, it was a day to celebrate. Seeing her mother in pain from the restraints and suffering from what seemed to be torture, was scarring for a child her age, to be sure. But a necessary evil must come to pass if all is to be well again. She remembered praying hard to the Almighty for her mother to be freed from the evil. She remembered hearing her father and the reverend praying in the name of Jesus for God to save her soul whether she survived or not and that everyone else be spared such a fate. She remembered her mother screaming and wriggling like a wounded animal while the men held her down with make-shift restraints like towels and blankets. But most of all, she remembered how traumatized and helpless she felt during the ritual. All the while they were performing the exorcism, she wanted them to stop. But as much as she wanted them to stop, she also recalled when her mother, in a fit of her 'madness', tried to hurt her with a broken bottle, not realizing that she might have killed her own daughter. So Myrna, even at such a young age, was able to reason that all of this torment was for her mother's own good. She wanted her mother to be normal again, so the beatings and all other measures for curing her would stop.

A few days after all the painstaking effort to make her well again, it wasn't long that Clement and his daughter realized Adella's condition hadn't changed. The evil 'madness' was still with her and in the home. There was no choice but to cope with Adella's behavior, and the attempt to beat the evil out of her, soon resumed at its normal pace. Clement, beating his wife to save her life, became more and more determined to administer punishment with greater conviction. So, the abuse intensified.

Myrna vividly remembered the day her mother died by his hands. It's true, the evil had to be beaten out of her mother come what may, even if the beatings should bring about terrible consequences of physical harm or perhaps worse. As it happened on a particularly quiet and overcast morning, Adella was in no small measure afflicted by her disorder more than usual; seeing pigs in her bedroom wanting to harm her, smelling foul scents from supposed defecation in her broom closet, eating dirt to nurse a few rotting teeth that were more painful than other days, talking, screaming, and cursing at people she thought sure were there in her midst but not at all seen by Clement or her crying daughter.

Being witness to such 'madness', Myrna knew what was inevitably coming next and was nowhere to be found in the vicinity of the beatings that took place, but still remembered that day and what happened. She was outside trying hard to not hear the beatings that were going on inside. She did notice, however, one of her neighbors going towards their cabin where the beatings were taking place to spy through their window. The neighbor, a widow by the name of Mrs. Helston, undoubtedly heard commotion that Myrna tried hard to block out of her ears with each hand. It was likely that the neighbor heard shrieks and cries of pain and terror, which were loud enough and terrible enough to justify her curiosity, as well as grave concern for someone's well-being. Myrna watched her neighbor grow pale with fright, bringing both hands to her mouth in disbelief; or perhaps it was to suppress her own gasps as she watched the murder through the window. Myrna wasn't sure which. Perhaps it was both.

When Mrs. Helston ran back to her home not five hundred feet away, she ran with a shriek of her own, crying bloody murder which alerted other neighbors to the unknown horror she had witnessed. That's when Clement ran out the door and called to Myrna to come home.

Myrna was still far off and running toward the cabin when she cried out, "Father, what happened?"

"Come here child!" he yelled.

As she finally reached him, he was resolute to not allow her to go in the cabin for fear of seeing her mother lying dead on the floor, bleeding from the nose, mouth, and ears.

He continued, "Something terrible's happened!"

"What is it, father?" she cried with fright in her eyes and tears running their course down the sides of her face, which had become bright red from running and fear.

Clement fabricated a quick story, which was plausible to this young girl and served his purpose well. He spoke frantically, "The devil was finally beaten and had taken his leave of your mother, but Mrs. Helston killed her directly with a most hostile stare from the window! It was a hex from that evil witch that killed your mother instantly!" He pointed inside the cabin, "Your poor mother is lying there dead! Now, that witch may well run off and place blame on us for killing your poor mother, but we need to stop her before more harm is brought down upon us!"

Myrna tried hard to get past her father to go inside and see if indeed her mother's life was taken away by this young, and if truth be told, beautiful neighbor. But Clement stopped her before she could get by him.

"Father, I need to see mother!" she cried.

"A lot of good it'll do to see your mother lying dead on the floor in no great measure! We must denounce Mrs. Helston as a witch before she takes her evil elsewhere or even perhaps here in this home again!"

Just then, a crowd began to gather a little further down the road around Mrs. Helston to find out the matter of the commotion.

"We must go there 'fore she elects to bring condemnation down upon *me* for this brutal attack!" he cried to Myrna.

"But she's so beautiful, father!"

"Do you doubt your own father? Do you not trust your own father, as your lifeless mother's body lies inside there?"

"No!" she answered with all loyalty.

"Then, come!"

He grabbed her hand and began to run towards the crowd, which had grown to a multitude around Mrs. Helston.

It must be noted here that a multitude of people may conceivably constitute a mob given the proper motivation to be such. Fear of evil and damnation, odd behavior, miscarriages, an untimely and mysterious death of one's husband, fascination with birds, building artifacts out of clay or mud, and so much more, were all reasons for the aforementioned motivation. A hysterical young girl having witnessed the murder of her mother at the hands of a neighboring witch was also enough to make the crowd wonder; a wonder that fueled the fire stirring within the mob-to-be, as they heard the accusations from father and daughter of the poor murdered woman.

Contrary to what the crowd heard and saw, was the story told by Mrs. Helston which didn't seem very convincing. *If Mr. Arington beat his wife to death, wouldn't the young girl fear her murderous father?* It seemed more likely and logical to any sane person that this widow was a witch.

Then, someone asked the question.

"What shall we do with her, this witch?"

Clement cried out in kind, "She must be hanged!"

At that, the mob cried out in agreement and was convinced the righteous act had to be carried out immediately. Clement was sure to have Myrna stay with a good Samaritan neighbor until the deed was done and he had time to take care of the body that he used to call his wife.

It was years later that Myrna had overheard her father talking to a client about the witch's demise on that fateful day; how he helped string her up on that oak tree and then planted a note that read 'witch' on her thigh with his buck knife.

Myrna had been living with that realization about her father most of her life. She had come to terms with what needed to be done and her contribution to that end; her contribution to that fateful day. However, this was something that absolutely should not be shared with Isabell or her family; much less Alexander for fear of jeopardizing their relationship, which was so dear to her.

Never in her life had she ever imagined the trauma her accusations and her father's actions could have caused to someone she had gotten to know, and in Alexander's case, had grown to love.

Chapter 5

The summer days were hot with clear blue skies most of the time. It rained often enough to irrigate the crops, but not too much to muddy the ground. The daily walks in the fields that Alexander and Isabell played in as children were now routine for Alexander and Myrna. Their relationship blossomed amid the secret Myrna kept tight-lipped about, concerning her and her father's involvement in the death of the hanging woman some eight years prior. They enjoyed each other's company, walking hand in hand and sometimes making love; albeit with the fear of being discovered as knowingly committing a sin out of wedlock against God. But it was obvious they had a relationship that was more than professional. They didn't fear being recognized as being romantically involved, but they made sure to not give any hint of committing any sin that could have them removed from the church. Acquaintances who knew better, however, did not approve of their relationship.

It also seemed there was disapproval of Clement and Amelia being together as well. Both relationships were well known and established within the family, but Clement's reputation gave the rest of the local folk reason to wonder why Amelia would allow such a man to enter their home. Because after the hanging of the woman eight years prior, there was an inquiry concerning whether Clement had told the truth about the witch or whether he had lied and indeed had killed his wife instead of the neighbor.

Still, Clement and Amelia were now married. It was an arrangement that seemed the logical and convenient thing to do. Regardless of what others thought, Amelia was okay with being a wife. As far as Clement was concerned, he was okay with having a wife again. The benefits outweighed the burden of being alone to raise a family and maintain a home. It was a that point in time when Clement sold the old home on the north end of town and moved into the Whitlock home with Myrna.

The wedding was private, simple, and happened quickly. There was no need for invitations, nor was there any want for wedding guests. If it were up to Clement, there wouldn't have been a wedding ceremony at all, but one had to be wary of what people talked about in town. Any unmarried couple living together was fodder for rumors of wrongdoing, and God-forbid their union produced offspring who would undoubtedly be considered spawns of Satan.

The union of Clement and Amelia was also problematic for Alexander and Myrna, since they were now considered siblings by anyone familiar with their new family structure. It mattered not if they weren't blood relatives. Just the mere fact that they were now brother and sister through a witnessed holy ceremony in the presence of Almighty God was incriminating enough to be denounced as the devil's work. Mumblings, rumors, and accusations soon found their way through the village.

Feeding this frenzy was Isabell's condition. Consumption was an illness that was considered extremely dangerous, justifiably. The normal progression of the illness almost without exception led many to their graves even if one found it difficult to believe such a fate could possibly befall them or their loved ones. The unfortunate truth was that everyone including family and Isabell herself expected her condition to deteriorate, but the very opposite occurred. Her coughs ceased dramatically, her body temperature gradually inched its way back to normalcy, and the chest pains that were so debilitating abated with the passing of days. This reversal was most uncommon in those afflicted with consumption, but Isabell seemed to be the exception to its seemingly inevitable fate. Isabell sometimes joked with her mother about the power of her grandfather's brooch, which was now hers to keep. She joked that it was the brooch, with its very special power, that restored her back to health. She knew it was an absurd thought, of course, but in the back of her mind she wondered if there was something special about that brooch after all.

She grew stronger in a matter of days from when she had a heart-to-heart talk with her mother and received the brooch to keep. Her appetite not only got back to normal, but took on a robust and fervent nature that, up to that point, Isabell had never experienced. The thought of beans roasting, and boiling duck made her salivary glands turn into fountains whose flowing waters were hard to contain within the confines of her mouth. Her long brown-reddish hair regained its sheen and luster, once again easy to maintain and fashion. The color in her face and eyes became more radiant, and she appeared to have lost the frailty trait she was cursed with at birth because of the body weight she had regained from her recovery.

All these changes were alarming to the town folk, given the circumstances and the usual fate of the illness. *How could she recover from such an illness as consumption when all others suffer a most unfortunate fate? What powers does she possess to escape its effects of doom? Is there an unnatural power at work? Is that the devil's teat on her neck; the mark by which Satan makes his pact with the living? And what about the parents' approval of their incestuous children?* These were questions at work in people's minds that quickly became the rumor mill of the town. To say there was potential danger to the new Arington family was not only based in truth, it also became evident that something needed to be done; something drastic and even life-changing in order to escape the anticipation of being accused of witchcraft or of being bewitched, which was just as devastating to the community.

Then came the news of a sixty-year-old woman named Bridget Bishop who was hanged on June the 10th of that year where they lived in Salem. Amelia had heard rumors of people being tried and punished for being accused of being witches or delving into such things as magic, crossing over, spirits of the afterlife, and other abominations. These incidents had happened across the ocean but up until that moment, they were only rumors in the mainland, not executable offenses. Even if the rumors were true, they weren't events sanctioned by officials of the church and court, as was the case eight years ago with the woman Isabell had found hanging from a tree. It was later reported that that woman was feared to be a witch and it was safer for a woman with her evil behavior to be removed than risk contamination among the residents of the colony. They were simply scattered incidents of hate or unwarranted accusations; until now.

Given everything that had recently happened with the family and now the church getting involved in the solutions of witchcraft accusations, the prudent thing to do according to Clement and Amelia, was to move away from the town to a place where they were unknown. A new family just moving into a small town where the community hadn't heard about Isabell's consumption and recovery, as well as the romantic relationship between brother and sister who had become such by their parents' lawful marriage, would undoubtedly be welcomed. The prospect of being welcomed as newcomers and escaping the inevitable accusations that were sure to manifest if they stayed in Salem, was more than enough to convince the new Arington family to move away.

In a short time, it was decided that Clement would move the family to a town called Brentwood in the Colony of New Hampshire, where witch accusations in Salem were just rumors, where birthmarks were not some kind of tool used by supernatural forces, and where one could live without fear of being accused by a child and sentenced to death for the sake of relief from paranoia.

Clement had the means. He had inherited a reasonable sum from his father, as well as having accumulated a comfortable nest egg from his labors. He also knew people with noble ties and could negotiate the purchase of land with the best of them. Clement was as insensitive as he was shrewd. So much so that in anticipation of the move, he had been working on having an old widower evicted from his home which was the perfect size home for the Arington family. The old widower's crime to warrant eviction was delinquency in attending church services as well as keeping his home in disrepair according to the local magistrate;

someone whom Clement knew very well and owed him a favor from past transactions.

Arriving at the *decision* to move to Brentwood was not as easy as the original *idea* of moving. Ideas are easy to talk about and the prospect of moving may even be exciting but the concepts of ideas to final decisions, are worlds apart. There were many obstacles to overcome and many other factors to consider.

Many times, it seemed that moving was not a good plan at all, since there were so many details to think about. The mere thought of leaving the old cabin in Salem often became exhausting, making them all wonder if they were overreacting to the rumors about them. It was often considered that perhaps the evil things they *thought* they'd heard about themselves might have been false, or at the very least, exaggerated. But the truth of the matter was that the rumors got worse and even led to witchcraft accusations from one or two elderly ladies in the community who they, themselves, had been accused of by others. Having been accused themselves, these ladies' accusations of the Aringtons held little credibility. Still, the accusations of witchcraft spread like wildfire since the sanctioned hanging of Bridget Bishop occurred, and too many poor souls accused of questionable looks or behavior, were locked up or killed. The Aringtons soon realized that if this witch hunt process could lead to condemning seemingly innocent people, it could conceivably affect them as well; even to the point of being killed by the very church officials they depended on for protection from such evil.

The announcement of Bridget Bishop's hanging also intensified Isabell's nightmares. Her screams in the night were enough to awaken a good portion of the neighboring population from their sleep and make them shake from fear as well. Some began to wonder if the screams were the result of a possessed soul from that cabin where unexplained healings were happening, and incest was rampant. *What else could it be but the evil possession of a witch?* All the while, Myrna knew where those screams came from and why. She knew they came from a frightened young woman whose nightmares were the direct result of her and her father's actions years before.

It soon came to pass that living among those people in Salem was extremely dangerous and there was no other decision to be made but to leave while leaving was still a possible option.

Réal Carpentier

*****

There was much to do in so little time. The men and women were extremely hard at work to get everything in order, and ready for the move; sometimes working through the night hours. Much was sacrificed for the sake of not having to move too many items. Some furniture, keepsakes, and such had to be left behind. Funds were also short in abundance. Some of Amelia's possessions were given away if they couldn't be sold, and some cattle and firewood was sold to the highest bidder. But Isabell never entertained the thought of parting with her grandfather's brooch. She wore it on a chain around her neck and kept it hidden from Clement for fear of his wanting to sell it. That brooch, she thought, was more valuable than money. And as difficult as it was to perform all the necessary moving arrangements discreetly lest they incriminate themselves by 'running away' to not suffer death through a tribunal decree, the family was able to maintain a low enough profile to not arouse any suspicions.

It was at this time that Amelia, Isabell, and Alexander became very dependent on Clement, as his daughter Myrna was. Clement, after all, owned the obligatory wagon that would carry all of the possessions from one cabin to the next. He was also well-organized enough to delegate and make the best of time management in order to carry out the move as expeditiously as possible. He seemed and was considered a trust-worthy individual who could carry out such an impossible task as moving an entire family and possessions within the short time they had.

It took approximately ten days from the time they started packing, to the time they were ready to make the move. In that time, many neighboring families loved to snoop because even though the Aringtons did most of the packing inside the cabin and tried hard to remain inconspicuous about the move, suspicious activities here and there were observed by passersby. Cordwood was being moved, some horses were sold, and other obvious activity was taking place. There were many who took the opportunity to mumble accusations and other derogatory comments under their breath, which caught Isabell's ears at times. She ignored this at first and tried her best to not be affected by such ignorance and malicious intent, but it soon angered her.

It happened one day when a young lady was walking by the Arington cabin with her father, since no one took the chance of walking near the place alone for fear of the evil that dwelt within. Isabell was sitting outside on the porch at the time mending a garment when the young lady spoke loud enough to be heard by Isabell.

"Look father, there's the witch that overpowered her terminal illness. She must be the one who screams in the night."

The young lady's father tried hard to not be embarrassed and was somewhat afraid of the comment his daughter had just made. Isabell looked up from her mending and stared at the young lady. The two girls looked into each other's eyes with glaring hatred.

Still looking into Isabell's eyes with contempt, she continued.

"She has the devil's teat on her neck, and it appears it's been used many times over."

"How dare you!" shouted Isabell

This made the young lady's father look at Isabell. It was indeed the devil's teat that he saw on Isabell's neck. It couldn't be anything other than the physical evidence needed to establish her as a witch and allow the church officials to carry out whatever sentence deemed necessary to rid the town of such evil.

"Mind your evil tongue!" the young lady's father replied, "Some of your fellow witches have been locked up with less evidence to work with. You, on the other hand, have plenty of proof working against you!"

"Yes," continued his daughter, "your devil deeds would have you locked up in short order!"

"My devil deeds?" returned Isabell.

"Yes, your devil deeds, and your supernatural cures, and your incestuous family, and God knows what else!" the young lady replied.

This infuriated Isabell. She put down the garment she was mending on the table beside her bench and stood up without breaking her stare from the young lady's eyes. Then she took a step forward, tightly clutching the brooch that hung around her neck. She was lost for words that could damn both of them to eternal hell but had plenty of hurtful thoughts. Her face was red, and her eyes were on fire as she focused those eyes onto the young lady's father.

What followed next was as much a shocking surprise to Isabell as it was for the harassing couple not fifty feet away. The father suddenly had blurred vision in one eye and began to feel a numbness in his face and his left arm. He tried to speak but his words were garbled and hard to understand. Then in a matter of seconds, he lost his balance and fell to the ground, hitting his head on a rock in much the same way as Isabell had so many years before.

The frightened young lady tended to him as best she could, but he remained unresponsive. She screamed for help, as Isabell just stood and stared. People started to gather and lend assistance, including Clement, Amelia, and the rest of the family save for Isabell who stood, still holding her brooch and watching; watching as people hurried to the man's aid, knowing full well there wasn't anything anyone could do.

This was the first incident that gave Isabell confidence in the magic brooch. She feared it was the devil's work at times but was also comforted by the notion that it could be used for good. But it was now clear to her that her family should move away as soon as possible, for there were too many reasons why she and perhaps anyone of her family might be considered dangerous.

*****

The move to Brentwood was a harsh reality for Isabell and Alexander. They were leaving behind all they knew as children and young adults, and everything of the old cabin in Salem was familiar to them which gave them comfort. But these were desperate times and they had to adjust to the new location, the new home, and all of its unknowns. Before they left Salem, however, Isabell wanted something to remember the old homestead by. The only thing she could think of that wouldn't get stolen or die, was an acorn. It had fallen from the oak tree that the witch was hanged from so many years before. Perhaps in some small way, she thought, it was her way of paying homage to the poor woman. She took it and kept it in her little trinket box. It would travel to Brentwood with her.

The new home in Brentwood was a place of Clement's choosing. He knew the family had enough confidence in him and he took the opportunity to make the proper decisions. It was hard especially for Alexander to adjust because until very recently, he had been the man of the family. Still, he knew his place and was happy enough to be with the beautiful Myrna.

The new cabin was a little bit larger than the one they had just left and stood on more land. The disrepair left by the previous owner was nothing that couldn't be fixed with a little time and the combined know-how of Clement and Alexander. A leaky roof, broken windows, as well as loose floorboards and steps were some of the repairs needed to be done. But once the work was prioritized, the repairs would be well on their way.

The women were amazed at the amount of space in the kitchen and the bedrooms. Gone were the days of sleeping in make-shift beds to accommodate everyone, and the dinner table was big enough to allow all to dine together. The decor needed work but the creative minds of the three women were already at work. Amelia had taken some of the curtains from the old cabin in Salem just to add something familiar to the new home. Isabell worked in the bedroom that would be shared between her and Myrna. The proper arrangement of furniture, after all, was paramount to the coziness of a bedroom. For her part, Myrna got familiar with the kitchen and acquainted herself with where to put utensils, silverware, and the like. All in all, it was going to be a nice place in which to live and most importantly, they wouldn't have to worry about people knowing the history of accusations against the family.

As much as it was a larger dwelling than what they were used to, it was a humble home in a nice neighborhood. Merchants were scattered about here and there on most days trying to make a marginal living by selling their wares. The kids of the neighborhood played in the fields as Alexander and Isabell used to when they were young, and nowhere were there any indications of people being hanged or accused of practicing witchcraft.

The climate seemed a little cooler than in Salem, but not by much; mostly influenced by what seemed to be a cooler steady breeze. The women certainly had to dress a bit warmer for the time of year, but the men didn't notice much of a difference in temperature since their function was mainly manual labor that made them wish it was cooler still.

Everyone was busy with the new home, whether it was the men planning and prioritizing what to repair next or it was the women planning and prioritizing what needed to be done for this new dwelling to become a home, for it certainly didn't seem to be at their arrival. But all were determined to make it work because the alternative was to stay in Salem and suffer all of the consequences it would bring.

As everyone was busy taking care of their priorities, Isabell was doing the same; hanging up home-made curtains, cleaning the walls and floor of any cobwebs left behind by the old widower, and generally making sure the new home was a reflection of her decorative flair. It was during these busy moments that she allowed herself to daydream as she was so used to doing since becoming a young woman and even more so after recovering from her illness.

She thought about this illness of hers that left so many dead, yet found herself not only alive but thriving in physical strength, motivation, and alertness. She tried to reason as best she could as to why she was spared and more importantly how it was physically possible but could not find any reasonable answers. All she had was her faith and that was enough for her. Yet she was still troubled by what happened to the young lady's father when they harassed her from afar just before the move. She had wished the man dead as she clutched her brooch in anger, and by some strange coincidence the father collapsed, and the word was that he didn't survive. *How could faith explain this anger?* Her anger to the point of causing death (if she indeed was the cause of it), had nothing to do with her faith, but rather some internal evil that she could not suppress at the time of the incident.

I hope the reader will now forgive the author and allow him the privilege of stepping out of the seventeenth century for a moment and fast forward to more contemporary times in order to speculate as to what might have happened to Isabell on a more scientific level than was available at that period of time.

There is some truth to the notion that we carry certain traits of our ancestors through DNA and whatever other chemical or footprint is passed down through family generations. It's very conceivable that one of Isabell's great, great, great grandparents suffered a miserable and terrible event. Perhaps even suffered a lifetime of anguish, poverty, disease, or maybe some kind of treatment that made them feel subhuman as in the treatment of the victims of the holocaust. Is it possible that she carried some DNA of someone in her past who felt enough anger to warrant vengeance at any cost, even if it meant for someone else to die for their pain? One might believe that this is a distinct possibility. If this is true, Isabell's anger for wanting someone to die to avenge her own humiliation might have been a result of an internal reaction from long ago. The notion that our makeup is the culmination of generations past, has merit; traits that are good and some that are not so good. It's up to us to try to suppress the not-so-good tendencies and build on the positive attributes gifted to us by our ancestors with all of their talents and faults. Isabell didn't have this information to work with and improve on. If she had, her anger might have been more in control and the young lady's father might have been spared a fatal stroke; *if* the brooch and Isabell's wish for his death had anything to do with the whole incident, that is.

Her recovery from consumption was most likely due to the basic principle in the treatment of pulmonary tuberculosis which is rest; that is rest of the lung or lungs infected and not so much rest for the patient. At the height of Isabell's illness, her infected lung may have collapsed, which in effect created a restorative condition known today as pneumothorax treatment. Her collapsed lung was at rest allowing the connected tissues to contract and bring the cavity walls closer together, which facilitated healing. Eventually the collapsed lung healed itself and became functional again, restoring normal breathing and resulted in reduced coughing.

As mentioned previously, this is all mere speculation on the part of the author. It's also very possible that there are no scientific explanations and that the incidents were in fact supernatural phenomena brought about by unknown powers. The fact that she recovered from a collapsed lung with more robust energy and improved physical attributes cannot be explained scientifically (at least not by this author), which leaves much to the imagination of those more inclined to believe in the power of the brooch.

Chapter 6

In the autumn of that year, the family had been in their new home for three and a half months and by that time, almost everything was repaired and arranged in a way that finally felt comfortable to them. The roof no longer leaked, the drafty windows were replaced, the rooms were properly decorated and felt cozy as a home bedroom should. There was even time to build a new fence for livestock and a small shed for firewood before the winter months arrived.

The fact that Clement and Amelia were still strangers when they were married wasn't cause for alarm. Marriage was always warranted when it was the convenient thing to do for financial or other important reasons. But eventually, the reality of living together and sharing a life becomes inevitable and the consequences of committing to a lifetime with a total stranger catch up with you. Such was the case between Clement and Amelia.

Clement had a chance to meet with some old and new contacts at the local tavern to discuss possible handyman employment opportunities. These rendezvous became more frequent and soon became meetings on a regular basis; not so much for the original reason of connecting with potential employers, but mostly to indulge in drinking in abundance. He was very successful at both since the offers began pouring in almost as frequently as the whiskey poured into his belly.

It soon became normal to have Clement walk in the cabin late at night heavily intoxicated and bursting with fury over nothing in particular. Everyone's new way of life with Clement involved putting up with fits of his rage that sometimes seemed they could escalate to physical violence. Alexander had to step into the middle of potential assaults more than once, which enraged Clement all the more. But still, he did what he had to do to avoid physical harm to his mother and sister. As far as Myrna was concerned, she had been used to seeing her father in all kinds of emotional states and she knew when it was time to stay away. As a matter of concern for her, however, she didn't like it when Alexander would get in her father's way for fear of having either one of them hurt. This state of living on eggshells around a drunken Clement got progressively worse and it was only a matter of time before threats became actual assaults.

A sober Clement was articulate, worked hard, and became the sole provider of the family. In fact, he was away most of the time, making him pretty much estranged from Amelia for the most part. In contrast, a drunken Clement was an aggressive, incoherent individual whose presence was feared and hated by everyone in the family including Myrna who stayed away but quietly wished *he* would go away. Among other obnoxious and sometimes dangerous atrocities this Clement would cause, Amelia still had to put up with his demands for carnal romps in the bedroom before nodding off into oblivion for the night. This, she hated most of all.

The Witch of Brentwood

It happened one night that Clement came home earlier than usual and drunk as usual. Alexander, having gone with Myrna to take a long walk down by the stream near the meadow in the village, had left Amelia and Isabell alone; not knowing they would be at the mercy of a drunken and angry Clement who at once upon entering, demanded his supper. This was the women's cue to jump and prepare something to eat. As they worked, Clement sat in his favorite chair and immediately caught a glimpse of something shiny around Isabell's neck.

"What ya got there?" he asked with a slur.

Both women looked at him in wonder.

"Where?" asked Amelia.

"Not you, you ugly sow. That one." he said, pointing to Isabell.

"Me?" Isabell asked.

"Yah. What you got there 'round that pretty neck of yours?"

Isabell suddenly realized what Clement was referring to and brought her hand up to clutch her brooch.

"Oh, this? It's a brooch mother gave me when I was sick." she replied.

"A Brooch? How come I never saw it before?" he asked angrily.

"No reason. I wasn't trying to hide it from you. Why should it interest you?"

"Because we could've sold it before we moved. You knew we needed the money."

"I couldn't have sold this. It's a present from mother and it's very old and priceless and I love it."

"It's a useless piece that we could have traded for something useful. You were trying to keep it from me?"

At that, Clement got up and staggered towards the women.

"Clement, please sit!" shouted Amelia.

But Clement kept coming towards them. He finally reached Isabell and grabbed her wrist to move her hand away from the brooch. She cried in pain as she felt her wrist twisting in his powerful hand. Amelia saw the pain in her daughter's face and tried to stop him, but he was too strong and resolute. He slapped Amelia which made her tumble and fall as he grabbed Isabell's brooch and ripped it from her neck that left a burning mark from the broken chain. The pain immediately reminded her of the dream she had where some faceless individual had ripped her birthmark from her neck with pliers before they tightened a noose around it. Isabell just knelt on the floor and wept.

"There, now it's mine!" Clement shouted at Isabell, as he put the brooch in his pants pocket.

Then he turned and went towards Amelia who had fallen to the floor holding the side of her face. "You should know better than to get in my way!" he said as he picked her up only to beat her as he had done with his 'mad' wife when she was out of control. With every blow to her face and head, he was reliving those moments when the demons who had possessed his wife had to be beaten out of her. Every blow and every cry of pain was more satisfying than the last until she finally fell unconscious to the floor.

"Mother!" cried Isabell.

"Yeah, you take care of each other now." he said, "Never mind about supper. Not hungry anyway."

Having said that, he went into his room for what seemed like thirty seconds. Isabell waited and listened for what he might be doing, while still looking at her mother lying unconscious. Isabell didn't dare move for fear it would make him angrier when he emerged from the room. She didn't hear much but wondered if he might be hiding the brooch. Then he came out again and slowly walked out the door, slamming it behind him.

Isabell immediately ran to her mother's aid. She held her in her arms and rocked her back and forth as her mother had done to her on so many long nights at the height of her illness. Amelia slowly came to and eventually came to the realization of what had happened.

"Are you alright, mother?" Isabell quietly asked with a trembling voice, trying not to alarm her mother to her own fear.

"Yes dear. Is he gone?"

"Yes. He left after you fell unconscious. Oh mother, he's an evil man."

"Don't say that, Isabell. He's been drinking a little much, that's all." Amelia answered, trying to sound convincing.

"Oh, I wish Alexander were here."

"It's alright, dear. He's gone now."

Suddenly, Amelia lifted her hand to gently touch the burn marks on Isabell's neck which had become bright red and noticeable even to a woman half dazed from being knocked out by a heavy fist.

"He took my brooch." cried Isabell. "He pulled and broke the chain off my neck."

"Oh, my poor dear girl."

"What shall we do?"

"I'm not quite sure, dear. I'm not quite sure."

The two women cried together and held each other for comfort and support, not only for the pain they had both suffered by Clement's hands but also because both knew the reality of what life would become, living with an abusive man.

The Witch of Brentwood

*****

Alexander looked up at the blue sky covered with brightness from the hot blinding sun occasionally hidden by a passing cloud. His hands were a pillow under his head as he lay next to Myrna in the thicket away from any passersby. His breathing was returning back to normal and so was hers, but they still felt satisfactorily exhausted from making love. They began to laugh at the prospect of having been able to again get away with unwed carnal pleasures that were so looked down upon by the hypocrites who committed the same sin; perhaps even more frequently than they.

"If mother could see me now..." he joked.

"And my father." she added, laughing.

"Oh no, that must never happen. I would find myself at the mercy of his wrath."

"He's not that bad, Alexander."

"Any man would protect his daughter from predators like me."

"Well, I should come to your rescue directly, then. No one would harm you. Not even my father."

He looked at the beautiful Myrna lying next to him for a moment, and then whispered, "I would suffer any kind of torture by anyone to be with you. One look in your eyes would be enough to cause me to feel no pain."

Overwhelmed with love, Myrna couldn't help but kiss him. It was unusual for her to initiate any kind of intimate move towards him, but his words worked a magic that touched her soul to the point of not being responsible for her own actions. For his part, Alexander didn't mind in the least. Any kind of affection from her regardless of who initiated it, would be welcomed anytime and anywhere as far as he was concerned.

After the kiss, they looked at each other in complete satisfaction and smiled.

"We should get back soon. They'll wonder where we are." she said.

"Let them wonder all they might." he replied. "I have no need to worry about what they may think. I would rather wish to remain here with you forever and stare up at the sky until we make love again." His words made her smile an enormous smile. "See the shape of that cloud over there?" he asked, pointing to a patch that was reflecting off of the river not twenty feet from where they lay.

"Yes." she replied.

"It looks exactly like how I feel at this very moment."

"How do you mean?"

"It's way up in the sky as high as *I* feel right here on this ground because of you. It's displaying its puffy chest because it has so much pride; as much as I have in you. The sun rays are shining through it to show the world how happy it is; as I am happy to have you by my side."

"That's beautiful, Alexander."

He looked back at her and softly said, "I love you."

"And I love *you*." she whispered.

They kissed again with more passion than before. Nothing but love was going through her mind, as she was completely absorbed in him. He, for his part, felt the same.

Suddenly, they heard a rustling nearby which sounded like someone running not far away and perhaps approaching in their direction. Upon hearing this, they immediately hurried to gather

The Witch of Brentwood

their clothes that were strewn about and made a dash away from the on-coming footsteps towards an abundance of trees where they could finish dressing. Hiding behind trees, they made haste to get dressed and waited nonchalantly together to see who the intruder might be. The rustling got louder as the individual got closer and they waited there hoping to be hidden by the trees. Then, they heard a voice crying from a close distance.

"Alexander!" cried the voice.

"Isabell?" shouted Alexander.

"Where are you?" Isabell cried.

"We're here among the pines."

Alexander grabbed Myrna's hand and started running towards the crying Isabell. Myrna could hardly keep up and for his part, Alexander felt weighed down and wished for a moment Myrna wasn't with him so he could run as fast as he could.

Isabell cried out again, only louder than before, "Alexander!"

He could see his crying sister running towards him. Even still a few hundred feet away, he saw her struggling to run. Her hair was disheveled, and her face distorted from crying and perhaps even from physical pain. He couldn't tell but as they got closer, he became sure there was something horribly wrong; something terrible had happened.

Finally, Alexander let go of Myrna's hand as they were close enough for Isabell to fall into his arms and hold onto him tightly as though they were lovers. She cried and tried to speak but her words were hard to distinguish.

"What's the matter, Isabell? What happened? Did someone get hurt?" He asked.

Still unable to catch her breath from running and crying, she gave no answer he could understand.

"What is it, Isabell?" asked Myrna.

Isabell looked at her with evil in her eyes and cried out, "Your father!"

Upon hearing this, Alexander released her from the comfort of his strong arms and asked, "What are you saying, Isabell? What about her father?"

"He attacked me and mother!" she replied, still leering at Myrna as though she was complicit in the attack.

"That's impossible!" Myrna shouted, "You're mistaken!" Her face showed obvious concern.

Isabell continued, "He tore the brooch from my neck and hit mother to the point…" She struggled to get the words out while Myrna and Alexander were trying to make sense of what they were hearing. "…to the point of falling unconscious to the floor!"

Alexander, not knowing what to do or say, turned to Myrna and asked, "Is that possible? Could he have done that?"

Myrna didn't reply but kept on with inquiries of her own to Isabell, "What could possibly possess my father to do such a thing? How dare you fabricate such nonsense?"

Isabell responded immediately by opening the collar of her dress, "Look at the mark on my neck! I feel such pain that the chafe must be visible to a blind man!"

Alexander and Myrna didn't respond but looked at her neck with great discernment.

"Do you see it, Alexander?" Isabell cried out.

"Yes, I see it."

Isabell continued, "And wait until you see the bruises on mother! I had to help her to bed and minister to her wounds before I could run out to find you! You'll see! Clement left both of us on the floor by his violent hand!"

Myrna became indignant and asked, "You don't believe a word of this, do you Alexander? Please tell me you don't!" Before Alexander had a chance to respond, she turned to Isabell to accuse her, "What do you have against my father you ungrateful girl? Why such lies? My father is a father to you both and a loving husband to your mother and I'll not stand for any more of these lies! Perhaps you should ask for his forgiveness for such accusations!"

"They are not lies! It's the truth so help me God!"

Isabell looked at Alexander for support or at least a look of acknowledgement that her story might have happened just as she described, but all she saw from him was disbelief and perhaps a look of concern for her mental state; a mental state so confused as to create such a fantasy for reasons unknown. His lack of urgent reaction to Clement's abuse left Isabell feeling furious and hurt. She stood looking at him.

Her incredulous eyes spoke a thousand words to him and made him wish so much that she was mistaken about this wild story. Even her fabricating the whole story to cause strife within the family would be welcomed if it meant it wasn't actually true. The way he felt, he would have accepted any reason other than the story being true because the truth would damage many things, not least of which was his love relationship with Myrna.

Seeing no hint of support from Alexander, Isabell began to cry again in frustration and turned to run back home.

After a moment of watching Isabell run away from him, Alexander turned to Myrna to console her. He held her in his arms as she asked softly, "You don't believe that, do you Alexander?"

He replied soothingly, "Of course not. Don't you worry."

"Why would she tell such stories?"

"I don't know. Perhaps she's not well. I'm sure everything will be fine. Let's go now and make sure everything is alright."

Myrna acknowledged with a nod as they began walking slowly arm in arm towards home.

*****

The cabin was dark and eerily quiet when Alexander and Myrna walked in, so it gave the feel of an abandoned or even a haunted house. However, everything was as it should have been. The table was set for five, the smell of pork filled the air, and the pictures of a smiling happy family were hung and undisturbed. Both held hands as they gazed around the room for any signs of abnormal behavior or incidents. There were none; no broken necklace pieces, no indications of blood anywhere, nor were there any signs of up-turned furniture or broken glass. Everything was fine. It gave Alexander a sickly feeling in the pit of his stomach to think that Isabell lied about the whole incident or even worse, imagined it really happened when nothing of the sort was apparent.

Myrna walked over to the stove and looked at the pots and pans sitting on top. They were filled with chops, potatoes, and an assortment of vegetables that were cooked and ready to serve, but there was no one there to serve, and save for themselves, no one to serve to. This, she found disturbing and any oddity as this, could be reason to suspect something was wrong.

Alexander saw the puzzled look in her face and asked, "What's the matter?"

"Where is everyone?" she asked, "There's food prepared but no one's here."

"Perhaps mother is in her bedroom."

"And Isabell?"

"In her present state, it wouldn't be surprising if she hadn't come back home but wandered off somewhere. I'll check for mother."

He quietly walked over to his mother's bedroom door and opened it quietly to not disturb her if she were asleep. The notion of her sleeping at this early hour was also disturbing to him but he tried not to be distracted by that possibility. The creaking of the hinges as the door opened made him think it was a wasted effort to try being quiet. When the door was opened enough to look in, there he saw his mother being tended to by Isabell; washing her mother's face with a cold damp cloth and trying to comfort and reassure her by shushing, as one would try to calm a crying baby. It was obvious to Alexander that his mother was crying as she tried to fight off the pain of the cloth touching the tender welts on her face. Her left eye was completely closed, swollen, and had a yellowish discoloration that Alexander guessed would soon turn black. There was a cut on the corner of the same eye that extended to the end of her brow. Her cheeks were also swollen and there were blood stains in her hair and pillow next to her right ear.

Alexander was overtaken with shock at the sight and remained speechless for a time. Isabell looked at him with a grimace as she washed her mother's face but didn't say a word because no uttered word was needed. No disappointment or deep emotion of hers could be expressed verbally, nor was there any need. Alexander understood.

"What is it?" asked Myrna who was now walking towards him.

He couldn't respond. Instead, he just let her walk to the door so she could see for herself. At the door entrance, she stood by his side and looked in silence. She didn't dare ask what happened because she knew. They both knew.

"Mother are you alright?" asked Alexander.

"Yes dear." she responded with a weak and trembling voice.

The Witch of Brentwood

He noticed she had trouble moving her head from one side to the other.

"Did my father do this?" asked Myrna.

"Oh, he didn't know what he was doing." Amelia replied, "He had been drinking a little and Lord knows the slightest thing can trigger a man in such a state. It wasn't his fault."

This completely took Isabell by surprise and her anger grew more and more as she had time to process her mother's response.

"What do you mean?" she asked her mother and immediately straightened up in her chair. "Look at you, mother! You're all bruised! He's the one who did this out of anger!"

"Now child, he wasn't himself. You have to forgive someone when they're not responsible for their actions."

"But he *is* responsible, mother! How can you say such a thing? He became angry for no reason at all and attacked both of us! You received the worst of it! How can you say that?"

"If my father was drunk, then he wasn't responsible for his actions." Myrna added. "Am I right, Alexander?"

"Of course." he replied, "No one of sound mind would do such a thing."

Upon hearing this, Isabell became speechless and didn't know what to do or how to reply to convince them that they were wrong. Their response to this violence was so beyond her comprehension that all she could do for the longest time was look at them in disbelief. Finally, she had processed enough of it to respond.

"I don't believe you; *any* of you!" Isabell said as she addressed each one of them in turn with an incredulous look.

As she looked at them, they were silent as though they wished the situation would come to an end. They seemed to Isabell like children blocking their eyes or ears to make something go away. Myrna knew the feeling all too well when she had blocked her ears as a child so many years ago to make the sounds of the beatings her father perpetrated on her mother, go away. But that was another time and place.

Finally, Isabell's eyes rested on her mother who was still in pain from the bruises and would be for a while to come. She looked at her intently with fury trying to figure out if her mother was protecting Clement for reasons she didn't yet understand. She wondered if perhaps love can be so strong that someone will gladly look the other way no matter how much pain is delivered. *Why is she so forgiving?* Myrna's forgiveness was understandable to Isabell and perhaps even Alexander's because of their relationship, but her mother's forgiveness was beyond the scope of her comprehension.

Finally, Isabell spoke again to her mother more gently, "He hurt you, mother. I was witness to the whole incident. He even attacked *me*. He wasn't drunk enough to *not* know what he was doing. He came at me for the brooch and when I resisted, he ripped it off my neck. See the bruises on my neck, mother?" she asked, exposing her visible marks. "He did this and he beat you when you tried to stop him. Had he been too drunk, he would have staggered and fallen himself, but he was steady and resolute. Why can't you see that?"

"We must forgive him, Isabell." her mother replied with a smile.

"Well perhaps you must." Isabell said as she turned to the others, "And you as well, but I shall never."

Having said that, Isabell stormed out of the room and ran out of the cabin to be far away so she could think and make sense of what she just witnessed. As she ran crying, she hoped she still had the brooch around her neck. If she was able to summon any powers from it, she would surely usher them to quickly punish Clement and make sure he never got the chance to hurt her or anyone else again.

*****

It was late when Isabell came back home that night. The air was cool, and everything seemed to be silent; all the birds, all the cattle, and all the world. The only sound she could hear as she approached the cabin she now called home, was her own footsteps which she tried hard to keep quiet. At times it felt as though she hardly touched the ground.

She took the time to see the sky and even playfully tried to count the stars she and Alexander had done on more than one occasion, remembering how he would try to cheat and count the same ones several times. Counting stars was only one of the ways she tried to escape the present and relive the past, but her thoughts kept returning to the intolerable events of the day. The red mark on her neck and the burning sensation from it, were also a constant irritating reminder.

She went into the barn for a while to pet the horses. She noticed that Clement's horse wasn't there which confirmed her hope that he wasn't home yet, although it was getting very late. Her wish was that he would never return, but that was unrealistic since he at least needed a place to sleep and eat. He would return. Of this, she was certain. The only thing she wasn't sure of was in what condition he would be. Considering this, made her seriously think about spending the night in the barn with the animals, if for no other reason than to be as far away from him as possible. Still, she wanted to be near her mother in case he came home in anger again to unleash his fury against her mother a second time.

While rubbing her neck to ease the burning pain, there were many thoughts running through her mind. She thought about that dream again in which someone had ripped the birthmark off her skin and called her a witch. It was a frightening dream, but the pain of that dream was only in her mind. The area of her neck she tried to soothe was real. It was real pain that lasted longer than a moment in the night and went away upon waking. She thought about the life she had in Salem; how terrible it was that some were being accused of witchcraft and even hanged for the mere mention of such accusations. She had heard of those being in a holding cell awaiting their trial in the hopes of being able to convince someone of their innocence. She longed for the days when she and Alexander were kids and life was carefree. But even *she* would admit that life had changed when she happened on the hanging woman; the one who triggered almost nightly recurring dreams to this very day. She tried to make sense of why everyone came to Clement's defense after his attack and her mother's beatings, but she knew in her heart there could never be a good enough reason on God's green earth. She thought about the brooch and tried to figure out a way to get it back. It was indeed a mysterious brooch, given what she experienced when it was in her possession. All during these thoughts, she petted Alexander's horse and her own neck for the comfort of both.

Finally, she suddenly became resolute to finding that brooch and taking it back at any cost; not only for sentimental value, but for the mystery behind it. Even if the mystery was only the fabrication of a young girl's imagination. She gathered her courage and made her way to the cabin where her mother and brother were most likely asleep.

The cabin was dark and quiet, which reassured her everyone was asleep. She knew she had to act swiftly before Clement came home, so she hurriedly lit a lantern on the wall near the stove still containing pots and pans of the night's uneaten supper, and very quietly removed her shoes and made her way to her mother's bedroom with lantern in hand to light her way. Even with no shoes, her walking was making too much noise for her liking, but she continued on. The snoring from Alexander's room assured her he was asleep and could only hope that Myrna was asleep as well. She felt like a burglar in the night because that's exactly what her intentions were. It didn't matter to her if it was wrong because she reasoned that it wasn't as wrong as what was perpetrated earlier in the day. *That* was *very* wrong compared to what she was now endeavoring to do. God would certainly forgive her. But at that moment, finding the brooch was more important than forgiveness.

She opened the door to her mother's room very slowly. The creaking of the hinges was something she knew would occur but didn't realize they would be so loud in such a quiet place. As soon as the creaking began, she stopped pushing the door and peeked in the room partly lit from the lantern she was holding. There on the table beside her sleeping mother, she saw a half-empty bottle of Clement's whiskey next to a small empty glass. It then occurred to Isabell that her mother would never wake from the screaming hinges after taking a couple of glasses of medicinal whiskey to kill the pain of her bruises. She suddenly felt relieved and considered herself lucky to be able to search the room for her brooch without fear of her mother waking from any noise.

Still walking on her tiptoes, she began her search. She went directly to the most likely place where the brooch might be; Clement's bureau desk, on top of where she laid the lantern to illuminate her findings. It would be a very desirable desk and I wouldn't mind owning it myself were it not containing his possessions, she thought. The top drawer filled with his undergarments and stockings, opened easily. She hesitated to touch the drawer's contents but finding the brooch was more important than her own modesty, so she obliged. Nothing was found other than a roll of bills under his stockings, obviously hidden from her mother lest she decided to use it for something useful like rye to make bread and cakes. She thought about taking the money. *That would serve him right.* But she decided against it since she wasn't there to rob anyone but rather, redeem what was rightly hers. Finding nothing that belonged to her, she closed that drawer and moved on to the one below it. There she found some shirts, pants, more stockings, and a few old pictures strewn about but nothing else that remotely resemble any kind of jewelry. As she arranged the contents so he wouldn't notice anyone had been rummaging through it, she felt something rigid in one of the pockets of a shirt that was laying at the very bottom of the drawer. She looked at it as carefully as she could with light being as dim as it was and couldn't recall him ever wearing it. Its pocket undoubtedly stored something; a piece of paper perhaps. She didn't know but it piqued her interest to where she couldn't help but retrieve it. Holding it up to the lantern on the desk, she began to unfold it until she was able to see the writing with some effort at first until her eyes adjusted to the dimness of the room. It read:

My dear Mr. Arington,

Regarding the unfortunate incident occurring approximately five weeks ago in the town of Salem, we the clergy and judiciary officials in good standing in the town of Salem in the Colony of Massachusetts, have found enough evidence to suggest that you rightly executed your duty as a citizen by hanging the woman found to be guilty of witchcraft.

We hereby vindicate any accusations of wrongdoing on your part and your party, and as such, we feel confident as well as grateful for your act of bravery in taking appropriate measures against witchcraft and witches.

We pray you shan't carry any further unduly guilt for your actions of executing by hanging, as this is the preferred method of cleansing. Henceforth, however, we respectfully admonish that you do not enact on your own behalf but rather allow the church and tribunal to make the necessary lawful determination and execution of such determination.

Everyday say your prayers on your knees, day and night with attention and devotion. God be with you.

The Honorable Reverend Bighamton
In the year of our Lord,
June Eighteen, Sixteen Hundred and Eighty-Four

Isabell stood holding the letter next to the lantern and read it over several more times before folding it back and replacing it in the pocket of the shirt so neatly tucked away underneath all the other shirts. Tears welled up in her eyes as she slowly closed the drawer and began to relive the nightmares that were more real now than they ever were.

"June, Sixteen Hundred and Eighty-Four," she whispered to herself, being mindful of her sleeping mother not six feet away, "I was ten years old then."

She thought for a moment with eyebrows furrowed in serious contemplation. To the best of her knowledge and recollection, there was only one execution by hanging eight years ago in Salem; that being the hanging woman who so frightened her when collecting a bouquet for her mother; the one who caused recurring nightmares to this very day. *Was Clement the one who helped kill that poor woman?* She tried to dismiss the idea, but it kept coming back to her as a great coincidence at the very least. Her mother being married to such a killer was almost too much for her to bear and she tried hard to talk herself out of the possibility. Yet...

Her thoughts were suddenly disturbed by the gallop of an approaching horse. She held her breath for a moment in order to better hear where the galloping sounds were and where they would stop. As sure as anything, the horse stopped near the barn. Isabell abruptly abandoned any further search of the room for her brooch, hurriedly picked up the lantern on the desk, and made her way out of the room before Clement came in. Quickly, she hung the lantern back on the wall near the stove and extinguished it before running to her bedroom and hopping into bed without waking Myrna she shared her bedroom with. There, she listened to every footstep he made as he came in and staggered into the bedroom where her mother was. All she saw was the blackness of night but could imagine his angry drunken face. Soon she heard him lie down in bed and the sound of silence was soon replaced with the sound of Clement snoring.

Lying in bed in the night and everyone being asleep, her mind raced with images of Clement hanging the poor woman who was most likely falsely accused. The thought made her cry. She cried in silence. Many times, in between tears, she tried to reason that perhaps she was mistaken; perhaps the letter was regarding some other incident that, as the letter stated, forced him to rightly execute his duty as a citizen. But the thought of him being a killer kept creeping in the back of her mind.

Moments passed. Her mind was racing so that she couldn't get to sleep, nor did she *want* to sleep for fear of having her recurring nightmares. She wondered if she should confront him about the letter from his past, but soon dismissed the thought. To talk about the letter would be an admission to rummaging through his belongings, which would undoubtedly unleash more fury on her, and Lord knows who else.

She lay in bed with eyes wide open until morning when the cocks crowed, the birds sang, and the sun shone for a new morning filled with hope; a hope that was as far removed from her life as her ten-year-old innocence.

The Witch of Brentwood

*****

Myrna was very young in her dream. The landscape was the same as she remembered it and the sunshine on her face made her happy to be alive with no responsibility except schooling and easy chores like keeping her room clean and helping around the kitchen. She was walking in the wilderness at first, meeting animals of all sorts; tame as could be, allowing her to pet them one by one as they scurried. Next, as dreams can be unpredictable, she heard her mother calling her to come home. As she turned towards her mother's voice, she saw a house where there was none before. She knew it was her home even though her childhood home looked nothing like the cabin in the dream. Still, somehow she knew it to be home and thought nothing of running towards it as she normally would. Her feet, only protected by skimpy sandals, were scraped all over from running through the thicket but it didn't matter.

As she approached, she could see her mother in the doorway signaling to hurry. Gone were the physical attributes of her mother's schizophrenic condition everyone referred to as madness. She seemed as stable as anyone else Myrna ever knew, which was unusual in her real life, but in her dream her mother's unfettered condition was normal to her.

Having arrived next to her mother, she noticed a frown from her mother's face and asked what the matter was. At this, her mother pointed to the inside of the cabin through the opened front door. Myrna looked in to see her father standing over an eighteen-year-old Isabell, whose body lay dead on the floor. There was a note on the body Myrna wasn't able to see closely enough to read, but she knew what was written on it just the same.

"Father, what have you done?" cried the young Myrna.

He didn't answer but rather ran towards the open door to grab Myrna's mother by the neck and drag her in the cabin.

"I told you not to tell anyone!" shouted Clement at his wife.

Myrna's mother tried to get away, but Clement was too strong and too intent on administering just punishment.

The young Myrna stood at the doorway crying and witnessing every unimaginable thing her father did to her poor mother. She tried again to reason with him.

"Daddy, the evil madness is gone now! It fled from her!" cried Myrna.

Clement didn't respond. He kept beating his wife. When her body went limp, he continued with blows to the head and torso until he was exhausted.

"Daddy!" she cried.

This made him look in her direction and started after her.

The last thing she saw was the evil fury in her father's face before she feverishly woke up and gasped in panic; perspiring from her head to her midsection, and heart beating like it never had before. She tried to contain herself as best she could to not wake Isabell sleeping in the next bed four feet away. Taking deep breaths and closing her eyes tightly, she was finally able to subdue the panic feeling but was very apprehensive about going back to sleep lest the dream continued.

After a few minutes, she was able to regain control and reasoned that it was only a dream. Possible reasons she had dreamt such a thing floated around in her head for a while until she decided to let go of it. *It was a silly dream*. She kept repeating this in her mind until she finally succumbed to the inevitable fatigue from her horrific dream experience and fell back asleep; twitching, moaning, and turning frequently because her nightmares would continue well into the morning.

Isabell was very well aware that Myrna was having a terrible night of sleep. They both were. She lay still the entire night listening to Myrna's moans of fear from her dreams and tossing to and fro. To the best of Isabell's knowledge, Myrna had awakened only once, but her night's sleep would undoubtedly leave her exhausted in the morning, which Isabell was happy with. *This night will be proper vengeance for denying her father's attacks.*

Isabell didn't try to sleep because she knew it would have been a vain attempt. She found herself satisfied to lie in bed waiting for morning; not really knowing what the morning would bring. It was quiet at times and other times Myrna would stir and moan from dreaming. Hearing this, made Isabell also feel sorry for Alexander. He was, after all, involved romantically with Myrna which Isabell thought was the reason he didn't believe Clement could perpetrate such attacks. She was sure he believed her but just went along with denying for fear of losing Myrna.

All these thoughts ran through her mind when suddenly the sounds in her mother's room began. They were the same sounds she had heard when her mother first became intimate with Clement. These sounds were different now, however. They were sounds not consistent with love-making, but rather the sounds of forcible rape, it seemed. She could hear her mother trying to suppress screams; perhaps screams of pain from whatever pain he was inflicting. Her sounds were not those of someone in love. She thought for a moment of bursting into their room and making him stop. In fact, she readied herself to get out of bed to do exactly that but as she was about to, the sounds subsided. It was over.

Isabell always thought that love-making was a long-lasting process of love between the two involved. Selfish and superficial sex never occurred to such a naive young woman as she was. But Isabell was beginning to learn a lot more than she wanted to.

Chapter 7

There was a chill in the air. The different layers of garments did nothing to help shield the coldness from tender skin. Whistling could be heard through tiny gaps of the closed windows, as the wind blew more than usual for this time of year. It was a fresh reminder that the summer temperatures would be over soon. The morning sun was hidden with an overcast which contributed to the fallen temperature. A few leaves were falling here and there as the trees they were previously attached to, swayed back and forth. The scene gave a feeling of a child leaving a parent to find its freedom and look for greener meadows elsewhere beyond the home. Anyone looking more closely at those falling leaves might have seen a hint of frost on them, much like the figurative frost that lay on everyone in the room that morning for breakfast. There was a chill in the air.

Last night's supper was cleaned up early and given to the livestock to make room for cooking the morning breakfast. The smell of the pork that was left out all night lingered even after it was taken out of the cabin and blended in with the smell of breakfast. Plates and eating utensils were placed in the usual manner, the wheat cakes were served, and the coffee was hot. It was just an ordinary day as far as an outsider would be concerned but the Arington family knew better, and everyone remained silent. They ate and drank without so much as a look in anyone else's direction lest a conversation might ensue.

The left side of Amelia's face was swollen considerably more than the right, and her eye had turned a darker shade as Alexander had guessed it would. The blood from her hair was washed away early in the morning so as to not bring attention to the severity of Clement's anger. She had some difficulty eating, and drinking a hot beverage was next to impossible because it greatly stung the cuts to her top lip. Still, she made no fuss and pretended there was no pain.

Myrna looked pale and had no appetite. The bags and creases under her eyes gave evidence of a nightmarish slumber that left her tossing, turning, and kicking the entire night. She picked at her food sporadically simply because she felt she had to, while looking up at Alexander at times to assure him she was alright despite her appearance. Frequently, she felt like she might vomit at the table, because the visions of the nightmare lurked in the back of her mind. She tried hard to control those thoughts by thinking about the day before when she and Alexander made love in the open field. But still those violent thoughts crept back in all too often.

Clement was a little hung over from a previous night of drinking but not too much to prevent him from eating his breakfast. He fully remembered what took place, since he wasn't the type to completely forget from drunkenness. As much as he remembered the night before, he felt no shame, remorse, or empathy towards the ones he hurt. In fact, he was happy to have the brooch in his possession, as well as having established his unequivocal authority. What he would do with the brooch, he still wasn't sure. But it was a valuable piece of jewelry and that was enough to possess it. If there were ever a time to have to sell or trade it, he would have it for that purpose.

Isabell was not as tired as she thought she would be, having been awake all night and being fully aware of what was happening around her; from Myrna's restless sleep to the sounds of an animal having his way with her mother, even as her mother was hurting from the cuts and bruises. Thinking about the love-making part of the night made her a little queasy so she tried hard not to think of that. She neither was hungry, nor did she pretend to be, and didn't care much if anyone noticed. She felt comfortable enough just sitting at the table with her head down looking at her food, resolved in her mind that if anyone mentioned anything about her posture or lack of courtesy, she would confront whoever it was without hesitation.

Alexander was torn. The fact that Isabell condemned Myrna's father whom Myrna loved was torturing him. Never would he hurt her by going along with Isabell's accusations of her father's wrongdoing. *He had been drinking. These incidents happen to many people especially when they feel the pressure of trying to provide for a family.* By the same token, he knew Isabell would hate him as long as he didn't support her in her relentless attempt to typify Clement as evil. He also had very little appetite, but he knew the importance of good nutrition. So, he ate in silence.

The sounds of the eating utensils clanking against the plates and bowls were loud against the silence of the room and made the lack of discourse that much more awkward. Finally, Clement spoke.

"The wheat cakes are dry." he said with disdain in his voice, which was obviously directed at Amelia who had made them.

Upon hearing this, Isabell looked up at him in anger, but he didn't look up to see her leering at him. He kept eating and not caring much if anyone was offended. She looked around the table to find that no one reacted to his insulting words, which angered her more. Finally, she got up from her chair and walked briskly towards the door to leave.

"Isabell?" her mother called to her.

But those words went unheard it seemed. No one at the table reacted for fear of Clement's anger as Isabell stepped out slamming the door behind her.

At first, she walked but her pace soon quickened, and eventually was running to somewhere she didn't know or care. What was important to her at the time was running as far away from Clement and her family as possible.

Isabell ran until she was tired and could run no more. Fortunately, there was a fence nearby that was welcoming her to sit on, to catch her breath and give her time to think. She was starting to feel tired from a sleepless night as the adrenaline rush from her anger was beginning to subside. She wondered if she'd be able to fall asleep tonight but didn't entertain that thought for too long. *I'll attend to that problem tonight. Now is not the time to be distracted by such trivialities.*

She walked to the fence that was less than five hundred feet away but didn't see a nearby cabin. There was a crest beyond the fence not far away, and she thought perhaps there might have been a house on the other side of the crest of that hill she couldn't see. Trespassing on someone else's land was not something she approved of nor was she the type to engage in such

The Witch of Brentwood

behavior, but her feet were beginning to hurt and the combination of running with no sleep the night before, wore on her almost to the point of exhaustion. She simply had to rest for a moment. So, she continued to the fence and wearily sat down on one of the rails.

There, she rested her head in her hands and would have cried were she not so exhausted. Instead, she let the outdoor sounds and fresh air restore her and clear her head. The morning wind that blew earlier had subsided to a gentle breeze now blowing through her hair and it felt wonderful. She felt rejuvenated to some degree and were it not for the breakfast encounter she had with Clement, happiness would not be far behind.

She sat daydreaming much as she had done before. Her daydreams were always of a young prince who might one day sweep her off her feet and marry her so she would be removed from the abuses of Clement and her family who had disappointed her greatly. Suddenly, she heard a voice cry out from a distance.

"Hey!"

She thought it was her imagination at first, but it came again.

"Hey there!"

Isabell lifted her head and looked behind her in the direction of where she thought the voice was coming from. There, she saw a young man walking towards her; someone she'd never met before, which made her realize just how far away from home she had run. *No wonder I'm so tired.* She wasn't lost, necessarily, but this was a place she had never been to during her daily walks.

The young man kept walking towards her and waved at her in a friendly manner, but she didn't return the salutation. She just looked, studying him as he kept walking in her direction. He didn't look intimidating in any way nor angry that someone had trespassed, so she remained sitting on the rail looking at him as he approached.

He was a good-looking young man, from her perspective. His short brown hair was disheveled a little but still neat and his thick eyebrows made his blue piercing eyes stand out in contrast. The short beard he sported was a perfect match for his face, which was in itself strong and rugged. He wore a white ruffled shirt and black slacks that very well defined the strong muscular shape of his body. The boots he wore were tall, reaching just below his knees and the sound they made on the ground as he walked was surprisingly quiet given the sturdiness of his physique. All in all, a pretty good specimen of a man, she thought. But she tried to control that thought as he finally reached her. He climbed the fence and jumped to the other side so they could be face-to-face.

"Hello." he said with a smile.

"Hello." she replied.

"I don't recall ever seeing you in these parts."

"I don't come here, usually. Forgive me for trespassing, but I was exhausted and had to sit for a spell."

"It's quite alright." He held out his hand. "My name is Derris; Derris Blackmoore. Pleasure meeting you."

"Charmed, I'm sure." she said, offering her hand but trying to remain coy.

"And your name?" he asked.

"Isabell."

"Do you have a surname, Isabell?"

"Isabell Whitlock."

"Well Isabell Whitlock, may I sit and entertain you?"

"Consorting with strangers is not the fashion my mother properly raised me to follow." she said with a smile.

He frowned and said, "Well now, consorting is such a distasteful word to use when two people are simply..." he paused to think of the right words to use, "...keeping company."

She giggled upon hearing that.

"Call it what you shall." she replied. "Where is your home, Mr. Blackmoore?"

"Derris. Please."

"Okay, Derris."

"Just beyond that hill," he answered, pointing. "My family owns a little cabin there. I'd love to show you someday and perhaps have you greet my family."

"I would be much obliged."

"Perhaps soon?"

"Perhaps." she said coyly.

They both smiled.

After a moment, he said, "Well, unfortunately, I must get on with my work before father becomes wise to my dalliance." He puffed up his chest, "*The grain won't gather itself, young man.*" he said with a stern voice, imitating his father in jest.

This made her laugh. She didn't think she would ever laugh again after her experience at home in the last twenty-four hours, but here she was laughing. It felt good to feel good again, and it was all because of this wonderful young Derris Blackmoore.

Knowing she was enjoying herself with him and was beginning to feel at ease, Derris felt confident about himself. So, he asked her, "Shall I see you again?"

She thought for a moment, which gave pause to his confidence. Then after a moment she replied, "I would like that."

Her response made him sigh a sigh of relief, which made her giggle again.

"Perhaps tomorrow?" he asked.

"I don't know. Tomorrow may be impossible, but soon."

"Alright, I'll watch this fence often for you."

"Very well, then. If you don't see me, I shall sit and wait until you do."

"Alright, until then. It was a pleasure meeting you."

"The pleasure was mine, to be sure."

He took her hand again before they said their goodbyes, then they reluctantly parted ways.

She decided to go back home feeling much better about herself, while still knowing in the back of her mind that life back home could never be the same. But now after meeting Derris, things were different for her. She now had something to look forward to; better days with a nice young man who would be there to protect her from the evils of the world. She recalled all the times she would daydream about a young man asking her to dance to a soft waltz and whispering things in her ear too daring for a young lady to even think about. She recalled how she felt when she allowed herself to daydream as such. That's how she felt on that day, walking home. It was as if those daydreams were wishes coming true, while their fleeting essence could suddenly become a reality.

The Witch of Brentwood

*****

The word around the neighborhood was that there was a cunning folk woman who lived among them. She was known for having the right remedies for the right ailment as well as being able to bring rain for the crops and foretelling the weather. It was just a rumor, mind you, but rumors are usually based in fact. Isabell thought this woman's position in the community would be very risky if she had resided in Salem. Still, the talk of witches and the demonic possession of Salem and its inhabitants were beginning to make their way to Brentwood and beyond. So, her position as a cunning folk was getting riskier with every passing day.

Her name was Flora Wemmick; a middle-aged woman who was never married and lived alone. Her gray hair was long past her shoulders and her eyes that were probably a hazel color in her youth, now appeared to be the same gray color as her hair. She wore a gray shawl over what probably was her only black dress that dragged on the ground and her damaged shoes were too tight for her rash-infested feet. She liked her fingernails long, because it was her only defense against predators who would try to attack her; not that anyone *did* attack her but then again, her paranoia was much more of a dominant character trait than her rationale.

Her home was a small one-room cabin which was probably built years ago as a shed for storing shovels, rakes, and those kinds of tools. There was no use in trying to decorate the place, nor did she possess the creative artistry to accomplish such a feat. So, everything looked somewhat dull and unwelcoming. She did put up some shelves, however, to store her medicinal herbs and other ingredients she used in her 'craft'. This ability of hers was established when she coincidently predicted some weather patterns for a few days and was able to later 'cure' someone's ear infection and cough. Ever since then, she was known as a cunning woman able to use her God-given gifts for good. There were always some who believed her gifts had nothing to do with God, but rather with the underworld. People usually tried to avoid walking past her cabin for fear of what she was capable of, but others seeking help for whatever ailed them were more likely to pay her a visit for a possible cure.

Isabell entertained the possibility of paying this woman a visit at one time. Perhaps she could cure her recurring nightmares and as a bonus, maybe even cure her fear of death and dead people. She hadn't really thought about visiting her, until the day she passed her cabin on her way home from her encounter with that wonderful young man, Derris. She knew Flora lived in an out-of-the-way place but wasn't sure exactly where. But on her way home from sitting on the fence where she met Derris, she passed a small cabin with an older woman outside who fit Flora's description as it was described to her by her mother. Isabell was sure it was her. She was told that she was a strange woman who did strange things. On this day she passed by her cabin, this strange woman was outside lighting torches that seemed equidistant from each other; five in a circle and one in the middle. She was doing this all while moving in what seemed to be some kind of ritualistic dance. This made Isabell quicken her pace. It also didn't help that there was a small cemetery not far from her cabin.

Having passed the place, Isabell slowed her pace and eventually came to a full stop. She stood there thinking about whether

The Witch of Brentwood

turning back to go see this Flora would be a sound idea. She thought for a good long time. Anyone watching Isabell from a distance would have been concerned for her well-being and wondered why she was standing there not moving. After a while, she slowly turned around but with no greater intention of taking another step towards the old woman's cabin. She could still see the cabin from where she stood but was well at a safe distance. If the old woman saw her and went after her, Isabell could still turn and outrun her. Of this, she was sure.

She stood looking for a while, and then saw the old woman go back into her cabin. Her torches were lit and everything about the place was quiet. In fact, things seemed more tranquil than quiet, which gave Isabell a good feeling about the old woman they called cunning by trade. So, she decided to pay the old woman a visit and started on her way back to her cabin.

Walking past the cemetery to get to the woman's cabin was difficult. She had visited the cemetery where her grandmother was buried, too many times for her liking. But this cemetery felt different. She felt more of a phobia as opposed to fear.

She walked past keeping her eyes closed, half opening them only occasionally to make sure she didn't trip over some rocks or walk head on into a tree. She could almost hear the dearly departed moaning and crying to be released from their underground prison. There was a chill that ran down from the standing hairs of her neck all the way down to the back of her legs and she began to hum a tune to herself that was hardly audible to the human ear, as someone would do in a dark forest just to calm and comfort the fear of the unknown.

Finally, the cemetery was behind her, and she was able to focus on meeting the old woman and what she would say to her that wouldn't sound too imposing. Since the woman didn't receive much company, *or is that too much of a presumptuous thought*, her visit might be deemed quite an uninvited imposition.

The outside door didn't appear to be shut correctly from a short distance, but upon reaching it she noticed it was loose from its hinges and couldn't close properly if someone tried. In fact, the entire outside of the cabin was in disrepair from what she saw, if one could even call it a cabin at all. She looked around at the torches' glowing flickering flame and wondered about their purpose, but then quickly decided it was the old woman's affairs only, not hers.

She knocked on the door. It moved back and forth with every knock, and it made her sad to think it would swing wide open with a strong wind. Hearing footsteps from the inside coming closer to the door, she braced herself. Suddenly, it opened.

Isabell was surprised to see what seemed like a very pleasant middle-aged woman looking at her with a welcoming smile.

"Hello, may I help you?" the old woman said.

"My name is Isabell Whitlock. I'm sorry to bother you, Ma'am."

"No bother. How may I help you?"

"I'd like a friendly conference with you if that would be alright."

"What about, dear?"

"I understand you have some remedies?" Isabell stated more as a question.

"Some." was the only response.

"I may be in need of something. I'd like to speak with you about it."

The Witch of Brentwood

The old woman looked Isabell up and down before inviting her in.

"Would you like to come in?"

Normally Isabell would never agree to such an invitation from a stranger but after all, she was the one imposing on *her*.

"If you wouldn't mind." replied Isabell.

Once inside, the old woman introduced herself.

"My name is Flora. Flora Wemmick."

"Nice to meet you, Miss Wemmick." Isabell said, extending her hand.

Flora shook her hand and said, "Please, it's Flora."

"Alright then, Flora."

"How may I be of service?" asked Flora, offering Isabell a seat. They both sat down facing each other and Flora saw the hesitation in Isabell's eyes. "Don't be shy, dear. What is it?"

"I heard you are one who can cure certain ailments."

"Well, that's what they say about me." Flora replied.

"Is it true?" Isabell asked.

"We all have the ability to help one another. I'm only more willing than many others who would rather not be troubled." Flora then noticed the birthmark on Isabell's neck. She reached out her hand to touch it. "May I?"

"Yes, of course. I've had it since birth." Isabell remarked.

"I see."

Flora closed her eyes but kept her hand on Isabell's neck. "I sense a great deal of healing power in *you*." Flora said.

"How do you mean? And how can you tell?"

"Oh, anyone with any insight can tell those things especially if it's apparent as in your case. What ails you, my dear Isabell?"

Flora still had her hand on the birthmark with eyes closed as if she were concentrating or perhaps reading it as a blind person would read braille.

"I've had terrible nightmares almost every night since I was a young girl and wondered if you could help."

Flora removed her hand from Isabell's neck and looked her in the eyes.

"You have the power within you, dear. Sometimes you need a little help from external sources, but the true power is within you. I feel it. But I must warn you, not everything can be healed. Dreams are exceptionally difficult because of their origin."

"What does it mean, origin?" Isabell inquired, with a curious look.

"Some dreams are random thoughts in your mind from the worries of the day and some are much more. Did something cause those nightmares; perhaps some unfortunate incident with family?"

"Yes."

"What was it?" Isabell hesitated. Seeing the hesitation, Flora added, "You need not say if it still burns your soul."

The reason Isabell hesitated was her uncertainty to talk about the hanging woman. She wasn't sure if Flora was not a witch herself.

"I'd prefer not to summon an experience so painful, if you don't mind." Isabell replied.

"That's fine, dear. The past doesn't have to be exposed for healing."

"What did you mean when you said I have the power?" Isabell asked.

"You have a very special gift; a gift that will be disclosed in the near future. You may even have a suspicion of such a gift."

Isabell thought about how her illness of consumption abated suddenly after she was given the brooch, and the time a man fell, debilitated after her clutching the pendant and wishing something bad would happen to him.

"Something has happened, hasn't it? Flora asked.

Isabell looked pensive and answered, "I think so."

"That is what I mean when I say you have the power. It shall evolve and you shall use it again." Flora responded with a smile.

"Do *you* have the power?" Isabell asked.

"Yes, I do, dear. We both do, and we're not alone."

Upon hearing this, Isabell felt compelled to ask her directly what she tried to avoid previously.

"Are you a witch?" she asked the old woman, hesitantly.

"Do you think I am?"

"Yes." answered Isabell, not meaning any disrespect.

"Then I am if you think so. Many people think so. I like to think of myself as someone who can help others."

"But you can also hurt others, correct?"

"We all have that tendency. You do as well, don't you?"

Isabell looked at her, recalling the fallen man.

"Yes, I suppose so."

"Does that make you a witch, dear?" Flora asked.

"I'd like to think it doesn't."

"Oh, it's not what *you* think that matters, my dear Isabell, it's what *others* think of you. That's what can interfere."

"Interfere with what? Interfere how?"

"Interfere by their being afraid. Fear can be very dangerous to the person they are afraid of. I gather you haven't lived here very long. Where are you from?" asked Flora.

"Salem in Massachusetts."

"Salem." Flora repeated to herself. "There's talk of witches in Salem."

"Yes, there *are* witches there. I saw one hanged when I was very young. I've had nightmares about it ever since."

"You were wise to leave there."

"Yes, I know."

"And now you must leave my home."

"So soon? But can you help me with my afflictions? Why must I leave?"

"We should not be seen together; much too risky. Did anyone see you come here?"

"I think not."

"It would benefit us both to be more discreet. You can return when the moon is high. It's for our own good."

"Our own good?" asked Isabell, hoping for clarification.

"Yes."

"But returning when the moon is high is unsafe. I've heard there was a woman in Scotland about a hundred years ago who was declared a witch because she would wander out of her home at night."

"It was her own fate. What do you think happened to her?"

"Well, I've heard tell that they burned witches in that part of the world."

Flora replied, "They *hang* witches in Salem where you come from, don't they?"

"Yes, they do."

"We need not bring this kind of punishment to Brentwood."

"No, of course not. I wouldn't want anything to happen to you."

"Nor you." returned Flora without moving her stare from Isabell's eyes. "If you come at night, be careful not to be seen, or do not come at all. Now go."

"But I have so many questions."

"Not now. In time we will meet together again. Now go." Flora repeated.

Not wanting to overstay her welcome for fear of not being invited to return, Isabell turned to leave. When she reached the door, she looked back at the old woman and asked, "Why are there lighted torches outside in a strange formation?"

"Some rituals are important for gaining knowledge. This is my way."

Isabell returned a puzzled look to Flora before eventually opening the door and making her way outside. She was no longer apprehensive, but rather more confused than anything.

On her way home, she thought about everything that had happened in the last couple of hours; the dreadful breakfast she ran out from, the wonderful meeting with Derris Blackmoore, and finally her encounter with the enigmatic old woman named Flora. Of the three, she thought mostly about Flora; thinking perhaps she'd met a true witch, complete with strange rituals and possible powers beyond comprehension. If so, their meeting would indeed be dangerous, but she didn't care. There were problems in her life to take care of. But most importantly, she also wanted to know more about her own powers if she indeed possessed them as the old woman believed.

Réal Carpentier

*****

The old woman stared at the cabinet to the left of the fireplace. There was no door to the cabinet, but rather, a brown blanket pinned up to hide the contents on the shelves. She liked Isabell's visit but was happy she was gone, for there was much that needed to be done. She sat in her rocking chair thinking and staring. What happened two weeks before was mulling in her mind and brought the anger back with a vengeance.

It was a day like any other when it happened. She was outside weeding the garden, if one could indeed call two tomato plants and some rhubarb a garden. She was bent over when she heard two young girls snickering. At first, she thought nothing of it but it soon became apparent they were laughing at her, or her backside to be more specific. Turning around to see who it was, would have made no difference. After all, she was that age once and had her share of ridiculing and being ridiculed; something everyone goes through to some degree. *Sometimes when you ignore them, they go away.* That's what her mother would say often when she was a little girl, even though she discovered early on that that little bit of wisdom was really far removed from the truth. They remained relentless, however, and continued their giggling that soon became much more.

"Hey lady!" one shouted, "This side of you is much prettier than your face, I heard tell! They were right!"

The girls weren't little kids. Flora could tell by their voices they were old enough to know better than to bother someone tending to their own affair. She tried to ignore them to appease her now deceased mother of many years, but their giggling gave way to laughter and more verbal attacks.

If only she had a dog or perhaps a vicious bore, she could unleash on them that would teach those nasty girls to remove themselves in a hurry and never return. But she had no such ally.

"You should bury that gruesome face in the dirt with your plants, witch!" the other girl added.

This made Flora turn to see their faces, hoping it might instill some level of intimidation and have them move along. But it didn't. They kept on.

"What are you going to do you old witch, cast your spell and turn us into toads?" one of them said, followed by a round of giggles.

What the young girl had said was hardly distinguishable because she had a mouthful of some fruit she was eating, but Flora had discerned enough to realize it was more of the same. It also looked like the girls weren't about to move along anytime soon, as they were becoming more and more daring. They even approached a little closer, which gave Flora reason to fear physical harm.

"You stay away from here! Go on, move along!" Flora shouted. "One more step and you'll be sorry! I swear to you, you'll be sorry!"

The girls kept up their intimidation anyway until Flora decided it was enough. She turned to go into the house to find something she could protect herself with. Suddenly, she felt something hit the back of her neck at a respectable velocity. She brought her hand up to where she'd gotten hit and turned around in anger. Upon having achieved their goal of making the old woman angry, the two girls ran off in a fit of laughter and shouted more obscenities and insults as they ran.

Flora kept her eyes on them until they were out of sight. She then looked on the ground for whatever it was the girl had thrown with such accuracy. She felt the back of her neck again, still wet from the projectile, and spotted an apple core not three feet from where she stood. Picking it up, she looked out again to make sure the girls were no longer in sight, then she went back into her cabin.

This incident happened two weeks prior, but it didn't matter. Her anger was what mattered now, as she sat in her rocking chair and stared at the blanket-draped cabinet. Suddenly, she convinced herself to do what must be done.

Getting up from her rocker, she walked to the cabinet, pushed one side of the blanket open, and reached in to produce a little hand-made doll. It was not the best-looking doll she'd ever fabricated. After all, she had completed it in only two weeks, but it would do nicely. What it looked like, didn't really matter all that much. It *did*, however, contain a very important ingredient essential to its purpose. During its construction, Flora had stuffed the apple core that the young girl threw at her inside the doll. It was carefully placed in the vicinity of where the doll's heart should be.

Flora knew there was something magical about using an item that contained a person's significant characteristic; saliva, a root of hair, a piece of skin, or whatever represented the essence of the person involved. What she didn't know was that centuries later, that essence would still be considered magical as the molecule that carries genetic instructions in all living things and come to be known as DNA.

She took the little doll outside and looking around to make sure no one saw, walked to the middle of the burning torches where the center one was. Placing the doll in a circular fire pit made with flat black slate rocks, she picked up a can full of kerosene and poured it all over the doll until it was drenched. She then took the middle burning torch and lowered it onto the doll and watched with satisfaction as the doll immediately became engulfed with blazing fire.

Not far away, a young girl named Clarinda was outside fetching water from the well to help her mother make a soup that her father loved so much. Suddenly after reaching the well, she felt strange. She sat on a boulder hoping it would pass. At first, she thought it was that nagging pain she gets in her chest every once in a while from eating too many spices and herbs. But this sensation became increasingly different and more painful. It was a burning feeling that took her breath away and built up into her throat. Her face eventually became distorted with overwhelming pain and fright as she tried to scream but couldn't. The pain was becoming too intense to bear and the smell of burning flesh filled her senses. Finally, she was able to cry out a tremendous scream as flames shot out of her torso. In a very short moment, she was unconscious and felt no pain as the rest of her body burned like a log soaked in kerosene.

The remains were found a while later by her father and a hired hand named Clement Arington who was helping him rebuild his roof. There was no doubt it was his daughter Clarinda, since a hand remained untouched by fire and was quickly identified from a ring he had given her for her birthday two days before.

There was an investigation with no conclusion. As much as the family grieved for the loss of a loving daughter, the incident would only become one of the many claims of spontaneous human combustion centuries later.

*****

The room was still silent as the women were clearing off the table and getting ready to clean the dishes. Still vivid in the back of everyone's mind was the incident with Isabell and how she walked out from the breakfast table without asking to be excused. Amelia wondered where her daughter had gone without a word because young women were vulnerable especially in a relatively new place. Brentwood was beginning to feel like home but there were yet many areas unknown to them. She hoped her daughter would be safe and come home soon. Not that she needed help around the kitchen, but simply for her daughter's safety.

Clement had left right after breakfast was done that morning. Before walking out the door, he mumbled something about the job he had to do in town, which no one could really hear or understand; something about a roof. If the truth must be told, Amelia and Alexander felt a little relief when he left, given the experiences of the previous day and the awkward moments and silence of the morning breakfast.

Alexander and Myrna were uncharacteristically quiet with each other throughout the entire morning. It was usual for them to play and flirt but this morning was different. It wasn't so much that they were angry with each other; they weren't. It was more or less a situation of not knowing what each other were thinking since hearing of the attacks and then seeing Amelia all bruised. It was obvious that Clement had beat her but the reasons why he did were unknown. No matter what their own interpretations were of the beatings, they knew they had to talk soon about it and dispel any misunderstandings they may have.

"Is there something else I can assist you with?" Myrna asked Amelia.

"No dear, thank you. You run off now and enjoy the day." Amelia answered. "I'll just finish a few things and then start mending your father's shirt."

Upon hearing this, Alexander wondered if the shirt was ripped from the struggle with Isabell before he ripped the brooch chain from her neck.

"Very well then." Myrna replied. Then she turned to Alexander and asked, "How about a walk?"

"That would suit me fine," he answered. "I'll get my hat." Then he turned to his mother. "Mother, you won't mind being alone?"

"No, of course not." she said, "I'll keep busy until Isabell comes home then I think we'll go into town for some purchases."

"Very well then." he said, retrieving his hat from his room and signaling to Myrna that he was ready.

Myrna waited at the open door as Alexander walked over to his mother and kissed her on the forehead.

"We won't be long." he whispered to her.

"Enjoy your day. It's a beautiful day for a walk."

"We will." he replied and then took Myrna's hand to lead the way.

As they walked, there was more silence until Myrna began speaking.

"What are your thoughts about what Isabell said?" she asked.

"Well, I believe her. Don't you?"

"Yes, I do but I'm certain there are circumstances she failed to mention in her story of how it happened."

"What sort of circumstances?"

"Alexander, you don't believe for one instant that my father did what he did without being provoked, do you?"

He thought for a moment, then said, "I'd like to believe there was a good reason but what sort of provocation would lead a man to beat a woman to the severity shown by my mother's bruises? And why would he tear the brooch from Isabell's neck? You saw the mark it left."

"There must have been something that happened or something that was said. I don't believe Isabell told us the entire story as it happened." she returned.

"Why would she alter the incident?"

"To protect herself, Alexander. To see to it that we don't think she could ever do something wrong and think of her as evil."

"I guess that's possible," he replied.

"Of course, it's possible. It's also possible that she hates my father and would like to turn you against him."

"I don't think Isabell is capable of that kind of thinking. She's a good person."

Myrna thought for a moment, which created an awkward silence. She was suddenly tempted to tell Alexander of the day Isabell revealed her nightmare to her and what had happened eight years ago to cause those nightmares. She knew Alexander had also seen the witch hanging on the tree when he rescued an unconscious Isabell. But he didn't seem to be affected to the same severity as his sister. Then he spoke again.

"Why the silence? Did I say something wrong?" he asked.

"Alexander…"

"Yes…what is it?"

"I have something to tell you that you may not like."

He repeated, "What is it?"

"Isabell revealed something to me when she was deathly ill that I kept contained inside of me for too long."

He didn't say anything but rather, waited until she got the strength to continue. Whatever it was she was troubled with, it was obviously serious enough to make her pause. He gave her time to gather her thoughts.

After a while, she continued, "The reason Isabell is having recurring nightmares is because she happened on a gruesome scene years ago when you were both only children."

"Yes," he said, "The lady that was accused of being a witch and was hanged because of it."

"That woman *was* a witch, Alexander."

"Are you sure?"

"Yes."

"How can you be sure?"

"Because it was my father who helped kill her." She waited for Alexander to process what she had just said, then continued, "He's the one who attached the note that read 'witch'."

His eyebrows furrowed as he grimaced and added, "That note was held in place by a knife driven into her thigh."

She gave a guilty look for a moment as though she were trying to apologize for her father's indiscretion, then said, "I know. He shouldn't have gone to that extreme. But she was a witch, Alexander. She killed my mother with her spells. I was there."

"Your father killed her?"

"The entire town did. My father was only taking part in what was right." Again, she let him process his thoughts and then continued, "That's why I believe Isabell hates my father."

"How would Isabell know he was involved in that? *I* didn't know."

"She may have found out somehow. Perhaps he mentioned it to your mother, and she told her."

"Perhaps," he replied.

"So, you see? It's possible that she provoked my father. Having had a few drinks, he might have lost all control and then did what he did despite himself."

"Yes, I guess that's possible." he said, still trying to analyze the logic. Then he continued, "I know those dreams plague her at night and I wouldn't doubt in the daytime as well."

Having planted that seed in Alexander's mind, she continued with her assertion, "My father is a good man. It's unfortunate that Isabell might think otherwise, but the nightmares are of her own fears and the manifestations of what she saw." She gave him a sideways glance that he didn't see, and then resumed, "I wouldn't want anything to happen to us because of her accusations. I love my father, Alexander, and I sincerely hope you respect him for the good man that he is. I love you, Alexander, and we should not allow her hatred to come between us. Please?" she begged.

"Nothing shall come between us, Myrna. I love you too much."

She gave a little smile and kissed him fervently in part to thank him for understanding such a volatile situation and to affirm her love for him.

After the kiss, she appealed to him, "Alexander?"

"Yes my love, what is it?"

"We shouldn't mention any of this to Isabell or your mother. It may make things worse where Isabell might seek revenge against my father and even me."

He smiled at her and said, "You're right. Let's forget all about it; as though it never happened."

They kissed again and then continued their walk.

In their travels, they laughed and giggled to make up for the lost time they experienced earlier that morning and stopped along the way in a deserted area where they were able to make love without being seen.

The Witch of Brentwood

*****

There was silence all around. Amelia sat in her rocker waiting for Isabell to return from wherever it was she went to after storming out at breakfast. She missed her daughter not because of the silence but because she had betrayed Isabell by making light of Clement's tirades the night before. She had told her son and his love they could take a walk and not worry about her being alone, even if she had preferred them to stay and keep her company. But how could she deny the opportunity for lovers to be alone together? Clement coming home was not something she wished for, however. Being alone was far more pleasant than getting beaten, although it wasn't something she feared at the moment since his work was always more important than being with family. So, she was alone and there was silence all around.

She didn't mind being alone when she was finishing up with cleaning and washing after breakfast, but now she found herself thinking too much with nothing to do but sit. The birds outside were unusually loud that day, so she decided to get up and go outside to watch them fly and bathe. To her, watching and admiring birds was a very natural pastime even if it had become something to avoid because of the stigma that existed with birds appearing to witches unwittingly. So, she watched her birds and did much thinking.

The beatings from Clement kept playing over and over again in her mind, as well as her making up excuses for him to Isabell. Keeping peace in the family was important to Amelia but was it so important to the point of risking her daughter's trust? This bothered her more than anything. She would have withstood twice the pain to make Isabell understand the importance of not making too much of the incident notwithstanding its severity. If only there was some way of making things right, she thought. If only she could make it up to Isabell so their relationship could somewhat get back to normal. She thought long and hard until she finally came up with something that would surely restore Isabell's faith in her.

Clement was a slob and the only reason his belongings were in order was because of the impeccable cleaning habits Amelia learned as a child. However, he did have some belongings he considered valuable enough to keep away from everyone else. It was a secret hiding place where he kept money, deeds, purchase receipts, and the like. He made sure Amelia didn't know about its location or what was kept inside, but she found it one day as she was cleaning without his knowing. If there was one place Clement would keep a valuable piece of jewelry like Isabell's brooch, it would be in that hiding place along with other valuables.

She stood straight as a statue watching her birds almost as if they were an inspiration, and let her mind explore all of the ramifications of what she was about to do. Her eyes shifted back and forth in total concentration, not seeing anything other than her thoughts. She wondered whether he would even notice its disappearance for quite a while, thinking that he might not look in his hiding place very often. She entertained the fact that he was drunk when he ripped it from Isabell's neck and perhaps didn't even remember where he might have hidden it. That was a possibility as well. But if he *did* notice it missing, there would be serious consequences. Of this, she was sure. This was the only reason she remained standing outside for so long. She thought about it long and hard and finally came to a decision.

The Witch of Brentwood

She worked up her nerve and then looked around the yard and down the road. Seeing no one in sight, she hurried to the back of the cabin and looked out at the backyard. All she saw were chickens with some scattered eggs on the ground, and the cattle quietly grazing. No one was around and she was completely alone to do what needed to be done. So, she walked back into the cabin, proceeded to her bedroom door, and opened it. She didn't know why the creaking of the hinges gave her fright, since there was no one there to hear her wrongdoing, but it made her wince anyway.

She closed the door behind her and walked to a closet opposite the bed. The closet door never closed properly due to a loose hinge that was never repaired. She guessed that he must have thought it was the perfect hiding location, thinking no one would ever suspect his valuable possessions to be stored in such a vulnerable place.

She opened the door slowly and looked in the back left corner of the closet floor. There was a section of floorboards that were lifted very slightly from the rest of the floorboards, which is what drew her attention to it when cleaning a couple weeks before. At that time, she had investigated it out of curiosity, thinking it was something else that needed to be repaired. But instead, she found it was a secret compartment that Clement had made to serve as his hiding place.

She listened very carefully for footsteps or idle conversations of people approaching. There were none. So, she lifted the compartment floorboards one by one to reveal what she had seen before; money, receipts, and other valuables. But there was one item there that she hadn't seen a couple of weeks before. It was a little pouch the townsmen carried with them that was mainly used to keep smoking tobacco to refill their pipes. She picked it up and immediately noticed the contents were not tobacco. It didn't feel like tobacco, and she knew at once she had found what she came for. The fact that he had hidden it in a tobacco pouch gave her renewed hope that he wouldn't notice its disappearance even if he looked into the compartment because it wasn't visible. He wouldn't notice its disappearance until he was ready to sell or trade it.

She carried the pouch to her own bureau desk and found a perfect piece of jewelry in her trinket box that could be put there in its place. It was expensive but not as valuable as the brooch, so she didn't mind exchanging one for the other. Carefully removing the brooch from the pouch, she placed it neatly on top of the desk. Suddenly, she heard what seemed to be Alexander and Myrna talking not far from the cabin. She ran to the window to spy and saw them approaching at a faster pace than Amelia would have liked. She hurried back to the desk and quickly placed the substitute into the pouch. Then without missing a step or a beat, ran to the closet and returned the pouch exactly in the same location of the secret compartment. She heard the front door opening as she replaced the floorboards, stepping on them to make sure they didn't stick up too much above the rest of the closet floor.

"Mother, we're back!" Alexander called out.

Amelia quickly shut the closet door as best she could despite the loose hinge, ran to her desk to grab the brooch, dropped it in the pocket of her apron, and ran to sit on her bed.

"I'm in my room, Alexander." she replied, trying not to appear out of breath.

"Are you resting?" he asked.

"Yes dear. I'll be out directly."

"No. You rest, mother. We'll be outside gathering eggs on the ground before the racoons steal them away."

"That would be very kind of you both. Thank you."

Then, she heard the door close.

After a moment, she got up and went to the window, making sure to not be seen by the two young lovers. Both were enjoying their company as they gathered eggs and pretended to throw them at one another. She looked on as she felt torn with emotions. Her happiness for them made her wish her youth was not so far behind her. She was always honest as a child but suddenly stealing from her husband, which was a sin, was now the right thing to do. As she watched the young lovers, she hoped so much that Isabell and Alexander wouldn't stray from each other because of the man she married out of necessity.

Réal Carpentier

Chapter 8

Isabell could see her home from a distance and approached with reluctance. She was sure Clement had not come home from work yet but wasn't sure of the way things would be with the rest of the family since having left the breakfast table so abruptly. But as she walked, she mostly thought about her mysterious encounter with Flora. The conversation she had with her was a bit scary, but it was also a bit intriguing. *What was it she said, 'You also have the power'? That's what she had said. What kind of power? And power to do what, exactly?* These questions kept her preoccupied. She no longer dwelled on Clement and his evil fits of violence.

As she got closer, she saw Alexander in the backyard with Myrna and decided to join them and perhaps have a word with Alexander alone.

"Hello!" Isabell shouted from a distance.

They looked up and saw she was coming their way. Myrna immediately said something to Alexander and then left to go back into the cabin with a bowl full of eggs. From where she was, Isabell couldn't hear what was said but perceived it to be more of a command than anything else; perhaps a warning of some kind.

Finally, Isabell was in the backyard alone with Alexander.

"Where did you go?" he asked.

"Nowhere in particular; just here and there."

"Why did you leave as you did?"

"I couldn't bear to be with Clement anymore. I thought I could pretend nothing ever happened, but I couldn't. His complaining about the food was the final insult, so I left."

"Well, you shouldn't have."

"Why not, Alexander?"

"Because it's not proper."

"Was it proper for him to beat mother unconscious?"

"He was drunk. He couldn't help what he was doing. What did you say to set him off, Isabell?"

She looked at him with anger. "I said nothing to him. He just came at me and ripped the brooch from my neck and when mother tried to stop him, he beat her."

"Why do you hate him so? Do you know something *I* should know as well?"

"I don't hate him. That is, I didn't until last night's assault."

"Myrna seems to think you might be unfairly blaming him for something from years ago."

"Years ago? Why would she think that? We didn't know him years ago. What is she telling you, Alexander?" He turned away and said nothing. She immediately grabbed his arm for him to face her again and insisted, "What did she tell you?"

"That perhaps you blame her father for the nightmares you've been having."

The Witch of Brentwood

Isabell looked puzzled. She tried to analyze what Alexander was saying but couldn't make any sense of it. For his part, Alexander saw the look in her face and was convinced it was sincere. *She didn't know about Clement's involvement in hanging that witch after all.*

"Do you know what those nightmares are the result of, Alexander? The hanging woman we saw as children. I'm sure you've had your share of bad dreams as well because of it. Why should I implicate him in any way? We didn't know him then."

Realizing Isabell didn't know about Clement's involvement, he decided to stop the conversation at once, as Myrna had instructed him before leaving.

"Well, let's forget about all that." Alexander said, "But try not to put so much blame on him. He's a hard worker and a good provider."

"What's happened to you, Alexander? Are you so much in love with Myrna that you'd turn your back on your own sister and mother just to not jeopardize your relationship with her? Is that what it is? Because if it is, you're no better than Clement. The pain you give is not physical, but it's just as bad if not worse. Your pain is emotional. There's no cure for that, Alexander. There's no medicine that will cure the emotional pain from someone you love who turns his back on his family for the love of someone we hardly knew just weeks ago."

Isabell didn't expect to cry just then. In fact, she had made up her mind that if she had the urge to cry, she would run away and cry privately so Alexander wouldn't see. But she wasn't strong enough to follow through with her plan. With his looking at her partly with anger and partly with some degree of guilt, tears began to streak down her cheeks. He opened his mouth to reply but she struck his face with her hand before anything could be said. They looked at each other for a moment without saying a word. They were both thinking the same. *How could this have happened to brother and sister? How was it possible for two who loved and supported each other so much, to be opposed to one another so quickly? Would things ever return to normal?* To those questions, neither one found the answers. After a while, she just shook her head in disbelief and ran off into her bedroom.

Myrna, who had been busy washing the dirt from the eggs, was suddenly surprised by a very distraught Isabell running into her room. Curiosity got the better of her and immediately ran out to meet with Alexander again.

"What happened?" she asked.

"I don't believe she knows about your father's involvement years ago. She insists she didn't hate him for any reason of the kind."

"What are you saying, my father just becomes violent and attacks women for no reason?"

"No, of course not."

"There's a reason she provoked him, Alexander. Don't let her make you believe otherwise. She's not the young innocent girl she used to be. Of that, I'm certain."

"I'm sure you're right." he replied.

At that, she kissed him passionately to assure him of her undying love. For his part, Alexander felt torn but his love for Myrna was too strong to allow sibling love to get in the way.

In her room, Isabell reflected on her conversation with Alexander as she cried. She tried to figure out what he meant when he said something about hating Clement for something he'd done years ago when neither one of them knew him; and Clement being the cause of the night terrors. Then she remembered the letter she'd found in his drawer that was tucked away inside an old shirt pocket. It was dark in the room, but she thought she'd read that the court officials had found him innocent of wrongdoing. She thought about it for a moment, then decided it was too much of a coincidence to give it any further consideration.

She then cried until she fell asleep.

*****

Sharing a bedroom with Myrna was becoming next to impossible for Isabell. Still, there was no other room and the luxury of having her own room simply didn't exist. She thought of asking Clement about the possibility of building an addition to the cabin but the mere thought of asking him to do her a favor was at once discarded as ridiculous. *I'd have a better chance at experiencing a virgin birth.* That whimsical thought crossed her mind spontaneously and then immediately asked for forgiveness from God lest it be considered blasphemous.

Since the incident of the beatings, things were very quiet in the room that was shared by the girls. Nothing was spoken, nor was there hardly any eye-to-eye contact. They simply went about their affairs as though the other person wasn't in the room. Any outside animal noise or thunderclap from electrical storms were preferable to a conversation with someone not willing to understand reason or give others the benefit of doubt.

On the night of Isabell's visit with Derris and Flora, she was awakened by dreams again. She didn't scream out as usual but rather grunted before waking. It was loud enough to be heard by Myrna and it woke her as well. She turned in the direction of Isabell's bed and was able to see her by the moonlight shining through the window. After a time, Myrna initiated a very rare discussion between the two.

"Another dream?" asked Myrna.

"Yes, another dream."

"Is it always the same?"

"Usually, but at times, with some variations."

"What was this one?"

"I'm sure you're very interested." she told Myrna, sarcastically.

"You're right. I am not. Just making conversation."

"I'm not in the mood for conversation, if it's all the same to you."

After that, there was silence in the room again for a moment. Then, Isabell started again.

"Myrna?"

"Yes?"

"Would you ask your father to return my brooch?"

"Why? Why is that brooch so important?"

"Because my mother gave it to me. It was handed down from her father. It has no value other than sentimental value. So it's worthless to him."

"It may be of value after all. Who's to say? Besides, my father knows what's best in the affairs of finance. If he needs it to support this family, then he should have it."

At that, Isabell turned her back to Myrna trying to end the conversation. Ignoring this, Myrna started again.

"Are the visions of that hanging woman with the knife in her leg still haunting you?"

Isabell very hesitantly answered, "Yes."

"Have you any idea who did it to her?"

Isabell turned to face her again. "How could I?" she replied.

"I don't know. Sometimes stories travel from one person to another."

"I don't know who did it. Why should that matter?"

"Just asking. I bet if you knew, you'd have a burning desire to hurt that person. Am I correct in assuming that?"

"Yes, you are. But this conversation serves very little purpose."

Myrna thought for a moment, then asked, "If I was involved in her death, would you hurt *me*?"

"Myrna, leave me be. I'm very tired and should like very much to try to sleep again."

Myrna insisted on an answer. "Would you?" she asked again.

Isabell replied angrily, "I may hurt you now without your involvement if you persist in keeping me awake."

Isabell turned her back on her again for a final time in an attempt to end this meaningless conversation.

What Myrna was trying to do with her inquiries wasn't obvious to Isabell. But they served a useful purpose. If Isabell knew that her father's actions were the cause of those sleepless nights, it would be reason enough for Isabell to provoke him. If not, there had to be another reason because her father, the one she depended on all her life, was not the kind of man to use violence against defenseless women unless, of course, if the woman was the victim of some evil possession.

This thought suddenly made Myrna's inclination come to a halt. Her mind took a turn, and she began concentrating in a totally different direction. Her eyes stared at the ceiling so removed from the moonlight that she couldn't see it. Seeing anything didn't matter, suddenly. What mattered was fixing her eyes in a particular direction in order to concentrate on something more important; the possibility that Amelia was possessed by an evil spirit much like her own mother was. Those beatings were necessary, she recalled. It suddenly became possible that her father had a very serious reason for the so-called attacks just a few hours before.

Myrna thought long and hard. She heard the steady rhythm of Isabell's breathing indicating she was asleep again. She let the thoughts of demonic possession whirl around in her mind. She thought of possible scenarios that might come to pass in the near future if the woman she now lived with was indeed inflicted; all the dangers associated with evil, living amongst her and her father. She thought of all the experiences she had gone through with her own mother that may have to be realized again. All these thoughts played and danced around in her mind, which made it impossible for her to get back to sleep. She thought also of Alexander and wondered if he would suffer the same fate as his mother.

Perhaps it was those evil thoughts running in her mind or something totally different, but she suddenly began to feel very ill. At first, she ignored it and rejected her feeling of nausea as just another passing moment like the ones she'd felt in the last couple of mornings. But this time, the nausea didn't pass. It got worse to the point of having to quickly get out of bed, leave her room, and stumble in the dark to feel around for the ash bucket that was kept near the stove. She found it just in time.

If this nausea persisted every morning, she would soon have to visit the local doctor and determine what the problem might be. She wondered also if it was connected in any way to having missed her last menstrual period. From what she knew, they were supposed to be on a monthly regular cycle.

Réal Carpentier

*****

Next morning, everyone was up bright and early for breakfast because it was Sunday and anyone with any conviction at all had to be in the meeting house for church services on time to worship and give thanks. The breakfast table was set very nicely, as that was the custom every Sunday.

It was quiet as it had been of late, with a few glimpses at each other to see if the other was looking at them. Isabell and Myrna caught each other at one point, eye-to-eye, but turned away just as quickly. Alexander and Myrna held hands whenever they didn't have to cut their food or butter their toast. Amelia was starting to look more like herself, save for a bruised eye that was slowly getting back to normal, so she tried to set the example of getting back to normalcy by making small talk that seemed more superficial than usual.

"I trust everyone had a good evening?" Amelia said. It was more of a question than anything.

Isabell and Myrna looked at each other, as Clement just grunted in acknowledgement.

"I did, mother. I hope you, as well?" Alexander replied.

"I did indeed Alexander. Thank you."

After that small exchange, everything went back to being quiet again for a moment. Then, Clement spoke. As he spoke, others around the table responded except Isabell who only listened and listened well.

"There was an incident that occurred where I was hired." he said to no one in particular, still looking down at his food.

"Do tell." replied Amelia.

"It happened yesterday."

"What happened?" asked Alexander.

"My client's daughter was burned to death."

There was a general reaction of astonishment around the table with a few gasps from the women.

"Oh my God! How might such a calamity have happened?" Myrna asked.

"They don't know. There was no evidence of combustible fuel to be found near the vicinity, nor were there any nearby areas that were burned."

"What do you mean?" asked Alexander.

"Nothing else was burned except her and some of her garments."

"That's not possible." Alexander replied.

"It's not possible but that is the reality. Nothing was burned except her. There were parts of her that were still identifiable but that was all."

"How might something like this have happened?" Myrna asked again.

"There are no answers," replied Clement, "but I think I know."

"What?" asked Amelia, "What do you know?"

"I think it was that old woman who lives close by in that shack she calls a home."

"How could she have anything to do with it?" asked Alexander.

"Because I believe she's a witch."

Finally, Isabell spoke, "She's a cunning woman who helps with ailments. At least I heard it said."

Clement replied in a stern voice, "They call her a cunning woman but that's only another name for witch, if you ask me. I believe she can hurt as well as heal."

Just then, Myrna began to wonder if perhaps he was right. They had encountered a witch before; the one that killed her mother. She immediately thought about how her poor mother died at the hands of that witch; a witch that her father had ultimately ridden the town of. Then she wondered if Amelia had anything to do with burning the young girl as well. Fear began to creep inside her along with a chill that slithered up her spine.

Clement continued, "How else would something like this happen? There was nothing to indicate there was a fire except for her body. It also seemed like the fire started from within."

"From within?" asked Amelia.

"From inside her. It seems that's where the fire started. That's what my client said. That's what was most charred."

Isabell became very pensive at that moment, as others around the table inquired more and more. She recollected her encounter with that sweet old woman. She even had a sweet name; Flora. *How could anyone like her be accused of such a thing as being a witch and setting fire to an innocent young girl?* It didn't seem right. Then as she thought further, she remembered her answer when Flora asked if she thought she was a witch. Isabell had felt bad about her response but still she had replied yes. She recalled the mysterious torches burning next to her cabin and Flora saying Isabell had to leave because there was much to do. She also called to mind her conversation with her about being able to heal and hurt. *But you can also hurt others, correct?* she had asked Flora. The old woman's answer was now resonating with her and beginning to frighten her. *We all have that tendency. You do as well, don't you?* That was the old woman's response. Isabell wished she hadn't had that conversation with Flora, but she had and that's what so frightened her; the fact that a witch had implicated Isabell of being the same.

Finally, Amelia said, "Enough of all this talk of witches. I'll not have any further discussion about this in this house. Let evil stay where it will, but it has no place here."

Myrna turned her head and looked at Amelia with a dubious expression. She didn't know if Amelia was sincere or only saying that to cover her own guilt of being a witch herself.

Totally ignoring Amelia, Clement commanded, "I forbid anyone from going near that place. If there's a guilty witch living in that shack, justice will be served somehow in its own time. We'll have nothing to do with her or her kind."

Everyone agreed, even Isabell. But she knew she would return to her, for there were many unanswered questions mulling in her mind. She had problems of her own to overcome and if Flora could be of some help to provide a cure of sorts, she would return.

Breakfast was soon over. The women had lost their appetite and the clinking of utensils against dishes became an annoyance. No one said much except for the obligatory mumbles necessary for practical communication. As soon as the kitchen was clean, Isabell went into her bedroom to get ready for the day's church services.

Myrna was already dressed for church since she could hardly sleep and woke up early enough to get dressed; anything to take her mind off of the fearsome thoughts she had through the night. So, she went outside to wait while the others were ready to leave and tried hard to not dwell on the evil that could possibly exist around her and her father. Sooner or later, however, she would have to have a discussion with her father to get his opinion on the validity of her fears. She still felt a little nauseous but attributed it to her fears.

The Witch of Brentwood

*****

Inside the cabin, Clement waited near the fireplace and at times tended to it while the others got dressed in their Sunday attire which was mainly black or somber colors to signify repentance and sanctified thought. The morning was cold despite the blue skies and the chirping birds. In fact, it was colder in the cabin than it was outside, which was a usual occurrence this time of year regardless of where one lived in the United Colonies of New England. The hot embers and flame felt good but any closer would undoubtedly result in the reddening of his skin.

Alexander came out of his room all dressed and ready to go. He asked Clement where Myrna was and Clement said nothing but instead, pointed in the direction of the outside door. Alexander gave a nod, thanked him, and proceeded out to meet her. Sometimes the less said, the better, depending on everyone's mood. This had become the most prudent way of thinking within the last few days.

"Isabell, do you have a pin for my hat?" Amelia shouted from her room.

"I have one, mother." Isabell replied. "I'll bring it directly. I'm not fully dressed yet."

"No, that's okay dear." Amelia said, walking towards Isabell's room, "I'll meet you there if it's alright."

"Surely."

Amelia opened Isabell's door and gave it a shove to close it again once inside. But the hinges, being worn and stiff as they were, prevented the door from closing fully. With the door ajar, Clement was able to see inside her room without any effort from where he was sitting. So, he looked and saw Isabell who was only partly dressed. She was wearing a chemise only, which showed her calves and her bosom free of a corset's restraints. Her hair had been let down to arrange it in a different fashion, which at once gave her the appearance of a woman with loose morals in his eyes.

Amelia took the pin from Isabell and then whispered so Clement wouldn't hear, "I have something for you."

"What is it?" Isabell whispered back.

"Not here." Amelia replied and then walked towards the door.

Almost immediately, Clement turned away as Amelia came out with her pin and proceeded to her room neglecting to shut Isabell's door. Isabell, with her back to the door, was unaware her door was not closed and once Clement was sure Amelia was out of sight, he once again turned his view towards Isabell's room.

Clement had never seen Isabell in that way before nor did he ever imagine her in such a manner. But for the first time, he saw how beautiful she was; the way her hair caressed her bare shoulders, and the silky look of her skin. Even her profile seemed to take on a new beauty he had never seen. She bent down to arrange her shoes, revealing the curvature of her back to her rear bottom. His stare grew wider, and he no longer cared who saw him looking. After all, the door was open, and he was only human; even on Sunday. He then had a side view of her as she sat in her chair and began to massage her right leg from her ankle to her knee, which lifted the bottom of her chemise slightly to reveal her thigh. She then proceeded to do the same with the other leg. Clement licked his lips from seeing something he hadn't even seen from his own wife. How beautiful Isabell was. His arousal became more intense until finally, she looked in his direction. They looked at each other for a good long time. For his part, he simply couldn't look away. As for her, she was too much in shock that Clement was looking at her with the most lecherous look she had ever seen or heard of. After coming to her senses and seeing so much pleasure in his face, she ran to the door to shut it completely.

Just then, Amelia came out of her room still adjusting her garments here and there for perfection.

"How do I look?" she asked Clement.

He was still flush from seeing Isabell.

"Just fine," he replied.

"Dear me, why is your face all red as a beet?"

"I had to bend down to tend the fireplace."

"Where is Alexander?"

Again, Clement didn't answer but only pointed towards the door.

Amelia turned towards Isabell's door, "Hurry Isabell. We don't want to be late."

Isabell didn't answer.

"You also Clement, come along." she said walking to the door.

"I'll be along directly. You go on and meet Alexander outside."

Once Amelia was outside, Clement once again turned to face Isabell's door which was now closed tightly. He couldn't see her but could imagine what she was doing behind that closed door and what she looked like doing it. The thought alone was enough to arouse him again. He saw nothing but still he stared at her door.

As Isabell hurried to dress herself, she couldn't help but see his burning eyes in her mind. She had never experienced such a look from a man but knew of it from her conversations and warnings from her mother. She hadn't meant to display herself only partly dressed, as that was certainly something only evil women did. Hurrying to get fully dressed, she prayed for forgiveness and hoped Clement would not hold her responsible for what he saw. She also prayed he would *forget* what he saw. She hadn't heard him go outside with the others, so she knew he was still behind that door. She could picture him still staring. There was a door between them, but she still felt violated.

Outside, Amelia, Alexander, and Myrna waited patiently.

The Witch of Brentwood

*****

The puritans held their day of prayer and worship in high regard and of the utmost importance, especially in those days when rumors of witches were much more than rumors. The meeting house was always full; standing room only. The men were seated on one side and the women on the other. It was an all-day affair, since the sermons usually lasted between three to five hours, and the prayers and hymns were also time consuming. They took a break for lunch and then resumed. This was a typical Sunday, and everyone attended the services for fear of being found at home when some of the officials conducted a search for anyone not attending.

Clement and the rest of the family took their places. Alexander sat with Clement on the left while Myrna and Isabell sat on both sides of Amelia on the right side. The place was full of people as usual, and the preacher was in the front near the pulpit where he would give his sermons and read from the good book. Myrna prayed fervently for protection from Amelia because she believed with all her heart that she was sitting next to a witch. Isabell would try to be discreet when she looked around to see who might be in attendance, hoping to catch a glimpse of Derris Blackmoore. Finally, she spotted him. They were both sitting halfway between the front and back, only he on one side and she on the other, but he had spotted *her* right away when she walked in. As soon as their eyes met, they both smiled at each other and this made Isabell feel a little better, given what had occurred in the previous days including that morning. When it was time to break for lunch, she couldn't see him because they were both with their respective families. This made her long to get back to the meeting house, and lunch felt like forever for the first time in her life.

During one of the hymns, Isabell felt her mother's hand reach hers. At first, she thought she simply wanted to hold hands in prayer, but then it became apparent that her mother was trying to give her something. To remain inconspicuous, both women remained focused with eyes looking in the direction of the preacher as they sang their hymn. Isabell opened her hand discreetly and once the object was in her possession, she closed it quickly because her mother's subtlety indicated that it must be kept a secret. Then she remembered her mother telling her she had something to give her but 'not here', as she recalled her saying in her room. After a moment, Isabell looked down nonchalantly to see what the object was. There she saw a star-shaped brooch; complete with an array of diamonds surrounding a white pearl. Her eyes grew wider but tried to remain calm. After a while of holding and cherishing it, she placed it carefully in the little pouch she carried on her wrist for such things as thimbles and beads. Isabell tried to contain her ecstasy at being the owner of her brooch again and glanced over at Clement every once in a while, to make sure he was oblivious to the entire transaction. She continued on in prayer and praise as if it were a normal Sunday, but this was no ordinary Sunday.

Soon, the church services were coming to a close and the sun was about to set. It dawned on Isabell that she had not seen Flora anywhere in the meeting house for the services. It gave credence to the possibility of her being a witch as Clement claimed, since no one on the right side of puritan ideology would dare miss the services; not on a Sunday. Still, she didn't want to dwell on such negativity too much since she now had possession of her brooch, was in the company of the young Mr. Blackmoore, and was finally filled with happy thoughts.

Everyone congregated outside for a while after the services which gave Derris an opportunity to walk over to where Isabell was, since she had made sure to stray far enough away from her family.

"Greetings," he said.

"Greetings."

"You look lovely as ever, If I might."

"Why, thank you." she replied coyly.

"I was hoping to see you this morning when I tended to my chores outside."

"I had to get ready for church, silly. A woman can't simply be expected to go out on a Sunday without some preparation."

"No, I suppose not."

"Besides, you would undoubtedly think terrible thoughts of me if I was forward enough to stalk you."

"I love bold women," he said.

This made her laugh, which made him smile in satisfaction.

"Shall I see you at the fence tomorrow?" he added.

"Perhaps."

"I would greatly love seeing you again."

She giggled, "Then, you shall. I'll see to it."

"Great! Until tomorrow, then."

"Until tomorrow." she returned.

Then to her amazement, he kissed her hand, smiled, and went his way.

Finally, she made her way back to where her family was and tried to behave nonchalantly as though it was just another ordinary Sunday.

"Who was that young man?" asked Amelia, much to Isabell's surprise.

"Oh, just someone I know." she answered.

"How do you know him?" Amelia persisted.

"Just an acquaintance." Isabell returned.

As she spoke, she could see Clement eyeing her from head to toe. If she was not mistaken, it appeared to be the same look she saw from him earlier when he saw her dressing with an open bedroom door. This made her extremely uncomfortable and wished he wasn't so physically close to her.

Then, Clement added, "I don't care for the likes of him."

At once, Isabell turned away from him and didn't respond. Amelia could tell her daughter was distressed about the whole conversation, so she simply didn't press the matter. She hoped at least that this young acquaintance was a nice boy to be respected and trusted.

Clement didn't like the looks of Derris, but he recognized him as the young man who worked for Mr. Berryman, a gun shop owner whom Clement had come to know well. Clement had a collection of guns he'd purchased from Mr. Berryman and had asked him to hire Alexander as an apprentice. To Clement's surprise, Mr. Berryman was all in favor. Business must be very good, Clement thought, if he was willing to hire two young men.

Finally, it was time to take their leave and go home. The women assumed their places in the buggy as Alexander sat next to Clement who held the reins. On the way home, Clement had good news for Alexander.

"I spoke with Mr. Berryman today during our lunch time." Clement told Alexander.

"Mr. Berryman?" Alexander asked.

"Mr. Berryman, the gun shop owner in town. Are you aware he's in need of help in his shop?"

"No."

"He's in dire need. We spoke about you."

"Me?"

"He's interested in hiring you as an apprentice for gunsmithing."

Alexander looked puzzled.

"Me, a gunsmith? Am I not too old to be an apprentice?"

"No. It's preferred that one starts at an earlier age to complete the seven-year training, but it is not necessary. You're a smart and capable boy. You would benefit from the three years until you're twenty-one."

"Was it you're doing?"

"He initiated the conversation. He asked about you. He said you are what he needs." Clement waited for a response, but none came, as Alexander was too astonished to respond. Clement continued, "Sounds like it should be of interest to you. You've been pretending with guns since you were a boy, your mother tells me."

Alexander smiled, "That, I have."

"Interested?"

"What would I learn exactly?"

"He needs someone he can train to repair, design, and build."

Excitement was becoming obvious in Alexander's face. "In his shop? In the gun shop?"

"Yes. He has a repair shop on the top floor."

"Indeed, I always wondered where those stairs led to."

"What do you say? He needs someone directly."

Alexander thought for a moment, then asked, "What do you think? Would you advise it?"

"I certainly would." replied Clement, "You can't be a child all your life. He assured me tools would be provided. I'm sure it would be a handsome compensation as well."

"It sounds very enticing."

"He's even willing to provide lodging for you. What do you say?"

Alexander didn't have to think very long before he answered, "I accept!"

He wasn't at all sure if he would take up the offer of boarding, but the prospect of working with guns and learning a trade was something that pleased him greatly.

"Great!" replied Clement, "I'll see him tomorrow and we can begin the process as soon as we can."

Since the apprenticeship was a legal contract between the apprentice and master craftsman, the process would include drawing up the contract to be signed before the courts which would be entered into a deed book and considered binding. Even the process sounded exciting to Alexander.

This was wonderful news and a great opportunity for a young man his age to make something of himself. *How proud mother and Myrna must be.*

Amelia and Myrna were proud indeed, having heard most of the conversation the two men were having. It also seemed to Amelia that Clement wasn't the monster she thought he had become in the last few days.

Isabell sat without saying a word, clutching her wrist pouch that now contained a very valuable item. She also heard the conversation and would have liked to be as proud as her mother but in her heart, something didn't feel right. She didn't know why and felt somewhat guilty for feeling that way, but she also knew that feelings don't lie.

*****

As soon as they arrived home, Amelia started making supper right away as was her usual practice on Sunday after church services. Myrna helped as usual, but Isabell went directly into her bedroom without a word. She closed the door behind her, and with her ear to it, listened for anyone who might be following her.

"Isabell, aren't you going to help in the kitchen?" Myrna asked.

"She'll be along directly." Amelia replied to Myrna.

Amelia knew full well why Isabell rushed to her room. There was a precious brooch to hide before something happened to it. She hoped Isabell would find a safe and secret place where no one would ever go, especially since that room was shared. Although she didn't know if her daughter had such a place in that little room.

Hearing no one approaching, Isabell looked around the room for the safest hiding place that would not likely be breached. *A bureau desk would be too obvious. Under the mattress would be too risky.* Finally she spotted the little trinket box her mother had given her on her birthday two years before. She loved that little box because not only was it beautiful on the outside, but also on the inside where it was cushioned with a soft burgundy liner.

She opened it and looked in. The first thing she saw was the acorn she had taken from the oak tree of the hanging woman. It didn't make sense but somehow, she was happy to know the little oak seed was still there. She had never tried to remove the liner before and hoped it wasn't glued or somehow fastened permanently. With a little tug, the liner came away from the wooden shell of the cover and revealed the perfect place for the brooch. She tucked it in carefully so as to not damage it or the liner, then put the liner back in its place showing no evidence of tampering or bulging. Just then, she was glad her little box didn't play a tune as she had wished for when she received it. She didn't want to give the slightest clue as to where to look, should Clement be looking for it someday.

She closed the box again without making the slightest noise and went back to join the others in preparation for supper.

While eating, the conversation revolved around the news of Alexander's opportunity as an apprentice. Myrna was ecstatic about the prospect of Alexander learning a trade while earning money on the job, but she was also preoccupied with thoughts of how she'd been feeling of late. It was not normal for her to be ill in the morning. Her preoccupation showed in her face.

"What's the matter Myrna?" asked her father.

"Nothing. Why do you ask?" she replied.

"You look concerned or worried about something. Do you not think Alexander's prospects are good?"

"Oh, I'm overjoyed at his prospects, father." Then she looked at Alexander with a smile. "I wish you only the best and I'm certain you will make a great gunsmith. Mr. Berryman is the luckiest man in the world to have you work for him. I'm sure his business will increase tenfold."

"I'll see to it." replied Alexander with a smile.

"What's the matter, then?" her father asked again.

"Nothing of concern." she said.

"Do you wish to speak with *me*?" asked Amelia. "Perhaps it's something that can only be shared with another woman."

Myrna didn't look at her at all as she replied 'no' with conviction in her tone. Amelia didn't pursue the notion and simply kept on eating.

The rest of the supper continued with Alexander's prospects on everyone's tongue in between bites. No one asked about Myrna's look of concern again and she was successful in not visibly showing any more worry.

Finally, supper was over, and they all followed their normal routine for a Sunday evening. The women cleaned, Clement smoked, and Alexander read from the bible. It was a routine they were all comfortable with. The men knew better than to get in the way of the women, while the women enjoyed hearing bible stories and even liked the smell of Clement's pipe.

Finally, the work was done, and everyone retired to their bedroom to change and get ready for an early bed; everyone but Clement, that is. He liked to retire later than all the others. His reasoning was that it gave him a chance to think about the following day's work. Only this night was different. He had seen Isabell disrobed earlier in the morning. He also saw how she looked at the young Blackmoore boy with what seemed to be lust in her eyes. These thoughts stirred something in him, and he sat alone near the fireplace with graphic images in mind.

After a while of Clement being alone and everyone else in their respective chambers, Isabell stepped out of her room, not knowing Clement hadn't retired to bed yet. As soon as she opened the door, she paused as they looked at one another. She was wearing a dressing gown, which was deemed more than appropriate for night wear.

The Witch of Brentwood

"I'm sorry," she said, "I thought everyone was in bed. I just wanted a bit of grapes before bed."

"It's alright." he said. "Get your grapes."

She closed the door of her room and proceeded to the table hurriedly. There, she took some grapes and had every intention to return to her room as quickly as possible. But Clement got up from his chair and stood behind her at the table. Feeling his breath on her shoulders, she could tell he was closer than he should have been.

Next, she felt his hands on her shoulders. She immediately shrugged them away, returned her nighttime snack to the bowl, and turned to face him with a fear that was apparent in her face. She tried to go back to her room, but he grabbed her arm with a firm hand and squeezed ever-so-slightly so as to not hurt her. He had the same look she had seen that morning as he leered at her from head to toe.

He brought his other hand up to her face in gentle form. There, he brushed her hair from her eye before gently caressing the side of her face.

"I saw how you looked at that boy tonight." he said softly enough to not be heard by anyone but her.

"Let me go." she commanded.

He squeezed her arm a little harder.

"You shall take orders from *me*! No woman commands me in my own home."

As she begged him to let her go, Amelia quietly opened her bedroom door to spy on what she thought she'd heard. She saw her husband looking at her daughter with lust in his eyes and holding her against her will. He had that look that she was well familiar with. She cringed at seeing him lick his lips not two inches from Isabell's face. Knowing she couldn't do anything about this without provoking his anger, she quietly closed her door again and hoped that what she saw would go no further.

Finally, Isabell was able to release herself from his grip and run into her room. Clement would have loved to follow her and display his authority over her, but unfortunately for him, she shared the room with his daughter.

Clement was mad as hell could be. He looked down into the bowl of grapes, grabbed a handful, and launched them against the door of her room.

Amelia sat on her bed and listened in fear. She heard Isabell running into her room, but no other sounds of chase or evidence of her being followed. She'd had this kind of encounter in her *own* life some eighteen years ago and remembered how frightened and terrible she felt about the incident. The rapist was successful in her case, and she became pregnant with the twins. At least the attacker was no longer in her life but in Isabell's case, the perpetrator lived under the same roof as the victim. Amelia surely expected it to happen again; perhaps several times, and perhaps leading to an awful outcome. She knew about the tendencies of men; *disgusting pigs*. She placed her own husband in that same category but also felt helpless. There was nothing she could do to help. There was no one she knew who could or would do something to stop it. Sometimes pretending something like this didn't happen at all was the best way to deal with it, Amelia thought.

Soon, Clement walked into his room and saw Amelia sitting on the bed.

"What's wrong?" he asked.

"Nothing, only waiting for you to come to bed."

The Witch of Brentwood

Clement didn't answer. He walked to his side of the bed and started undressing to don his nightshirt. Just then, Amelia got his attention by removing every piece of garment she was wearing as he looked.

"What are you doing?" he asked.

She didn't respond, but rather got into bed trying to lure him in. She thought his incident with Isabell was only a passing mood that she could alleviate with a good night of intimacy. But she was wrong.

He looked at her in bed completely undressed and waiting for him. She thought she was enticing, but all he saw was the contrast between her and Isabell at that moment. He mulled over the juxtaposition of the two.

Isabell's skin was smooth and tight. Her body was shapely with obvious curves. Her hair was delicate and smelled as a young woman's hair should smell. Her voice was soft as an angel's, and her touch was the flutter of a butterfly.

He looked at her for a while, then finished changing into his nightshirt, blew out the lantern, and plopped into bed with his back to her.

She said nothing but understood what was happening as she stared into the darkness. His desires for her had grown cold. It didn't matter why. It didn't matter if it was because she was no competition for Isabell or any other woman he encountered in his travels from day to day. In fact, as she slowly went to sleep, nothing mattered to her at all anymore.

The rhythmic breathing sounds of sleep filled every bedroom. No other sounds were heard except for an occasional creaking of the cabin's structure as it settled due to temperature changes;

not loud enough to wake anyone. Dripping water was also heard from the kitchen as well as incidental crackling from the embers of a dying fire in the fireplace. Occasionally, there were the usual sounds of moaning from Isabell's room as a result of the ever-recurring nightmares, but otherwise, the cabin was dark and silent.

Some had dreams of great success in the gunsmithing trade, complete with rich partnerships and dining with dignitaries from all over the world; dealing and bargaining for a better position and pay.

Some had dreams of fear of living with witches that could make their menstruation come to a halt, jeopardizing their ability to bear children, and making their twilight years very lonely.

Some had dreams of lust, complete with dominance and degradation of younger women who were vulnerable and defenseless. Crying and pleading made it all the more satisfying and insatiable.

Some had dreams of being discarded like useless cattle too weak to perform much needed work, complete with disrespect, public ridicule, humiliation, and shame; being compared to a much more desirable woman full of vigor and zest for life.

Some had dreams of frightening women being dragged on the ground with a noose around their necks and screaming for mercy. Those frightening dreams, however, were intertwined with other more pleasant dreams of love and laughter, complete with a handsome prince, a fence, and a brooch around her neck that reflected the sun rays into her lover's eyes.

Still, as all these dreams came to pass, the cabin was dark and silent.

Chapter 9

The following day was quiet as usual. It was a normal morning with no time for any formal breakfast, as that was reserved for special days like Sundays and holidays. But it was an exciting day for Alexander. The process of apprenticeship had to be done soon and this particular morning was as good a time as any to begin. Clement and he left early to meet with Mr. Berryman to get the proper paperwork, bring it to the officials of the court authorized to approve such an undertaking, and then return to Mr. Berryman to begin training. Once done, Clement would proceed to work on the roof of the poor family whose daughter suddenly and unexpectedly was scorched beyond recognition for apparently no reason; unless one believed in witchcraft, that is.

Isabell did some cleanup work in her room and then went outside to feed the animals and replenish the water troughs. Her mind was filled with images of what happened the night before with Clement. This was her first experience with men behaving like the very animals she was tending to at the moment. *How unbecoming.* She'd had daydreams about young men and their bold whispers that made her blush, but animal behavior was never part of such fantasies. She wasn't sure what she would do if this happened again. For that matter, she wasn't sure if she *could* do anything because he was much stronger than she. She was also torn about telling her mother about the incident. But finally decided that her mother had to know.

Just then, her mother came out to wash and scrub the garments she and Isabell wore at church the day before. Isabell thought it was the perfect opportunity to discuss it, as much as she cursed at the thought of doing so. She looked at her mother sitting at the wash tub from a distance. The poor woman's hair was disheveled from a night of sleep, her ragged clothes indicated this would be a day of work, and she looked tired. Perhaps tired wasn't the right description Isabell would have used. Her mother was more dispirited than tired; as though she had no ambition to face the day, or any other day for that matter. So, she hated to add to whatever was bothering her mother, but she needed to tell her what must be said. She approached her.

"Good morning, mother."

"Rather a chill in the air today." replied her mother. "What shall you do with yourself, Isabell?"

"Go for a stroll later, I suppose."

"Good. Take advantage of the days before winter comes. Lord knows the mild days are coming to an end."

Isabell had so many things to tell her mother just then. She didn't want to spend any more time with trivial discourse of the weather and such talk. She wanted to tell her the good things in her life; the boy she'd met, thank her for the brooch, and tell her where she'd hidden it. But these things were of secondary importance. The discussion of Clement's advances had to be a priority so something could be done.

"Mother, something happened last night after you went to bed."

Amelia knew full well what Isabell was about to say but didn't want to hear it. There was no way to avoid it. It was the way of human nature. It was wrong for a man to make such advances towards his daughter, this she knew, but Isabell was not Clement's daughter. So as wrong as it seemed, it wasn't really all that bad as far as Amelia was concerned. What was bad about it was her own ego; her man making advances towards another woman. She didn't fault Isabell for the incident, because she couldn't help being attractive to *any* man, but how unfortunate it was for Clement to lust after her own daughter.

"What happened, dear?" asked Amelia

Isabell hesitated, then said, "Clement made advances towards me when we were alone."

Amelia thought for a moment. "You must be mistaken, Isabell."

"I'm not mistaken. He grabbed my arm and had an awful look of desire in his eyes."

"Oh Isabell, it's easy for women to interpret the looks of a man. We mustn't fall prey to garbled notions."

As Amelia said this, she didn't dare look at her daughter.

"Garbled notions? There was no confusion whatsoever. Mother, Clement attacked me last night. If I hadn't gotten away, I shudder to think what he would have done."

"I'm sure it was nothing. Sometimes men get in moods much like we do, Lord knows."

"He's your husband, mother!" Isabell exclaimed. "How can you take this so casually?"

"I'm not taking it casually, Isabell. I saw what happened last night. I opened the door to my room and saw. It was nothing. You're confusing this with something which doesn't exist."

Isabell couldn't believe what she was hearing. "If you saw him, mother, then you know what happened. It couldn't be interpreted any other way. Didn't you see what your husband was doing to me, and what's more, what he wanted to do?"

Amelia couldn't answer because she was holding back tears; tears that would convince Isabell of how serious this really was. Instead, she turned and casually walked back into the cabin without a word as if she were too busy with other things to carry on so about nothing. By the time her mother reached the door, tears were streaming down her face. Isabell called out to her one more time in desperation but there was no response.

Isabell knew all the responses from her mother about this not being something to worry about, were all lies. *Why would mother respond so? Surely, she knows how grave this all is. Why is she trying to protect him over protecting her own daughter?* Isabell tried to make sense of it all, to no avail. She would have liked to ask her mother why she considered the incident a trivial matter.

After a while, a very confused and disappointed Isabell went back to her work in the yard. When she was done, she looked somberly in the direction of the cabin before leaving to meet with her young friend, Derris.

The Witch of Brentwood

*****

Each step was a step closer to her independence. The further away she walked from home, the more she felt free from harm and despair. As she walked, she thought about how different things were, from when she was younger, and life was carefree. It's true she was frailer and sicklier in her younger days, but there were no secrets to keep from family, no risk of being preyed upon by lecherous drunks, and there was no lack of trust between her and Alexander. Even as a child, she knew the twins couldn't be kids forever and that things naturally had to change. That was part of life. But she also felt she wasn't ready for the change. If she could have remained a little kid forever, it would have suited her just fine.

As she walked, she noticed the clouds rolling in and gradually covering the sun. It got chilly suddenly, and she was glad she'd brought a light overcoat just in case. It didn't look like rain just minutes ago but now she wasn't sure if she'd have to run for cover under a tree at any moment. The sky grew darker with gray clouds as she rounded the corner. She knew where she was, having been here just a couple of days prior but the familiar surroundings still didn't calm her anxiety. The gray clouds didn't help her discomfort either. There she was in plain view of the cemetery next to the cabin belonging to the old woman, Flora Wemmick.

She picked up her pace in order to pass quickly by without looking, if she could. But she couldn't help it. It may have been sheer curiosity, much in the same way she was mesmerized by hearing scary ghost stories around a fire when she was younger and even now as an adult, if she were honest with herself. The sight of the gravestones was as scary as it had been two days ago when walking home from meeting the old woman and she couldn't imagine walking by them at night. Finally, the cemetery was behind her as she got closer to Flora's home. She was now able to slow her pace a little and gradually come to a halt, looking at the dark cabin under that gray sky.

She stood waiting and listening for any sounds of life from Flora's dwelling. She saw and heard nothing. The only sense she felt was the smell of imminent rain, which she felt would come soon. And even though she was still a good way away from the fence where she'd met Derris as well as an even greater distance from her own home, Isabell didn't move despite the impending rain. She only looked at Flora's homestead for a good long time; longer than she wanted.

The rain didn't start gradually. It was a waterfall that came down on Isabell in an instant, completely leaving her drenched in a matter of seconds. Still, she stood looking.

Finally, she ran to the cabin and knocked on the door. Waiting for Flora to open, she looked around to see the torches that were in place the other day were no longer there. They've served their purpose, whatever that was, she thought. She knocked again, while still being rained on. Getting no response, she called out to her.

"Miss Wemmick!" *Nothing.* "Flora!" *Nothing.* "Are you home?"

It was hard to hear anyone approaching the door because of the enormous racket the rain was making, hitting the ground and the roof of the cabin. Then, the door opened.

"Isabell!" Flora exclaimed. "Come in out of the rain, dear." Isabell entered as Flora ran for a towel to give her. "What were you doing out there?"

"I was on my way to meet my young man but when I passed your cabin, I felt I had to see you."

"You shouldn't be here in the daytime, Isabell. Do you remember what I said? You should only come at night."

"I don't believe you're a witch. Also, I don't care what people think. If they spread negative rumors about me, then so be it."

"You don't understand what you're saying, dear. Did anyone see you?"

"I'm sure not. Who but I, would be fool enough to be in this rain?"

The sound of the rain on the roof was as loud inside as it was outside. Isabell also noticed a few leaks in the roof. Drips came down in a plop where some bowls were strategically placed to keep the floor dry. Flora motioned for her to sit with her at the table.

"You *are* a foolish girl." Flora said with a stern look.

Isabell ignored that comment. Perhaps it was meant as an affront, or an expression of endearment, she thought. Either way, she wasn't about to argue with the truth.

"I have something to ask," said Isabell.

"Go on but be warned. You may not like the answers."

Isabell paused to formulate what she was about to say very carefully. Then, she began.

"There was a young girl who died two days ago not far from here. She died by fire."

Isabell stopped to see how she would react. Flora didn't say a word and looked willing to let Isabell finish what she wanted to say.

Isabell continued slowly and with deliberate intent, "They say the fire started from within her and burned outward. Nothing was found to start a fire near where she was. It was as though it started on its own. Nothing else burned around her except for a few charred patches of grass. Some people accuse you of such an evil deed." She waited again. Flora said nothing. Isabell resumed, "Yesterday morning at breakfast, I recalled what you said to me; how we were all capable of hurting others as well as doing good. And you didn't deny the notion when I asked if you were a witch."

"Nor did I admit to being one." Flora added.

"That's true. But I saw the torches just outside this very spot as I walked past. They were in such a strange formation, and they didn't seem to serve any useful purpose."

"Oh, but they *did* serve a purpose, my dear." Flora responded.

"What purpose?"

"*My* purpose."

The two looked at one another and waited. The conversation had been conducted in a very cordial manner despite specific and rather blunt language. Both were still very friendly with one another, and their intent had no ill will. They were only interested in the truth. Isabell *did* wonder, however, why Flora seemed to be so vague; almost avoiding to give direct answers. But then again, she *was* warned that she may not like the answers. So far, Flora was correct in saying that.

"Flora?" asked Isabell.

"Yes, dear?"

"Did you kill that young girl?"

Flora paused, then asked a question of her own, "If you wish someone dead and they die, are you the killer?"

Isabell just stared at her and said, "No but if I have the means of wishing them dead, I am. Wishing they were dead and wishing them dead are different from one another." There was a silent pause, then she added, "Did you wish her dead?"

"Yes. Yes, I did." was her response.

"And that's what killed her?"

"Most probably."

"How?"

"I had her essence in my possession, and I burned it."

"Her essence?"

"It was an apple she ate. She threw it and I picked it up. Her saliva contained her essence. When her essence burned, she burned."

Isabell felt an uneasiness in the pit of her stomach. She wasn't afraid, necessarily, she was more stunned at Flora's candor.

"So, you *are* a witch." There was no response. Isabell tried again, "Are you a witch?"

"Yes."

Many things went through Isabell's mind just then. She could hardly keep focus on what she wanted to say next. Then, she remembered what Flora had told her on their first encounter.

"What did you mean when you said I have the power too?" asked Isabell.

Flora responded, "You're *also* a witch, my dear."

Isabell stood up.

"That's not so!" she exclaimed.

"You have powers. I know it. I feel it."

Isabell began to cry, "I made no deal with the devil. I attend church every Sunday." Then she darted for the door, shouting, "I'M NOT A WITCH!"

Isabell ran out into the rain headed for the young man who seemed to be the only solace in her life. As she ran, the rain started to abate slowly until it stopped completely. Next, the clouds began to separate, and the sun shone through again. Finally, she was able to stop to catch her breath.

The fence which had become their meeting place was around the corner, but she had to catch her breath before taking another step. She rested a while before starting to walk to the fence again. That's when she noticed the ground was completely dry. She stopped again. Looking around, she saw nothing but dry ground. Yet, she was still dripping from the harsh rain; the rain she had encountered past the cemetery as she approached Flora's cabin and had started with such force as to make her run for shelter.

The Witch of Brentwood

*****

Amelia had cried so much from her talk with Isabell that there were no more tears to shed. She still felt like crying but simply couldn't. The last time she felt such an ironic situation was when her mother died. Given an hour or two, however, she was sure her eyes would well up again.

It was now afternoon, and it was a nice day weatherwise at least. As she had expected, it hadn't rained. As such, she wondered why Myrna was still in her room since the morning. *Surely a young girl such as she was full of vigor and bloom, should be out taking a walk at the very least.* Amelia cleaned herself a little to make sure her swollen eyes didn't give too much away. Then came out of her room and knocked on Myrna's door.

"Myrna, it's me, Amelia."

"I'm not feeling very well. I wish to be alone." was the response behind the closed door.

"What's the matter, dear?"

"It's nothing. I'll be alright presently."

"Perhaps I can help?" Amelia asked.

There was no response. So, Amelia took it upon herself to impose uninvited. She opened the door and found Myrna covered up in bed and appeared to be shaking.

"What's the matter?" inquired Amelia.

Myrna didn't respond nor did she look at her. Seeing Myrna obviously suffering from more than just a simple ailment, she entered and sat facing her on Isabell's bed.

"Why are you shaking? Did someone hurt you?" Amelia asked.

Myrna paused before answering. She wished Amelia would go away. Finally, she responded.

"Why did father beat you?"

"Oh, he had been drinking, that's all. I thought that was made clear when Isabell was so upset. You even agreed."

Myrna didn't acknowledge her. She just kept staring at her door wishing Amelia would go away. Finally, Amelia became more resolute than sympathetic.

"I shan't leave until you tell me what's wrong." she said.

Myrna finally looked at her and began to speak. Amelia listened intently without interrupting.

"My mother died when I was very young." She told Amelia, "I was devastated when she died but I was also relieved because she had a madness in her; a madness that made her do horrible things and she frightened me terribly. But the fault wasn't hers. She had a demon in her which drove her mad. Some even said she might have been bewitched by someone or perhaps was yet a witch herself. Father would beat her."

She paused again to see whether Amelia was affected by what was being said. Amelia gave very little reaction for fear that Myrna would stop talking to her. By and by, she continued.

"Surely you must regard him as a brute for the beatings, but he was not. It was the only way to rid her of the evil since an exorcism was not successful. Eventually, she died at the hands of a true witch; a witch that met her end in the most gruesome manner. But it was well deserved."

After saying that, Myrna looked away again.

Amelia looked at her still, then asked, "It's a gruesome story, yes, and I thank you for confiding in me. But why tell me this?

What relevance does your past have to do with now; how you're trembling so?"

Myrna answered, "Why did father beat you? Are you also mad, as mother was?"

After the shock of hearing this, Amelia smiled at her and shook her head, saying, "No child. I'm not." After seeing no relief from Myrna, Amelia asked, "Do I behave as your mother did? Do I do horrible things? No, dear. I do not. You must believe I am not mad, and I am not bewitched by anyone, nor do I have a demon that controls me."

Myrna didn't respond or acknowledge what she had said, so Amelia stood up from the bed and gently took hold of Myrna's hands in hers. They looked in each other's eyes as Amelia softly said, "You must trust me. I am not afflicted. I do not have a demon. I am a child of God. This you must believe."

Myrna's lips curled a little, displaying a hint of a smile.

"Do you believe me?" Amelia asked.

Finally, Myrna gave a smile and nodded saying, "Yes I do."

"Great! I wish to have a close relationship with you as my daughter, and you must confide in me always. Whatever may worry you, I insist on knowing so I might help. Agreed?"

"Agreed." replied Myrna.

"Good. Now, go and enjoy the day. It's lovely outside."

As Amelia got up and walked to the door, Myrna called to her.

"Amelia?" Amelia stopped and looked back at her. "There *is* something else."

"What is it?" asked Amelia.

"I've been getting ill almost every morning."

"How long has this been happening?"

"Many mornings, now."

"Well, perhaps it's nothing. We should let the doctor examine you soon."

Amelia turned towards the door, took another step then stopped. She turned to face Myrna again and asked, "Is there anything else which is not right?"

"Yes." was the response.

"What is it?"

"I haven't had my bleeding cycle this month."

Amelia's eyes grew almost twice their size, and she brought her hand to her mouth.

"What is it?" asked Myrna.

Amelia walked to her and held her hands again.

"What is it?" Myrna asked again.

"I believe you're with child, my dear."

"What?"

"These are the symptoms when you bear children. You're with child."

Once the shock of the news had faded, the two women embraced and welcomed the joyous occasion. It wasn't right that the two were rejoicing, for being with child out of wedlock was a grave sin. Amelia felt guilt for being happy and knew Myrna should be on her knees asking for divine forgiveness. Myrna knew this as well, but the news was too wonderful to think otherwise.

Then, a new look of concern came over Myrna's face as she asked, "Do you think Alexander might be happy?"

Amelia took the question to mean that Myrna hadn't been with any other man but Alexander. Knowing this was good news indeed.

"Of course. He shall jump for joy. I'm sure of it."

Earlier, Amelia wondered how she would survive the day in her sorrow. Now, it was as though she was a new person without care. All she could think of is the new arrival into the family. Myrna, for her part, was more than elated. She'd dreamed of carrying Alexander's child one day, and now that dream had come true.

"Must we tell father?" asked Myrna.

"Oh yes. We must tell him before he realizes it on his own when he sees your growing belly. We mustn't keep any secrets from him."

"Do you think he'll be happy to hear it?"

"I'm sure." Amelia replied with some reservation.

There was a hint of hesitation in her voice just then. Any reasonable man would be happy about the announcement of a new baby for his daughter. That is, provided she was married.

Réal Carpentier

*****

Derris Blackmoore was not finished with his chores. There was much to do every day; tilling, harvesting, digging, cultivating, and everything else required for his family to survive. His father was crippled from a terrible disease years ago and his two sisters depended on Derris to take care of the manual labor since he was the only capable man of the family. But every morning since he'd first met Isabell, he would wander away from his chores and walk to the fence to see if she was there.

On this particular day, he walked to the crest of the hill beyond which was the fence where they'd first met. As the fence came into his view, he stretched his neck to see further down in hopes he would see her there sitting and resting as he had seen her the other day. She didn't disappoint. There she was with her back to him, waiting and taking in the beauty of the horizon.

He didn't call out as he had done previously, but rather walked quietly to surprise her. By and by, he was close enough to stop and admire her. Finally, he spoke.

"What is this beauty?"

She turned immediately to face him with a smile.

"It's only me." she said timidly.

They both smiled and then he walked down to sit with her. Then he touched her hair.

"Did you bathe with your garments?" he asked half-jokingly.

"No silly, I was caught in the rain."

"The rain?"

"Yes, don't you know about rain?"

"I know about rain, but I dare say it hasn't rained."

"Of course, it did. How else should I get wet?"

The Witch of Brentwood

He looked at the ground and at once she knew what he was thinking. She had thought the same just beyond Flora's cabin when she encountered dry ground.

"Everything is dry except you," he said.

"I know. I see that as well. It must have rained briefly where I was but not here."

"Well, I still say you shouldn't bathe fully dressed." he replied with a smile.

"I'll try to remember."

She smiled back at him but was also troubled inside. She began to tremble a little because her encounter with Flora and unexplainable rain left her fearful. He noticed her trembling and assumed it was from being in wet clothes.

"Can I offer you an overcoat? I'm sure my sister has one to spare."

"No thank you. You're very kind, but I shouldn't tarry too long. My mother should wonder where I am."

"I see. You walked all this way to leave." he said.

"No, I walked all this way to see you."

She didn't stay long but long enough to have him fall in love with her. The way she spoke and the things they had in common as well as her beauty were too overpowering to resist. If one didn't know better, one would have surmised it was as though he was under her spell.

They spent the short time they had together talking and laughing and at one point, even held hands as lovers often do. There was no one around for miles it seemed, so Derris felt at liberty to sit very close and even gently brush her face with his hand. When he did this, she recoiled from him a little, because his hand felt exactly the way Clement's hand felt the night before. She tried to block it out of her mind, but the feeling was too strong. She apologized for her reaction, but he assured her there was no need for apologies; that it was *he* who should apologize for being so forward. This was the only awkward incident, though and beyond that, they enjoyed each other's company to the fullest until it was time for her to leave.

They bid each other goodbye with a kiss. As he got closer, she offered her cheek, but he gently turned her face with his hand and kissed her lips. As they kissed, she felt the same elation as when she would daydream about such things. Only the sensation of a real kiss was a hundred-fold. She now felt fulfilled and surprisingly happy considering all that had happened of late. She left him with a smile on her face that would remain until she reached Flora's cabin again.

However, Derris was hiding something from Isabell, as much as he was an honest man. The one thing he had kept from her up to this point had to eventually come to the forefront if he was to continue seeing her. The truth of the matter was that he was betrothed to another. They were to be married. Her name was Evelina Kenwig. He had been in love with Evelina and she with him since childhood. It was more than love, in fact. It was as though they had been married all these years. They knew everything about each other and felt the greatest comfort in being together. They held no secrets since they cherished honesty to the fullest and had recently made plans to marry in the presence of God and family. But God forbid, Derris loved Isabell.

It didn't rain on her way back home but as she passed Flora's cabin, she felt every bit of the fear she'd felt before running out of her cabin into the pouring rain. It was an evil place to be avoided, of this she was convinced. She looked down to the ground looking for wetness but found none. Where the rain had poured just one hour before, was completely dry; as dry as could be. The whole incident was very odd and gave her fright again. But as soon as she quickly passed the cabin and the cemetery, the fear subsided.

Isabell thought to herself on the way home. She was accused of being a witch by Flora who was a witch herself. The mere thought of being a witch had been frightening but as she walked further from Flora, the entire incident now seemed to be in such a distant past as to almost convince herself the visit with flora never happened. She assured herself that it had not rained despite her wet garments, hair, and skin. *It must have been a dream.* She kept telling herself this but never became convinced.

*****

Most of the supper conversation that evening revolved around Alexander's new position as an apprentice. Mr. Berryman was a tough but fair man and as far as the work itself was concerned, Alexander couldn't be happier. There was no news concerning the young girl who suddenly burned which Clement said proved his suspicions about the 'old witch' living in that broken shack she called a home. So all-in-all, supper was relatively uneventful.

Amelia and Myrna kept looking at each other during supper, wondering if now would be the right time to disclose the news about the new baby soon to be born into the family. There never seemed to be an opportune time, however. It was a delicate subject which could conceivably spark some unwanted responses and Amelia would have none of that at the table.

Once supper was done, everyone proceeded with their normal routine of reading bible verses, cleaning, and such. Alexander's day was still the topic of conversation, but it was winding down. As soon as Amelia thought the time was right for the news, she got everyone's attention.

"Alexander, please put the good book down for a moment and everyone please listen. Myrna has something to announce."

Everyone looked at Myrna, but she kept looking at Amelia for support. Amelia simply nodded her head to give her approval.

"What is it?" Clement asked.

Myrna hesitated for what seemed forever to everyone else, but finally she spoke.

"I believe I'm going to have a baby."

The room was silent. Everyone needed time to process what was said. The initial thought that went through everyone's mind was that it was sinful, and worthy of some form of divine punishment. After that, each one accepted the realization according to how their own lives would be affected.

Alexander would become a father with the responsibility associated with being such. He was also perplexed since they had only engaged in sexual activity twice since living together. *Surely, twice isn't enough to impregnate a woman.* He wondered if Myrna might be making a mistake in thinking she was pregnant.

For her part, Isabell suspected the father to be Alexander, although that hadn't been declared yet. She hoped he wasn't, but she was almost sure he was, despite the surprised reaction on his face. But there was a part of her that was a little jealous as well as happy there would soon be a baby to hold and love.

Clement, on the other hand, was headstrong in his thoughts that this situation was unacceptable and would only bring him shame with his clients. Never had he thought his daughter would grow to be a whore. He also assumed Alexander to be the father but didn't place blame on him. *A man is not responsible for what a woman does to him.* She, his own daughter, was to blame for bringing shame not only to him but to the entire family.

"I hope you all welcome this news as I do." Myrna said, looking at her father solemnly.

"Myrna is this true?" asked Alexander with concern. He wanted so to learn if he was the father.

"Yes it is, Alexander. We shall have a child soon."

A sudden pride overtook him as he rushed to her embrace.

Just then, Clement rushed in to separate them somewhat more violently than he intended. Amelia thought of stepping in to stop him but knew better.

"You've disgraced the family!" Clement exclaimed.

"Father, I didn't mean to. Alexander and I love each other. I thought you'd be happy for me."

"You shall always be my daughter, but this cannot go unpunished." he said.

"Father, please don't."

"I love you too much not to. Come with me outside." Then he turned to Amelia, and said, "Follow us."

"Please Clement, do not do this," said Amelia.

He ignored Amelia, then looked at Alexander and Isabell and said, "You both shall remain here."

Myrna proceeded outside and was followed by Amelia and then Clement. Her cries were in vain, as Clement was resolute in what had to be done to atone for his daughter's sin. They walked about two hundred feet from the cabin where there were plenty of tree branches on the ground to choose from. Then he ordered the women to stop.

"Expose her back," he said to Amelia.

Then he walked around to find a fitting branch with which to administer punishment. Amelia looked at Myrna apologetically and then approached her to begin removing her shirt, but not her corset.

Clement stood up with a branch in his hand and seeing his daughter was not fully exposed, said to Amelia, "All of it."

Amelia hesitated as Myrna cried but then complied. She removed everything on top to completely expose her back and front.

Then Clement stood behind his daughter and began to whip her with the branch.

With each stroke, she screamed. Each stroke was a knife to her back, leaving superficial cuts and scratches. There were scars on her back from previous punishments, but now there would be more. Amelia saw Clement's face as he whipped his daughter and recognized it to be the same look he had when he administered *her* punishment. That look along with the sounds of the blows and Myrna's cries, made her shiver. She thought she might have told him to stop after so many blows, but she couldn't be sure if she'd said anything at all. It was all so surreal.

Alexander and Isabell were still in the cabin hearing what was happening. At first, they were frozen in shock but after a while, Isabell ran to her room and snatched her brooch from the little trinket box. She held it close to her heart and gently squeezed it. She didn't wish for anything in particular but only that the beatings would stop. She wished hard; as hard as one could wish. Suddenly, the beatings stopped.

Outside, Clement was now in pain. He had a few more blows to deliver to his daughter but unexpectedly had to stop and get down on one knee. His back was in agony. It had happened before when straining a little too much to lift something heavy, but whipping was not that strenuous, he thought. Still, it took some time before he could stand and walk again.

While still down on one knee, he commanded, "Take her in and draw a bath for her."

"Are you alright?" asked Amelia.

"Do as you're told. I'll be in presently."

Amelia quickly picked up Myrna's shirt off the ground so she could cover her front and proceeded to take her back to the cabin.

Still crying, Myrna looked back and asked, "Are you alright, father?"

"I'm fine. Go in and clean yourself. And Amelia, tend to her cuts."

Amelia did as she was told. Once inside, she got a bath ready for Myrna who was moving most gingerly. Isabell inquired about Clement.

"He's still outside. Something happened to him suddenly. I'm sure he's alright." Amelia said.

"Are you alright, Myrna?" asked Alexander.

"I will be. Just a few bruises."

"What happened to Clement?" Isabell asked again.

"I'm not quite sure." replied Amelia. "He suddenly collapsed onto one knee and couldn't move. Divine justice was served, it seems. No offense to you, Myrna."

Myrna simply nodded.

Isabell clutched her brooch upon hearing this. She wasn't sure if she was the cause of his pain, but she was becoming more and more convinced of what the strange old Flora had said. "*You have the power. It shall evolve and you shall use it again.*"

From that point on, Isabell resolved to give serious credence to the possibility of having special abilities, much like Flora the *'witch'*. (It was the first time she'd allowed herself to call her that and believe it.) Although there was no tangible proof, Isabell's experiences with the brooch were too real to be a coincidence. It was then she decided to keep the brooch in her possession, whatever she did and wherever she went. Hiding it from Clement would prove to be a challenge but she would somehow make it work.

Réal Carpentier

Chapter 10

Morning was heavy and damp. Owls hooted as the sun began to rise. The room was still quite dark where Myrna lay still on her belly, trying not to move lest the pain resume shooting across her torso as it had all night long. Care had to be taken so her cuts didn't stick to the sheets of the bed, as that was much more painful than the normal pain of bruising. She had the entire night to think about Amelia and how wrong she was to think the woman was a witch. It seemed likely that the reason for the beatings Amelia received from Clement was exactly as Amelia said; he had drunk too much and was set off by something or other. It didn't matter what.

She didn't stir when she heard Isabell getting out of bed and apparently getting ready to leave. Answering fool questions about how she was feeling and how or if she slept the night, was not something she wanted to engage in, especially when Isabell knew the answers to those questions already. Where Isabell was going at such an early hour of the morning, was *her* affair only. Myrna had troubles of her own.

Not having slept at all for the entire night, Myrna had ample time to think about things; her situation with Alexander being of the utmost priority. That was very important to her. The relationship between her and her father was the same and she knew it wouldn't change. It wasn't the first time he had to administer punishment not only to her, but Lord knows her mother needed it even more than she. But she wanted to make sure Alexander and she were okay.

"Can you ask Alexander to come see me, please?" Myrna asked Isabell who was ready to leave.

"Of course."

"Only him. Try not to wake anyone else."

"Alright."

Isabell stepped out of the room very quietly and proceeded to Alexander's room where she found him sound asleep. She shook him gently until he woke and then whispered, "Myrna would like to see you in her room."

"Where are you going so early, and all dressed as you are?"

"I have something to do. Don't worry yourself about that, I'll be alright. But please see Myrna. She's the one in need."

"She's awake?" he asked.

"Yes, I doubt if she slept the night."

"Alright."

Alexander waited until Isabell was out of the room, then proceeded to Myrna's room.

There, he saw her lying on her belly with her back uncovered. The stripes from Clement's whip were bright red even in the early sun. A sudden sick feeling hit his stomach and it took all he had to not cry or get sick or both. He walked to her bed and sat next to her so she could see him without turning or moving too much.

"Good morning." he said.

"Good morning." she replied with a smile.

"I'm sure you didn't sleep last night."

"No. I was thinking most of the night."

"About what?"

"Us."

"So was I before falling asleep."

"I wish not to lose you, Alexander."

"Why should you lose me?"

"Because what we did was wrong, and the fault is mine for leading you."

"The fault is not yours."

"But now we have the responsibility of parents and we're mere children ourselves."

"We are not children and I welcome the responsibility. I shall be a good provider. Mr. Berryman is happy with my work and I'm happy also."

Hearing him speak like this made her feel so much better. The pain was still there but the worry about the future without him was gone.

"Thank you." she said.

"I wonder how it happened, though. I thought bearing children was difficult."

"For some it is but for others, it isn't. I even took very hot baths every time after we were done making love so it wouldn't happen. But it happened anyway. I'm sorry."

"There's no need to be sorry. You did everything we discussed."

He bent down to kiss her as they held hands.

"What should we do now?" she asked.

This was a question that Alexander had been thinking about since first hearing the news of her pregnancy. There weren't too many options open to them but of the most reasonable ones, getting married was the one that made the most sense. It was true that things were different since they'd move to Brentwood. Then, people didn't know them and couldn't judge or accuse them of evil influence. However now, they had gotten to know almost the entire congregation of the church. Myrna and he were considered brother and sister and a marriage between such, would certainly be deemed inappropriate at the very least even if they were indeed not related at all. Still, they resolved to get married in the quietest way if it was alright with Clement and Amelia, that is.

Being in agreement, he bid her good day and went back into his room to get ready for the day as an apprentice with a renewed sense of responsibility to do well for Mr. Berryman and to be the best gunsmith in Brentwood.

After he stepped out of her room, she began to cry again. It might have been a reaction of relief from knowing she still had Alexander in her life and that he was accepting of her current situation. But then again, it might very well have been the burning feeling she felt from the torn skin. Soon she would have to speak to Amelia about possible remedies to relieve burning pain. As soon as Clement left to go to work for his client, that is.

The dark of the early morning was soon replaced with the dim brightness of an overcast sky. In that time, Myrna heard Alexander and Clement leave for work almost at the same time. The puttering of Amelia around the kitchen was also heard, but because of the shame Myrna felt, she didn't bother asking Amelia about any remedies. Suffering through pain was less humiliating.

The Witch of Brentwood

*****

Isabell didn't have to knock on the door to let her presence known. Flora, who was outside tending to her garden, saw her coming when she was still far away. Isabell was not walking with any great urgency, but rather seemed to be coasting as one would when their mind is preoccupied and not paying much attention to where they are going. But Isabell knew where she was going, and her preoccupation was on the presumed reality of Flora's words when she'd said, 'you have the power'.

As Isabell approached, the purpose for her visit became obvious from the look on her face. And as she got closer still, they locked eyes and Flora knew immediately why Isabell was coming. There was no fear in Isabell's eyes, at least not the same fear as Flora had seen before. Her look revealed more of a concern for what would happen next since coming to terms with who she was.

It was still early morning, and the rising sun was hidden by the overcast. So, it was not as bright as it should have been for this time of day, but they could still see each other clearly. Isabell's slow pace came to a halt when she was close enough to Flora. They stared at each other for a time, and then Flora spoke.

"Come on in, child." she said, gesturing to the door.

"I wish to remain outside."

"But someone might see us even under this cloudy sky."

Isabell thought for a moment, then decided that she was right; going inside to not be seen with Flora was more prudent than ever. So, Isabell led the way into the cabin with Flora following behind.

"Would you like some tea, dear?" asked Flora.

Isabell nodded and got comfortable at one of the table chairs. There was no need to hurry or even run out today. It seemed Isabell was determined to learn the truth about Flora and herself. This was an inevitable point in time that Flora knew had to come sooner or later.

"I came as soon as I could this morning. Please accept my apology for having run away from you last time. I wasn't thinking clearly."

"It's quite alright. I understand. The unknown can be quite frightening."

"So can the truth." Isabell added.

Flora looked very seriously in Isabell's eyes and said, "Especially the truth."

"But I'm no longer frightened. I'm ready to hear the truth now. What do you see in me? What do you know?"

"I know nothing. What I feel is more revealing."

"Tell me."

"You have great abilities."

"Am I a witch?"

"You have cunning abilities. It seems you've come to terms with the notion."

"Am I a witch?" Isabell asked again more fervently.

"Witch is a very unfortunate name used by others as a reason for revenge and violence. Do not despair if you should be so accused."

"Alright then, we are both cunning folk?"

"Yes."

"But I've never cured anyone of any ailment."

The Witch of Brentwood

"Think back, dear. Are you sure?" Flora asked as she poured Isabell some tea.

It didn't take long before Isabell recalled her bout with consumption and how she was one of the fortunate souls to be cured almost miraculously.

"I had consumption." Isabell said.

"What cured you?"

"I always assumed the disease went away on its own and I recovered naturally."

"Think back, dear. Was there something in your possession you wished upon?"

"Yes. My mother had given me a lovely brooch. I remember clutching it so close to me. But that was a coincidence, correct?"

"There are no coincidences." Flora replied. "Were there other coincidences, as you call them?"

"I believe there were."

"Tell me."

"There were some people teasing me before we left Salem. I remember wishing terrible things and the man collapsed suddenly onto the ground as good as dead."

"What were those people saying?"

"They called me witch."

"Why do you think they would call you such a name?"

"They mentioned too many reasons to recall."

"Did they mention the birthmark on your neck as being a tool for evil?"

Isabell looked pensive and recalled what the young girl had said about the devil's teat having been used many times over.

"Yes." Isabell answered.

"That brooch is very dear to you, isn't it?"

"There was another coincidence just last night."

"Were you clutching the brooch at that time?"

"Yes."

"We all need the proper tools to get our work done. I wouldn't start a fire without matches, would I? There would be no fire started with a pail of water."

Isabell then thought about the young girl who without reason burst into flames and was burned alive.

"And I couldn't kill a man with a brooch, could I?" asked Isabell.

"That's correct."

"But it *did* happen, didn't it?"

"There are many strange things that occur with no possible explanation. But everything that happens has a cause. If *we* are to be the cause, it's best to realize what tools to use."

"My tool is the brooch, isn't it?"

"It seems so. You must take good care of your brooch. May I see it?"

Isabell untied the buttons of her collar to reveal the brooch around her neck.

"Lovely thing." said Flora. "Lovely thing indeed and very precious."

Isabell gave the brooch a little squeeze before replacing it under her collar and fastening the buttons up to her neck. She then sipped her tea.

"What else must I know?" asked Isabell.

"You must practice your powers. They've been given to you and you shall use them."

"Very well, but why?"

The Witch of Brentwood

"Powers are like muscles. Unless they are used, they will begin to atrophy. One is not whole without the sum of the parts. Your powers are part of you."

"But I refuse to do harm." Isabell said.

"Seems you've already done harm, dear. Practice your powers." Flora commanded.

Isabell thought deeply about this which was apparent in her expression. Flora gave her the time she needed to contemplate all of what was happening to her.

Finally, Isabell said, "I must be off now."

"To visit your young man?" Flora asked.

Isabell looked surprised that Flora knew of her intentions to hopefully meet Derris by the fence, although she knew she should no longer doubt any of Flora's abilities by now.

"Yes." she answered. "I hope to see him again today."

"There is something you should know, and I'm surprised you have no knowledge of it currently."

"What?"

"The young man you speak of is to be married soon."

"What? I don't believe it."

"You must believe it. But you have it in your power to change his mind."

"How do you know this?"

"I have seen him with another. Pretty young thing."

At once, Isabell felt jealousy. It was a sin but also a very powerful emotion to overcome.

"I must go now." Isabell said.

"Yes, by all means my dear, and please come visit again."

Isabell thanked her for her hospitality and soon was on her way to hopefully meet Derris at their meeting place. She clutched her brooch on her way. She didn't wish for anything in particular because she didn't want to manipulate her young love, but if she had a wish, it would be to have Derris to herself and have him be done with the other young girl; whoever she was.

*****

The sky was still covered with gray, but the day was bright. She waited at their meeting place much longer than usual. It was normal for her to wait for only a short while but today she seemed to wait forever before she finally saw him walking down the grassy hill. He was alone as usual but today Isabell felt a jealousy that wouldn't abate.

She looked at him as he approached with a smile. Perhaps what Flora believed about his intentions to marry was wrong. *How would a fine young man as he, be capable of being hypocritical? And how could he not think I would eventually find out?* There were many questions troubling her mind and she was resolute in finding sensible answers.

They exchanged usual salutations and proceeded with small inconsequential conversation that only tried her patience. She loved him so much, however, that she was willing to wait and find the right moment to confront him. But she resolved to do it in a most gentle manner. The truth was more important than exposing him for being someone with a quality she detested. How she hoped he didn't possess such a quality and that Flora was wrong about him.

"How be my fair lady on this fine day?" he asked as he sat beside her.

She couldn't help but smile. He was so handsome and charismatic, any lady with the slightest sense in her head would be a moth to a flame, willing to risk life and limb.

"Your fair lady is very well, thank you."

He then took her hand and kissed it. Just then, perhaps out of pity for his betrothed, she pulled her hand from him and looked away.

"What's the matter?" he asked. She didn't answer but continued looking away. He asked again and still got no answer. Finally, he gently put his hand on her cheek and turned her head to face him.

"What's the matter?"

She could now see the concern in his eyes and decided he deserved to know as much as she deserved an explanation.

"I know there's another in your life." The look of surprised guilt overtook him. "Why did you not tell me? Did you not know I would eventually find out?"

He thought for a moment, not so much as to think of what to say but rather he seemed to analyze the gravity of having been dishonest.

"I'm truly sorry." The sincerity in his face was obvious. "If you want me to, I'll go."

"No Derris, I don't want you to go. But I'm confused as to what to say or do next. Do you love her?"

"I did love her."

"Do you no longer?"

"Since I've met you, things have changed for me. You are all I think about in the morning through the evening. I dream of you most every night.

"But it's wrong of you to be with both."

"I only want to be with you, Isabell. If you feel the same, I'll tell her of us, and it shall be you and me from this moment on. What do you say?"

"I'd very much like that, Derris."

Upon hearing that, he kissed her. Thereafter, many things entered Isabell's thoughts. She wondered if the powers Flora believed she had, had anything to do with Derris's infatuation of her. If so, it certainly wasn't intentional even if she was ecstatic over the outcome. She also wondered if his feelings for her would last or if they were simply a temporary desire born out of boredom from being with the same person for such a long time. She'd heard that married couples often feel that way. Regardless of these things she wondered, the reality was that he truly loved her and she was determined to keep it that way no matter what needed to be done to sustain their feelings for one another. But Isabell knew what to do. *Doesn't every woman?* Her mother had done it. Myrna had done it. And now, she felt it was *her* turn.

After their kiss, she unbuttoned her collar and whispered, "Make love to me, Derris." She said this all the while she was clutching her brooch.

"It would be wrong," he said. "We're not married and it's a sin to even think of such things."

She clutched the brooch tighter and wished so much to change his mind. She undid another button, exposing more of her slender neck.

Suddenly he took her hand and without saying a word, led her behind a stone wall not a hundred feet from where they were. There, he laid her down gently in the thicket and they made love; sometimes slowly and passionately and at other times, more furiously as though they were both on fire. At times he looked in her eyes and at other times his eyes were drawn to the brooch just above her breasts. Her body lifted to meet his and the feel of his heart pounding in his chest made hers beat just as fast and hard. It was the first time for Isabell, and she loved every minute of this new experience. Now she finally understood the risk Myrna had taken. The risk was worth any punishment Clement or anyone else could possibly deliver. But she also knew she didn't want to be with child, not because of Clement's punishment but because she felt she wasn't ready to care for a baby. Suddenly, Derris looked to be in agony and his breathing labored greatly. Isabell didn't expect this and thought something bad had happened, but soon he collapsed in her arms and his breathing began to return to normal.

"Are you alright?" she asked.

It took a moment for him to gather his strength to answer, but soon he answered, "Yes."

As she lay with Derris in her arms, she was the happiest she'd ever been in her life. There was plenty of time to ask for forgiveness for their sin but for the moment, her love for him was more than enough to bring a joy she'd long for. It was as though her fears and nightmares might finally disappear.

It was a time of awakening for Isabell. She was beginning to understand the strange powers she'd experienced. She was beginning to learn about her own body and how it felt to be a woman. She was beginning to feel satisfaction from being invincible.

What she didn't know, however, was that at the height of passion with Derris, her necklace had broken, and her brooch fell to the ground. Neither one noticed it was missing even as they dressed and walked away hand in hand as lovers often do.

Chapter 11

It wasn't easy for Clement and Alexander to sit alone and have a man-to-man talk about Myrna's pregnancy, and not so much what should be done but rather how and when. But they were able to talk one night after work when they met at a local saloon. There, they were honest with each other about the grave situation that existed. They discussed how Alexander and Myrna had to get married, since Clement would not tolerate his daughter living in sin. But it had to be a private wedding with no congregation who would recognize them as brother and sister. Next, Myrna would not be able to attend church services for quite a while, and that a plausible reason had to be given for such absence. Finally, the baby, when born, had to be hidden from sight or possibly given away to another family, because its mere existence would invite public embarrassment and Clement was not willing to risk his position as a result. Only under these conditions would Clement allow them to stay where they now lived and not have to worry about finding a new home amidst scandal.

Alexander was in agreement. He was in no position to resist since he also had prospects for a promising future in his apprenticeship. He told Clement that he and Myrna had discussed marriage and that they were both looking forward to living together as husband and wife, albeit with no change in their current living arrangements. The church services could be missed given the right reason as long as the reverend didn't take it upon himself to visit their home unannounced. The only point Clement and Alexander didn't agree to was giving the baby away, as Alexander and Myrna were overjoyed with the prospect of being parents, caring for a little one, and watching him or her grow into a young child and eventually a young adult. There was no arguing between the two concerning this, but Clement secretly knew he would get his way.

That night, Clement and Alexander brought in plenty of wood for the fireplace, as the nights were getting colder. Isabell cleaned and Amelia made butter and the necessary bread for the next day. Myrna was in the washroom bathing in water that could have been a tad warmer for her liking. It was almost time to read some bible verses and it would have been a quiet and normal evening if Clement hadn't accidentally walked into the washroom to see his daughter's back all raw and tender from the blows of his whipping.

Clement stood there watching her bathe with her back in his full view. He was finally able to see how bad the bruises were and was struck with guilt at how excessive the punishment was. Punishment was necessary for her, this he knew, but now wished he had stopped whipping her a lot sooner than he had. She moved gently as she bathed to avoid bleeding again, frequently wiping tears from her face.

The Witch of Brentwood

What Clement was about to do next was not something he planned to do. But given the circumstances of her pregnancy and the imminent marriage to Alexander, he thought it would be a nice gesture despite their sinful act. He slowly closed the door to the washroom and went into his room as the women were still working in the kitchen. It was an opportune time to do this and the more he thought about it, the more he knew it was the right thing to do. He opened the closet door and lifted the floorboards inside to reveal his hiding place where the brooch among other items was stored. He thought perhaps the valuable piece that he'd confiscated from Isabell would make a nice wedding present for his daughter and hopefully make up for some of the punishment she'd endured. He picked up the little pouch where he'd carefully hidden the brooch and opened it to pour out its contents. But instead of the brooch, out came a worthless piece of jewelry that he'd seen Amelia wearing from time to time, although he hadn't seen her wearing it recently. Now he knew why. It was obvious Amelia had found the brooch and either kept it to eventually give it back to Isabell or she'd given it back to her already. Either way, she had stolen from her husband. So, he called for her to come into the room.

He sat on the edge of the bed as she closed the door behind her.

"What is it?" she asked.

He didn't answer. He got up from the bed and lodged a chair under the door latch to prevent anyone else from entering. Then he showed her his little pouch and turned it upside down so that her worthless piece of jewelry hit the floor in front of them. He never took his eyes away from hers, as she looked at the piece on the floor and then at him with fear of what was to come.

The first time Alexander and Isabell heard the commotion coming from behind the closed door of their mother's room, they thought something had fallen; perhaps a chair or a drawer from the bureau desk. But then they heard their mother scream and the commotion continued and got louder. Realizing Clement was beating their mother, they rushed to the door but couldn't open it. Alexander knocked on it for a response. None came.

"Please open the door!" Alexander shouted.

Alexander and Isabell pleaded for Clement to open the door to no avail. Soon, they were joined by Myrna who had heard the commotion and came running with a towel around her.

"Alexander, you must force the door open! Break it if you have to!" Isabell cried.

"Father, stop it!" Myrna cried out.

Isabell then reached for her brooch to see if it indeed had the power to stop Clement, but somehow couldn't get hold of it. She felt all around her neck but couldn't grasp it. She thought it was perhaps due to all the excitement.

Alexander moved the two women out of the way and took a step back to lunge at the door. He tried a few times before being successful but by then, it was too late. As they entered the room, they saw Clement sitting on the bed exhausted from the assault, and Amelia crying in a fetal position in the furthest corner from where Clement sat. They ran to her, but Clement grabbed Isabell's arm and tore her dress at the collar to expose her neck.

Not seeing the brooch, he shouted, "Where is it?"

Isabell raised her hand to protect it, and that was the first time she'd noticed it wasn't around her neck at all. She began to look frantically on the floor around her to see if she had dropped it, but it was nowhere to be found.

"WHERE IS IT?" he shouted louder.

"I don't know!" she replied.

Then Clement looked at Amelia and said, "Did you give it to her?"

Amelia couldn't admit to having given it to her, as he would as sure as day, beat her as well until she surrendered it to him. So, she thought quickly and answered, "No! I threw it in the pond where no one will ever find it!"

Clement was indignant. "Why you…"

He went after her again but was stopped by Alexander who by now was strong enough to keep him away.

"GET OUT OF MY WAY!" shouted Clement

"NO!" Alexander shouted back.

"Get out before I hurt you, Alexander."

"If you raise a hand to me, you shall lose it!" Alexander responded with authority.

This made Clement pause. Seeing how sincere Alexander was, he retreated, looked at Amelia, and said, "Your humility for stealing from your husband shall be on full display soon." After saying this, he stormed out of the cabin and didn't return until the following day.

Later that night after nursing her mother, Isabell had the chance to be alone with her.

"Are you alright, mother?"

"Yes dear, I'm fine."

"What happened?"

"He found that I'd taken the brooch."

"Thank you for saying you threw it away. If he knows it's no longer in our possession, he shouldn't want it back."

"That is sure." Amelia said, "I hope you're keeping it safe in a proper place."

"I'm afraid I lost it, mother."

"You did? Well, that's alright dear. It was only an old brooch. It's better lost."

Isabell knew better. This wasn't just an old piece of jewelry; it was so much more.

As they talked, Isabell was preoccupied with mentally retracing her steps to find where it might be. *Perhaps it was left in Flora's cabin.* She remembered showing it to her and her comments about it being lovely and precious. But she also remembered giving it a little squeeze before buttoning her collar, so she still had it when she left her cabin. Of this, she was sure. Then it came to her that there was only one other instance when it might have been lost. It was the moment that changed her life.

Flora had said that her powers were a part of her. If that was so, Isabell had lost more than her virginity, but a part of herself as well.

The Witch of Brentwood

*****

Everyone has a special place, especially if it is a place where lovers first meet. Such was the case with Derris and Evelina. Their favorite place was a corn field not far from where they lived. They had met there when they were only children playing and running between the corn stalks. They had no care of being seen trespassing, as it was a large field far removed from the owner's farmhouse. As it happened by chance one day, they ran into one another without any foresight, knocking Evelina down and giving her a bloody nose. Derris grabbed the dirty handkerchief from his back pocket and tended to her nose until the bleeding stopped. They had been friends ever since and later became lovers with plans of always being together. They visited their special place on occasions like birthdays, anniversaries, and such memorable days.

It was there they met on this particular day to tell her of Isabell. He wanted to meet elsewhere but she had insisted on their special place. Upon meeting, he shied away when she tried to kiss him.

"What's the matter?" she asked.

"I didn't want to tell you here."

"Tell me what?" The concern in her face was quite obvious.

"I've met someone."

"Someone? I don't understand."

"I met another woman." He still loved Evelina, but he was always the kind to be honest even when honesty could hurt.

"Derris, this kind of joking is not funny at all."

"It's true, Evelina. I still love you and I always will, but we can't go on with the way I feel now. It wouldn't be fair to either one of us."

Evelina searched for ways of changing his mind even if it was wrong to do so. So, she remained silent for a while just looking at him in disbelief.

"Please say something," he said.

She couldn't hold back the tears as she started reminiscing.

"We were always together since we were children." She said, crying. "You always came to my aid when I was hurt and later when I was sad for one reason or another. We schooled together and worked together. We did everything, and now *this*? What did I do wrong?"

He hugged her as she cried on his shoulder.

"You did nothing wrong," he whispered.

She pulled away and looked at him. "When I was twelve years old and boys used to tease me, you gave one of them a good beating. They never bothered me thereafter. When I was afraid of the horrible sounds the wild beasts make in the night, you held me and I felt safe. I need you, Derris. So much so that when the slightest hair is out of place on your head, I run my hand through it to make it right again."

Derris replied, "I know. I haven't forgotten anything we've gone through together. But I need some time to figure things out."

"Are you trying to give me false hope by asking for precious time?"

Derris didn't answer. She took that to mean that there was no hope at all. *How could someone else have so much power over him as to disrupt what was sure to be their destiny?* It was hard for her to make sense of it all since it seemed such an irrational decision on his part, and he was the most rational, sensible, and trusting person she had ever known.

Feeling completely defeated, anger built up inside her. She had heard enough and was no longer sure what was being said was true and what wasn't. Overwhelmed with anger and sadness, she slapped his face and ran off. He called to her but was met with complete silence except for her sobs as she ran.

As much as he didn't want it to end this way, it wasn't unexpected. He was bright enough to know better. Hurting Evelina was the last thing he wanted to do but his new-found love for Isabell was undeniable, and he was at least happy that the act of telling Evelina was over.

Evelina ran until she could run no more. Her tears were also depleted. *There are only so many tears a woman can cry*, her mother used to tell her as a little girl. Now, she knew what her mother meant.

She slowed her pace when she reached the area where Derris and Isabell had made love just hours before. Had Evelina known the significance of this spot, she wouldn't have stopped but rather kept going over the fence and beyond. She rested against the fence and prayed for divine intervention. As she prayed, bright sunlight reflecting off of a shiny object on the ground hit her eye. Looking down to where the reflection came from, she saw a broken chain wrapped around a beautiful brooch. In her sorrow, she untwined the chain, picked up the brooch, and held it close to her heart. Perhaps it was an omen from God to tell her everything would be alright, she thought. Perhaps in giving Derris enough time to think things over, he would come to his senses and return to where he belonged. Since receiving what she believed to be a sign, she vowed to be patient and give Derris time.

She then decided to return home. On her way, she clutched her new brooch. It was a fine piece of jewelry that she would wear around her neck every day to remind her of God's mysterious ways. She would have to find a chain for it, however, since the broken one was useless and was left behind on the ground. It was a shame though, she thought, that someone else less fortunate than she, had been separated from such a beautiful brooch. She wondered how such a thick chain could possibly break from someone's neck but then decided that it really didn't matter after all. What mattered was her belief that there was a reason God gave her a brooch; a brooch that probably had little value before her finding it, but now was invaluable as far as she was concerned. She found solace in that and felt a stronger faith.

The Witch of Brentwood

*****

On the same morning that Evelina found the lost brooch, Isabell was the first to awaken. The cabin was silent as usual when waking this early but at times she could hear the moaning from her mother who hadn't slept at all. Myrna must have gotten used to sleeping in a position that prevented the wounds on her back from rubbing against the bed sheet and sticking to it, because she seemed to have an undisturbed night; once she got to sleep, that is. Isabell knew this because she had again awoken during the night screaming. The nightmares were getting worse in frequency and in horror. In her dream, she was not only killed by hanging but then dragged to a cemetery that looked a lot like the cemetery next to Flora's home. Her fear of the dead had now evolved into a fear of her dead self.

The good thing about that morning was that Clement hadn't come home the night before. No one really expected him to after his confrontation with Amelia and Isabell, for that matter. Where he had gone or spent the night was a concern only to Myrna. He was her father, after all, and she loved him as a daughter should.

The reason he hadn't come home was obvious. Where he went and what he did, was another story that Myrna and the others didn't know but would soon find out.

Clement had met with a group of men; a former client, the town magistrate, the clergy and two others. The purpose of the meeting was to make his case against Amelia, his disobedient wife who not only was insubordinate to her husband but had stolen from him as well. Insubordination from a man's wife was not tolerated in that time period and neither was stealing from him. Everyone there was well aware of the gravity of her behavior and discussed a proper punishment for her. Clement made sure to mention that he had already delivered some form of punishment on his own, lest they considered him derelict in his duties as her husband. But the truth remains that her actions warranted some form of *public* punishment and that she would be made an example of, in order to send a message to other wives that this kind of behavior will simply not be tolerated. The men agreed. Before the meeting was adjourned, they had established a form of punishment that was appropriate for the behavior. One of them then offered Clement a place to spend the night so the men could be together in the morning to carry out what needed to be done.

Morning came. Isabell, being the first to wake, heard Alexander eventually leave for his gunsmithing apprenticeship. She also heard him talking to their mother before leaving. She couldn't hear what was said but the tone of their voices made her want to cry. It was hard to believe that her mother suffered another beating from Clement, but Isabell also struggled with the fact that the precious brooch her mother had given her was lost. As soon as she could, she would have to go back to the place where she had made love with Derris to see if it could be found.

The women had just begun to get out of bed and make the best of the day, when they heard the sound of approaching horses and what sounded like a group of men. Isabell went outside to see what was happening, only to see Clement and the others with him.

"What's happening?" Isabell asked.

Not a word was said in reply. Instead, Clement went into the cabin and then came back, practically dragging Amelia out with him. Isabell could see the grip he had on her mother's wrist was hurting her. Myrna followed behind with the same curious wonder as the other two women.

Then, the magistrate spoke, "Amelia Arington, you have been accused of disobedience against your husband. Further, you have been found to have stolen a precious jewel from your husband which is punishable by public humiliation. You are to disrobe and be tied to this wagon forthwith where you will be paraded throughout the neighboring homes as an example to the importance of being obedient and to atone for the sins you have committed against your husband and against God."

Clement then began to undress Amelia in front of all who were present. Isabell spoke out in protest and was immediately warned that she would join her mother in the punishment should she continue her disobedience.

"I don't care! This is wrong!" she cried.

She continued protesting not only verbally but also tried to interfere with her mother's disrobing. Finally, it was decided that Isabell should join her mother in the punishment.

Isabell was not undressed but was tied by her hands inside the horse-drawn open wagon. Amelia, however, was completely naked and tied to the rear of the wagon where she would have to walk behind it as both women were paraded through the neighboring homes.

The man with the reins started the horse moving and the embarrassing parade began as Myrna was forced to watch and learn a valuable lesson. Clement reminded her that she was fortunate to have been punished by only *him*. He made sure she knew that she could very well have joined the other two, were it not for his mercy on her.

The sounds of the horse and cries from Isabell and her mother were enough to attract the attention of curious neighbors. They came out to witness the punishment and denounce the women being punished, saying that they deserved the righteous consequences that befell them. There was a makeshift sign that read '*Disobedient and Thief*' so everyone knew what their crimes were. Some threw things like rocks, sticks, and buckets of water at the criminals. But all shouted evil accusations and curses. Most laughed at the naked Amelia, saying her body was that of an old witch, not worthy of the husband she had.

The punishment did indeed serve the purpose it was intended to serve. There was embarrassment. There were outcries of hate from neighbors. There were tears. But mostly, according to the punishers, there was atonement for their sins.

Once the punishment was over, the women were untied and allowed to go back to their homes, while Clement and the rest of the men resumed their normal day activities of working in the community.

Isabell took care of her mother once in the cabin and Myrna went to her room shaking from fear.

"Why did you get yourself punished, Isabell?" asked Amelia.

"I didn't want you to suffer alone."

"You foolish child. Didn't you know they could have stripped you as well?"

"I knew but I didn't care."

The two were silent from that moment on.

Once Isabell was satisfied that her mother was safe in bed and sleeping, she went back to look for her brooch where she and

The Witch of Brentwood

Derris had made love. She was optimistic all the way there until she reached the area. She looked everywhere; behind the fence, and in the thicket. She searched for a good long while because the grass was so high. While down on her knees looking on the ground, she took the opportunity to say a little prayer and asked God to reveal the precious jewel to her, but her prayer was never answered. All she found was the broken chain which she picked up and took with her. The brooch was nowhere to be found.

It was getting to be midafternoon before she finally gave up, thinking she must have lost it somewhere else. She walked away grieving at the prospect of never finding it again; not only because it was a family heirloom given to her but mostly because if it *was* the source by which to invoke some strange power she had, her power was also lost. Perhaps it was further punishment for thinking evil thoughts about Clement and what she would do to him if the brooch were to ever reappear.

As she got closer to home, she noticed people still pointing and cursing her for the crime of disobeying her father, but that made her more angry than ashamed.

Réal Carpentier

Chapter 12

Alexander had no knowledge of the shameful parading of his sister and mother as his future bride watched in horror. Having left early that morning for his apprentice position, it was nothing but a normal day for him. He loved his new position as gunsmith. It was everything he'd dreamed of since he was a child playing soldier on his make-believe battlefield. He still remembered all the fun he and Isabell had out in the field pretending to be the good guy and sometimes bad. This type of work seemed to be in his blood, and he was very happy with his new job at the gun shop.

He had visited the shop a few times since having arrived in Brentwood, but he'd only seen the section that only customers see. Now, he was able to see the entire shop; the backroom, the stockroom, the basement, and he was allowed to have access to every one of those rooms. As such, he felt privileged and was in awe at how Mr. Berryman had arranged and maintained the place. There were racks and shelves behind a counter with a bear head mounted on the back wall. The racks were loaded with different styles of guns and the shelves with accessories and ammunition. To the left of the bear head was a frame of Mr. Berryman's father who had started the business by first cleaning guns and then expanded it to include repair and then design. One could tell his father was a no-nonsense man simply by his photo. Mr. Berryman *himself* was serious and organized much like his father had been. His hair was never out of place and his attire gave him the appearance of being a very good businessman one could trust.

Gunsmithing hardly gave Alexander enough time for daydreaming, however. This was a position that demanded total concentration lest something was overlooked, and mistakes were made. He was not the type to allow himself to fall prey to such neglectful habits. Vices of this kind were more likely left to weak-minded individuals who allowed themselves to be preoccupied with unnecessary distractions.

On this day, however, his mind wandered. Since he'd got out of bed to start the day, he'd been thinking about Myrna and the fact that she was carrying his baby. His life was changing. What went through his mind was the baby, getting married and when it should happen, where they would live as husband and wife, and such worrisome things. What was also distracting was the whole notion of having committed a grave sin, the lashing Myrna had to endure for being so careless as to get pregnant, what people would say about her not going to church and how such a thing could be explained in such a way as to leave her blameless and not have her become fodder for suspicion. Indeed, everything that was happening in his life within recent days would be enough to distract anyone capable of the slightest thought.

As he was sitting in the backroom thinking about all these things, he was busy cleaning guns that had been used recently;

mainly by hunters who were out for game. In a rare moment of preoccupation, Alexander neglected to check the flintlock he was working on to see if it was still loaded. Not long after he'd started cleaning it, the hammer was triggered, and the gun discharged a musket ball no larger than a half inch in diameter. But it hit him just right. The lead ball entered the side of his torso just below the ribcage and fractured his lumbar vertebrae, missing the bottom of the stomach by one eighth of an inch. There was no exit wound as the pellet was lodged in the bone.

He fell to the floor on his back. He would never be able to recall if he lost consciousness but what he *did* remember was that he tried to scream or yell or call out, but he couldn't. He could reach up with his hand to assess how bad the wound was but there was no way to get up or even sit up, try as he might. It then dawned on him that he had no feeling or motion ability from the waist down. He panicked and at least tried to stop the bleeding by pressing his shirt against the wound, but he didn't have the strength to apply enough pressure.

Fortunately, Mr. Berryman had heard the shot and ran to the backroom and began administering aid at once. He tore off Alexander's shirt. The gunshot wound was not large, so he was able to apply pressure with a towel and control the bleeding a little. He then made a make-shift bandage by strapping a clean towel to the wound with his belt around Alexander's waist and told him not to move. Next, he ran out of the shop and alerted someone to get the doctor, who fortunately had his office not far from the gun shop. Mr. Berryman then went back in to be with Alexander to make sure the bleeding was still somewhat under control and to wait with him until the doctor arrived.

Many things went through Alexander's mind as he lay on the floor not knowing the extent of his injury. He hoped the lack of feeling and movement was not a permanent condition, as he had a future wife and baby to support and take care of. He feared not being able to work anymore. Even if he were to regain movement again, there could still be some permanent damage to prevent him from being efficient at his job. And being efficient was of the utmost importance to Alexander ever since he could remember. He was also disappointed in himself for being so preoccupied while at work. The issues that preoccupied him were important, but he had learned early on that there was a time and place for everything. There were no excuses for being lazy or undisciplined. Those attributes only resulted in unwanted consequences that could conceivably alter your life in a fraction of a second.

The Witch of Brentwood

*****

Clement had rushed home upon learning of the accident from Mr. Berryman. His heart was pounding from not knowing enough information about what had happened. It was one thing to cope with the reality of an accident and the assessment of how severe it was, but it was torture not knowing and letting your imagination run away with itself.

He rushed into the cabin to find Alexander lying in bed as the doctor was working over him, making sure the clean bandage was secured over the entry wound. Myrna and Amelia were crying hysterically beside his bed. Isabell was not home yet from searching for the brooch.

"What happened?" Clement asked no one in particular.

The women were too upset to speak so the doctor answered, "He accidentally shot himself at the gun shop."

Clement remained calm. He knew the importance of being strong especially when others around him needed someone to be strong *for* them. He kept inquiring of the doctor, "How bad is it?"

"There is no exit wound, so the pellet is still inside his body. He has no feeling anywhere below the waist so it seems it may have penetrated his spine somewhere above the pelvis."

Clement looked at Alexander's face and didn't see evidence of too much pain. The doctor noticed this and then added, "I gave him opium in some alcohol to drink. His state of mind isn't recognizing the pain and he won't be coherent for a while. I'll tell you what I know."

"Can you remove the pellet?" he asked the doctor.

"I don't dare. The pain would be too much even in this state of mind and we would run the risk of the area getting inflamed and contaminated. If this happens, it will affect his entire system and eventually his organs would fail and die."

"What can we do then?"

"He won't be able to walk. This most likely will be permanent. When the pain subsides in a few days, we'll try to get him to sit in bed and eventually help him sit in a chair."

Upon hearing this, the women started feeling weak with sorrow. So Clement ordered that they leave the room and lie down for a while. The women protested that they wanted to stay but Clement insisted and led them out, closing the door behind them.

"Will he work again?" Clement asked.

"If he doesn't walk again, I don't know how he could work. Invalid chairs are only available in Europe and only for the very rich. I'm afraid he'll have to be carried from now on. But staying in bed or in a chair may be the best thing for him. Fortunately, he has family who can take care of his needs." Clement pondered this new reality for a moment. "Any other questions?" asked the doctor.

"No."

"I'll check on him in a couple of days. In the meantime, mix this powder with some whiskey if the pain gets too unbearable." the doctor said.

"What is it?"

"Opium. He's too weak to smoke but he can swallow."

"Alright."

The doctor then got his things together and made his way out. "Come get me if you need me," he said before leaving.

Clement stayed in Alexander's room for a while just looking at him. He had come to consider him a son he never had, and in many ways, admired him. But now he was practically a vegetable lying in bed, having to be taken care of for perhaps all of his life. It gave Clement a sense of loss and now wished he hadn't introduced him to the prospect of apprenticeship with Mr. Berryman.

Just then, Isabell walked in and found her mother and Myrna crying. Her first thought was that Clement had done something to them again. She ran to her mother who was sitting by the fire.

"What's wrong, mother?"

Amelia answered, "Your brother has suffered a terrible accident, Isabell. His flintlock accidently fired and pierced his side."

"No!" cried Isabell. "Where is he? Is he alright?"

"He's injured and may not walk again." replied Myrna.

"Go see him, dear." her mother said, "he's in his room."

Isabell ran to him and didn't even notice Clement was in the same room. She held Alexander's hand as he lay, not sleeping but unaware of his surroundings. She called his name and got no response.

"He's medicated." Clement said.

She had heard him but chose to ignore him. Her focus was on her brother whom she'd grown up with and loved beyond anything or anyone else. She began to cry and held him as they had held each other so many times before.

Eventually his pain had abated so the remedial concoction that he was given was no longer necessary. However, he soon suffered from a new pain from the withdrawal of opium. It didn't last long and wasn't as severe as a longtime addict, but he'd gone through some very painful days; vomiting, shaking, and wishing he were dead.

Those days were now behind him. No longer was he suffering in pain but the realization of his condition was now something he had to face. Much like anything else he dealt with, he accepted his new fate for what it was and tried to be as practical about it as he could.

There was a time when he had to be fed by someone else; liquids at first and eventually worked his way up to soft solids. But he now could eat on his own. At times, he chose to sit up in bed and eventually swallowed his pride enough to ask to be placed in a chair near the fireplace so he could read his bible. Going to the outhouse was impossible, so someone (usually his mother) had to take care of that business as well, making sure he was clean afterwards. Occasionally, he bathed with the help of his dear bride-to-be, but mostly he had someone bring water and a cloth so he could wash himself in his room.

He hadn't heard from Mr. Berryman other than when he asked Clement 'how the boy was doing' and that he 'looked forward to having him back', knowing full well that that would never happen again. Alexander missed working and going about here and there, but he tried not to dwell on it.

Myrna would bring him food regularly. That was her job and she insisted no one else do it in her place. Everyone obliged her. It was at this time that Alexander wanted to have a serious discussion about what the future would hold. She placed the tray on the bed, and before eating, he began.

"I shall never walk again, Myrna." he said.

"Now, silly, don't say such nonsense." she said as she tried to look optimistic.

"No, dear, it's time to face it. This is what is left of me, and you know it for sure. I want you to know that I shan't hold you to your promise of marrying me. That was a promise made when I was well. Now things have changed. You're young and beautiful and anyone would be happy to court you."

"I don't believe what I am hearing with my own ears!" she replied, "We are to marry and that shall not change."

"Then you condemn yourself to a life of misery, caring for an invalid whose needs are that of a baby's needs. I won't allow it."

"And I shall not allow my future husband to dictate whom I should marry." She said, smiling at him which made him smile as well. Then she continued, "I love you and I want to take care of you as you would have taken care of me. There is nothing I want more than to be your wife. I want to be Mrs. Whitlock."

"Are you quite certain?" he asked.

"Yes." she replied without hesitation. "Now you eat while I draw you a bath."

Before she left the room, he grabbed her hand and pulled her down to kiss her. Then he said, "I have no feeling."

"I know." she replied.

"What I mean is I have no feeling down there." he said this as he looked down below his waist.

"We already have a baby on the way, Alexander. I need nothing else."

They kissed again before she left the room and he considered himself truly blessed to have such a strong woman by his side.

The days were long for Alexander. His sleep schedule was disrupted because he was always in bed and at times just fell asleep during the day. Because of this, he sometimes had sleepless nights and would lie awake just thinking about his situation. So, there was a time when he became depressed and asked God to take him home. But eventually, he got used to his new life and made the best of his condition. After all, he was still looking forward to being the father of a newborn baby.

As for Amelia, she had lost all hope for a happy life. She became more and more depressed with each passing day, seeing her son crippled by something that happened in a fraction of a second. Her relationship with her husband was also non-existent. She soon began to wish she wasn't alive to bear such pain.

Chapter 13

Unbeknownst to Isabell, Derris Blackmoore had become a close acquaintance to Alexander from working at the gun shop. Alexander and he had talked often about different types of guns during their workdays as well as their accuracy and the way they were designed. The two boys found they had much in common and were it not for the accident, they could have become good active friends doing things like target shooting, hunting, and the like; especially when Alexander knew of Derris's love for Isabell. They could have become like brothers. But it was still quite a surprise to Alexander when Derris came to visit him at home to see how he was feeling, much to Isabell's pleasure.

Isabell saw him walking down the road when he was still far away. She had been outside taking care of the livestock while Myrna was tending to Alexander. As for Amelia, the afternoon was always an opportune time to take a nap. She had been depressed of late and who could blame her. Her husband beat her, she was publicly humiliated, and now her only son whose career had just started to take shape, was paralyzed from the waist down, lying in bed all day and not being able to live his life as she imagined he would.

Isabell ran to Derris and into his arms when he was still far off. After they kissed, she led him into the house and to Alexander's room. She rapped on the door, then opened it slightly to stick her head in.

"You have a visitor." she said.

Alexander lifted his head and looked surprised. In all the time he'd been in bed recovering from the initial accident, he'd received no such visitations. Then Isabell opened the door to reveal Derris.

"How are you, old boy?" asked Derris.

Alexander looked overjoyed. He had come to know Derris quite well and wished to become close friends. "I've been better." Alexander replied, "but I've been worse also. I hope *you're* doing well."

"That's the spirit. I've always admired that about you; how you're able to be so optimistic. I'm sure your situation will improve soon."

"I'm sure you're right." Alexander said, convinced full well of the opposite. "This is my bride-to-be, Myrna Arington."

"Pleased to meet you, Myrna. My name is Derris Blackmoore."

They shook hands and all four exchanged pleasantries before Isabell and Myrna left the room for the boys to talk for a while.

The boys had a good meeting and Derris vowed to come back often. This came as a surprise to Alexander and thought that perhaps they could become close friends after all. Then Derris went to meet Isabell outside. As much as Alexander wanted to go out and enjoy the day with them, he was still happy to know someone with such empathy, and found himself smiling at the fact that he had found love in Isabell.

Isabell led Derris to a make-shift swing hanging from a branch of an old oak. She sat as he gently pushed her swinging back and forth for a time, then she stopped and began to talk about the horrors her mother had to suffer. She didn't mention her own humiliating parade for fear of what he might think of her, but she was sure to tell him about the abuse her mother had to take. The conversation then led them to talk about the other day when they made love and how it was wonderful even if it *was* a sin. They were both in agreement that they had to practice self-control from now on, but it was something that brought them closer together and he had every intention of not going back to Evelina. Isabell felt sorry for her because she had lost a good man in Derris, but now he was hers and she would make sure to keep it that way.

"Did you happen upon a brooch near where we made love, Derris?" she asked.

"No. I didn't."

"It was lost in that area, I believe. It had a white pearl with diamonds around it."

Upon hearing this, Derris' expression changed to one of recollection.

"Was it star-shaped?" he asked.

"Yes, it was. Have you seen it?"

"Yes, around Evelina's neck."

"What do you mean? She has the same brooch?"

"I believe it's yours. She said she'd found it on the ground on the day we ended our relationship."

"When did you have a chance to talk with her after that day?"

"There were some things we had to return to each other. That's when I asked about her new jewelry around her neck since I had never seen it before."

"Oh, Derris! You need to get it back to me."

"I don't see her anymore, Isabell. We're through."

"Still, you need to get it back. It's very old and it was handed down to me. It belonged to my grandmother."

"I can try but I'm doubtful of how successful I shall be. She said it's very special to her; that it was a sign from God when she prayed. But what does it matter? I'll buy one for you that will put that one to shame."

"I need *that* one, don't you understand?" she pleaded.

"Why, Isabell? Let's not dwell on a jewelry piece. Let's think about us instead. I would rather focus on us than chase Evelina. She might assume I want her back. We shouldn't have that happen. It shall only create more anguish."

Isabell knew he was right. It was too much of a risk for him to go after Evelina. *She may very well find his weakness and win him back.*

"You're so right." Isabell finally said. "What we have together is so much more than a brooch could ever be."

One would think she'd come to her senses. But the truth was that she had another way of retrieving that brooch and she promised herself that she would. So, she vowed to him she would never mention it again as long as he stays away from Evelina. He agreed.

The Witch of Brentwood

*****

There was a knock at the door. Flora recognized it right away. It was customary for Isabell to knock five times fast and as soon as she heard it, she thought it was wise of Isabell to visit her at night, finally. Usually Isabell came during the day, which Flora warned her about. She thought perhaps Isabell was at long last taking the risk of being seen with a witch, seriously.

"Come in, child." Flora said without going to the door.

Isabell opened it and walked in without a word. They sat near the fireplace.

"Why such a serious look, Isabell?" Flora asked.

"I've come to terms with what we discussed before."

"We discussed many things."

"I know. One thing in particular was the question of being a cunning folk, a healer…" she hesitated.

"Go on, child. Don't be afraid to say it."

"A witch."

"You've accepted that truth?" Flora asked.

"Yes."

"About me, or about you?"

"About both of us."

"So, you admit to being a witch?"

"I admit to having some sort of power over others. If that makes me a witch, then I accept it." Isabell said with conviction.

"What convinced you?"

"I've been able to carry out my will on occasion with the power of the brooch I showed you not long ago." Flora remained silent and let Isabell continue. "We've talked of coincidences and of magic. I believe in the magic of the brooch and the things I can do with it. You've said before that we need tools to accomplish what needs to be done. I've come to recognize that the brooch is my tool much like the tools *you* use to carry out what *you* need to do. And now it's lost, and I need it back. I've looked everywhere it could possibly be to no avail. You can help me."

"How?" asked Flora.

"By using the powers you have. You've said before that the essence of something, or someone is important."

"That's correct."

"I have the chain I used for the brooch to place around my neck. Perhaps the chain is the essence of the brooch. Isn't that so?"

"Perhaps."

"Oh, I hope." said Isabell.

"If I may, Isabell. It seems you wanted nothing to do with your powers or any tools associated with it. You've said so in no small measure."

"My mind has changed."

"What made that change?" Isabell didn't answer. Flora persisted. "Why are your powers important now?"

"Someone must be stopped from doing harm to others."

"And you mean to stop that someone?"

"Yes." Isabell replied.

Flora looked at Isabell with a smile as a mentor would look to a student with pride. There was no doubt Mr. Berryman had looked at Alexander in the same manner frequently.

"In that case, Isabell, we must try to retrieve your brooch. Let me have the chain."

Isabell retrieved the chain from her little pouch she kept on her wrist and carefully gave it to Flora. Flora then brought it to a table that contained such strange artifacts as seashells, bird wings, what looked like herbs, candles, cloth material, and wax. She placed it delicately on the table and shaped it to have five equidistant points from one another, much like the strange formation of Flora's outside torches Isabell had seen. The shape resembled a pentagram minus the inside pentagon. She then lit five candles around the chain, hovered her hands over the chain pentagram, and began an incantation of words unknown to Isabell. Flora's eyes were closed as the candles flickered in the dark. The whistling of the wind could be heard, and a chill was in the air from the drafty door, which made Isabell clutch her shawl and tightened it against her shoulders. She wasn't sure if she was cold or trembling from the strange ritual she was witnessing.

After a while, the ritual was over. Flora opened her eyes, picked up the chain, and returned it to Isabell, who carefully replaced it in her little pouch on her wrist.

"You must bury it in the ground for nine days." Flora said.

"Why nine days?"

"Because nine days will be what is necessary to complete the manifestation."

Isabell felt silly about asking the question. *Of course, the protocol must be followed precisely to the letter. What possible reason would there be to arbitrarily choose a number of days?* She was still naive, but she was learning.

"How deep?" Isabell asked.

This made Flora laugh.

"It's not a body, dear. Bury it in the ground in your backyard for nine days. After nine days have passed, retrieve it."

"Then what?"

"Then you can carry out what you need to do with this person who must be stopped."

Isabell was confused but she also had confidence in Flora. Whatever happened after nine days, she trusted she would be able to stop Clement from beating her mother and hurting his own daughter again.

"What about the nightmares I have? Will I be able to make them go away?" Isabell asked.

"As I said before, dreams may be difficult because of their origin. But you still have the power within you. The best approach is to remove any fears you may have from your childhood."

"But how is that done? How will I remove such a fear?"

"Sometimes fear is caused by someone. You will eliminate the fear when you recognize who is the cause."

"But how…?"

Flora didn't let her finish her question. She knew the answers would come in time.

"Go and bury your chain." Flora said, "Make sure no one sees where it is buried lest they go and dig it up and ruin what was done here tonight."

"What do I do until nine days are done?"

"Do nothing." Flora replied. "Only wait."

Isabell acknowledged and thanked her. Then she left.

Flora closed the door behind Isabell and had a feeling it would be the last time she would see her. She wasn't sure why the feeling was so profound, but she knew well enough to never argue with a feeling, as feelings never lie.

The Witch of Brentwood

*****

Isabell went home late that night with her broken chain and did as she was told by Flora. First, she went directly to the shed in the back of the cabin, listening intently to make sure there was not a sound from inside the cabin to indicate someone was still awake. Then, she fumbled in the dark to find a spade and had to feel all the way down the handle to make sure what she had was not a rake, or something else. She took the spade to the backyard and found an area that was soft enough to dig up, while not being too muddy. The light of the moon illuminated the work area enough for her to see what she was doing, so for that, she considered herself fortunate. She knew her shoes were getting dirty while she dug, even though it was still too dark for her to notice. She was sure she'd have to clean them before someone saw them and started asking questions. She felt she was a grave digger hurrying to bury the evidence. The hole was not very big in diameter, but she made sure the depth would prevent anyone from accidentally kicking up dirt and exposing the chain; not that anyone would be walking in that part of the backyard anyway, but it was better to err on the side of caution. Finally, she placed the broken chain in the hole and began to cover it making sure (to the extent that she could see) that no part of the chain was exposed.

What she had no knowledge of, was that Clement was lying in bed awake and had heard a noise in the shed. He would have been asleep were it not for Amelia's incessant crying for a good part of the night. He commanded her to stop her whimpering before he gave her something to really cry about. The last thing he remembered was her leaving the room and going outside, saying she needed air. Still, he was wide awake. Isabell's digging was too far from the cabin for him to hear from inside the cabin but there was definitely something going on in the shed; perhaps a small critter or perhaps something more dangerous that needed his immediate attention; like an intruder.

He got out of bed and got partially dressed. Taking a lit lantern with him, he went out by the backdoor to make his way directly to the shed. One his way, he heard noises coming from the backyard. Thinking the critter or the intruder had moved onto another area, he began to walk quietly towards it.

At first, he saw the outline of a person in the moon-lit darkness. As he approached, the outline began to take shape and soon his lantern made it bright enough to see it was Isabell holding a spade. She had finished burying the chain by then but still, the spade was in her hand.

"What are you doing out here at this time of night?" he asked.

"I felt like being alone to think."

"With a spade?"

"I thought I saw something, so I went to the shed and grabbed something for protection."

"Protection? Why didn't you just come in and go to bed?"

"I don't know." was the only response she could think of; not that it was any concern of his, she thought.

Clement put his lantern on the stump of a cut tree and approached her.

"Put that down," he said, referring to the spade.

"I think I'll just bring it back and go in now."

"Put it down, I said."

"Why?"

The Witch of Brentwood

At that, he lunged at her. She tried to hit him with it but he was too fast for her. He grabbed the spade with one hand and her arm with the other. He then threw the spade to the ground a few feet away so he could handle Isabell with both hands.

"Let me go!" she exclaimed. He didn't respond. "Let me go or I'll scream!"

"If you scream, it shall be the last thing you do," he replied.

Then he placed one hand over her mouth and forced himself on her. He tore the buttons of her blouse with his other hand and exposed her breasts as she struggled to get free. When it seemed she was freeing herself a little, he moved his hand from her mouth to her throat and squeezed until she gasped. He threw her to the ground and fell on top of her, trying to lift her dress to gain access to her undergarment and ultimately to herself. In her struggle, she was able to lift her knee and hit him in the groin. This was something her mother had taught her if she were ever in a compromising position with a forceful man and until that point, she couldn't imagine how that would allow her to escape. But it worked.

She stood up and looked at him while he lay rolling on the ground in pain, wondering if she should run or call for help. But the pain didn't last. When she saw him get up, she started running towards the cabin. He then picked up his lantern and followed. Her intentions were to run to her room and hopefully be able to block the door so he couldn't come in, because she knew there was no one who would be able to protect her.

It was dark. She could hardly see where she was going but kept running. Finally, she reached the front porch of the cabin and ran into something that stopped her most abruptly and made her fall. Clement soon arrived and the lantern was bright enough to expose what Isabell had run into. She looked up and screamed, while Clement also looked in disbelief. Amelia was hanging from the neck by a rope tied to one of the rafters of the porch roof. The color of her face was enough for them to be certain she was dead. There was no rape that night.

Myrna ran outside when she heard Isabell scream. It was a more intense scream than the ones she was used to hearing from Isabell in the middle of the night. Myrna couldn't bear to look, as her father lowered the body down from the rafters, so she went inside to gently break the news to the bed-ridden Alexander. On her way, she found the last note Amelia would ever write. It was only addressed to Isabell and Alexander. It read:

> *My dear Alexander and Isabell,*
> *I love you more than any mother can love a child. But I can no longer bear the burden of life under these current conditions. Living a life knowing my son is an invalid and my daughter fears for her innocence is no longer tolerable. I neither can bear any more pain from Clement; therefore, I am leaving this world. I pray you will forgive me for leaving you. And if it is God's will and at all in my power to do so, I will protect you and be your guardian until we are reunited in heaven.*
> *Love you always,*
> *Your loving mother.*

Chapter 14

Amelia's funeral was private and no one except Derris Blackmoore was invited. Really, who would want to attend the funeral of a disgraced disobedient thief anyway? There was no means of Alexander attending either, as his debility prevented any travel unless he was carried. He was, however, able to see her one last time to say goodbye. They had carried her body into his room for that purpose before proceeding to the burial.

Now, she was gone. Her absence created a void in the home. As much as Isabell and Myrna tried to own her chores and act motherly with Alexander, her wisdom was no longer there. Isabell would frequently look to her mother's favorite chair, which was now always vacant, and recall the conversations she'd had that seemed to make an impact on both of them. But now, she was gone.

Soon, the normal routine of life continued. It had been eight days since Isabell buried the broken chain of her brooch and she would not be able to dig up whatever was in there for another day. Flora was adamant when she emphasized that it should be buried for nine days, so nine days it would be. Isabell was not about to question proper procedures especially when it came to the mysticism of a witch's spell.

She stayed away from Clement as much as possible by usually spending most of her time in Alexander's room even when he was asleep. She wore more layers of garment and neglected her hair and appearance so that Clement would hopefully find her repulsive enough to discard any sexual thought that could cause another attack on her. She considered herself lucky to have been able to avoid rape so far, but something needed to be done soon.

As to Clement, he didn't miss Amelia's presence. In fact, her recent behavior and appearance were something he was becoming intolerant of. And quite frankly, he was more interested in what Isabell had to offer physically. But what occupied his thoughts most since Amelia's death was the cause of it. He simply didn't understand, or perhaps refused to acknowledge the pain she had gone through of late, including her being humiliated in front of an entire neighborhood; a humiliation which was sanctioned by the very clergy who at one time respected her as a God-fearing Christian. The reason for her death had to have a root cause, Clement thought. He assumed the perpetrator to be that old witch, Flora, who had recently burned an innocent young girl to death. *It had to be her. Who else could it be?* It was time for another meeting with the men who had approved Amelia's and Isabell's humiliating parade. And so, he organized such a meeting that very day.

It was determined that the accusation was valid, and the perpetrator was worthy of the same punishment as was practiced in Salem to rid the town, and indeed the colony, of this evil. It was also determined that the punishment should be executed as soon as possible. They thought it would be appropriate and less dangerous for them to have the witch burn much like the young girl she killed not long ago.

They arrived at Flora's cabin in the middle of the night with an abundance of lanterns and quietly blocked her door from the outside to prevent her escape. Next, they lit as many lanterns as the cabin had windows. There was a man stationed at each window as they wanted to prevent any means of escape for her. And although the windows were closed, they threw the lanterns through, shattering the glass and igniting the kerosene as it spread all over her floor.

It was the sound of the breaking glass that woke her. At first, she thought it was more of the same vandalism she was accustomed to but it soon became obvious her home was on fire. She rushed out of bed and noticed the several fires at every window and instinctively ran for the door. Try as she might, the very door she always had a hard time to keep closed, wouldn't open. She didn't have the strength to break it down and soon the fire spread into other areas of the cabin, engulfing furniture, and curtains. Soon, the smoke rose everywhere, and it became impossible for her to breath without coughing. She screamed and banged on the door until bones in her hands were broken but there was no response and no relief. A burst of wind came through her windows creating an immediate combustion in the rest of the cabin. She was engulfed in flames in an instant and fell to the floor rolling and kicking to relieve the pain, but it wasn't long after that she lost consciousness and burned to a skeleton along with the cabin and her possessions.

Isabell and Myrna were in Alexander's room when Clement walked in the following morning. It was unusual for him to do that since he normally left for work directly after getting out of bed. But that morning was the start of a new special day. It was the first day since getting rid of the town witch, but it was also day nine since Isabell had buried her broken chain.

"We need to worry no longer about that witch," he said.

Isabell and Alexander immediately thought he was talking about their deceased mother.

"Whatever do you mean?" asked Isabell.

"The old woman further down the road; the one who killed that young girl with fire. We took care of her last night in the same manner."

"You killed her?" cried Isabell.

"We all did. Why so concerned?"

"Why?" Alexander asked.

"To avenge your mother. She's the one who led her to her end."

"You have no proof," said Isabell.

"All the proof we need." Clement responded. "I only wish I could have labeled her a witch as before."

"Before?" asked Isabell.

Myrna and Alexander knew exactly what Clement meant by that. Myrna recalled the time she had overheard him saying how he'd attached a note to a witch's thigh eight years prior. She braced herself for what her father was about to divulge.

"A few years ago, now," Clement said, "we had to rid the town of Salem. The very same witch who killed my wife. We hanged her until she was quite dead, but it was not enough as far as I was concerned. I pierced her thigh with my knife to attach a note that said exactly what she was; a witch."

He said this matter-of-factly and with some pride, then laughed on his way out to go to his job.

Isabell and Alexander looked at each other but Alexander didn't look surprised. In fact, she was the only one who seemed to feel the shock of what was said.

"I didn't want you to know." said Myrna to Isabell. "I was afraid you would blame my father for the nightmares that have been plaguing you all these years."

Isabell had to process all she'd heard. It now made sense that Clement would be involved and even went a step further to humiliate the hanging woman she had seen in real life and in her dreams since she was ten years old. She hated him more than ever. The note her mother left was very specific about her not being able to live with the pain Clement inflicted on her, and now it was Flora who was the victim of his hatred. Isabell thought it was now her turn to avenge.

Hours before Clement came home from work that day, Isabell took a walk to see what was left of Flora's home. Where it once stood, were ashes and a few articles that would not burn including her bones. She imagined it wouldn't be long before a group of people got together to clean up the mess left by the fire and Flora would never get a proper burial, but rather her bones would become fodder for dogs during the day and wild animals at night. She went back home after a while of reflection and prayer. For some reason, she no longer feared the cemetery as she passed it.

She found the spade she had used nine days ago to bury the broken chain and used it in haste to open the hole again before

Clement got home. She moved delicately to not damage the chain any further but was anxious to find if anything had changed under that ground. She dug so far with the spade and then decided to move the rest of the dirt with her hands. Finally, she felt something. She pulled on the chain gently and removed it from the hole.

It was still daylight so what she saw was clearly visible, if not believable. The chain was no longer broken and as she held it up, her lost brooch was swinging back and forth on it like the pendulum of a clock. She brushed the dirt off and quickly put it around her neck where it belonged. She kept her hand on it for a long time, thinking about Flora and her powers. She was also now confident in the ability of her own powers, even if some would consider *her* a witch.

After a while, she hurried inside to talk to Myrna about all she knew of the hanging woman and her father's involvement since the truth was now revealed. Myrna now felt it should no longer be a secret but apologized to Isabell for the way the incident had affected her life from childhood to the present. After quite a while of talking about the incident, Myrna was starting to come around to the possibility that the hanging woman was not a witch after all, much like how she was convinced that Amelia was not a witch. It was hard for her to believe but perhaps her mother died at the hands of her father as some had accused at the time.

Not far away, the young Evelina Kenwig searched high and low for the brooch she'd found, for it was no longer hanging on her chain. It was the strangest thing, she thought. The chain, still around her neck, was not broken nor was it unclasped. The brooch had simply disappeared.

*****

When Isabell and Myrna were in Alexander's room discussing the past incident of the hanging woman, it was clear that Myrna was upset. All accounts from then until now pointed to Clement being guiltier than Myrna thought. With an open mind, she was able to recall some of the moments of her childhood when her father had come home drunk and beat her mother even when she was not acting 'mad' as she sometimes did. There were no explanations nor did Myrna care to hear any, since the important thing for her to do at the time was to run, hide, and block her ears. She was now able to see that the recent attacks from her father, including her own punishment for being pregnant, were not warranted. She didn't know about the incident with Flora since there were so many involved in her demise but was open to the possibility that it was not warranted either.

This revelation was devastating. Myrna cried perhaps more that night than all the tears she'd ever shed since she could remember. She wasn't sure how she could survive with the internal conflict of loving her father all her life and now feeling like he doesn't deserve her love. To make matters worse, she feared him. It wasn't the type of fear one feels from the consequences of disobeying their father, but rather a real fear of what he was able to do at will; right or wrong.

It was obvious to Isabell and Alexander that she needed time alone.

"You should go rest for a while, Myrna." Alexander said.

"I wish to stay here with you." she replied.

"I'll be here when you feel better. Please, go rest." he said.

Isabell then added, "Yes, it would be good for you. In fact, I'd like to talk to Alexander alone about mother. Do you mind?"

Myrna wiped her tears and agreed, "No, I don't mind at all. Maybe resting would be best for me." Before she left the room, she kissed Alexander and hugged Isabell.

When they were finally alone, Isabell showed Alexander the brooch around her neck.

"You found it?" he asked.

"I didn't only find it, Alexander, it was given back to me."

"Who had it?"

"That's not important. What *is* important is how I got it back." Alexander waited for her to continue. "I sought the help of Flora. She performed some kind of magic and it appeared."

"What are you saying? Have you imagined all this?"

"No. It's real, Alexander. And this brooch is as powerful as Flora's magic." Alexander just lay there trying to make sense of what she was saying. She continued, "Do you remember when I was deathly ill?"

"Yes."

"How is it that I was made well again? No one knew how. Not even the doctor, but it was the brooch mother gave me."

"You're a loon." was his response.

"No. The man who collapsed just before we left Salem; I wished him that way and it happened. And when Clement was flogging Myrna, I made him stop."

"He stopped because of a strained muscle in his back." Alexander said.

"I'm the one who caused it." she replied.

"Why didn't you stop him from beating mother, then?" he asked sarcastically.

"Because he had taken the brooch from me, remember? He ripped it off my neck. But now I have it."

"Hogwash." Alexander said in disbelief. Isabell also saw concern in his eyes, perhaps for her mental state. But she completely believed in the power of the brooch.

"Flora said I also have the power to heal and hurt people." Isabell revealed.

"And you believe her?"

"Yes, I do. And it would please me to prove it to you."

"How?" he asked.

There was no response. Instead, she unbuttoned her collar to expose the brooch around her neck and clutched it as she'd never done before.

"What are you doing?" asked Alexander, but he received no response.

What he saw was Isabell with her eyes closed so tight that tears appeared and rolled down her cheeks. Her teeth were so clenched that her jaw muscles became hard as rocks, and he feared she would break her own jaw by clenching so.

Suddenly, Alexander felt something he hadn't felt in a long time. There was a tingle in the toes of his right foot.

"Isabell," he said very quietly.

There was something different about how he'd said her name, so she opened her eyes and relaxed her face muscles.

"What is it, Alexander?" she asked.

"I feel something."

"What do you feel?" There was no response. She asked again, "What is it you feel?"

He looked at her with wonder. "My toes," he replied.

She smiled while he still had an incredulous look about him. He was afraid to be optimistic, she thought.

"Try to wiggle them." she said, looking down where his feet were covered under the blanket.

Alexander closed his eyes and concentrated like a poet searching for the right phrasing. He was still concentrating when Isabell saw the blanket over his foot move. He wasn't aware that it was happening, as he still only felt tingling.

"IT MOVED!" shouted Isabell. He opened his eyes and looked down but by then the movement had stopped. "Try again!" she said.

He didn't close his eyes this time but kept them on the blanket over his right foot. There, he saw what he thought to be a miracle. He saw the blanket move. It didn't move much but it moved. Isabell and Alexander laughed with elation, as she held him in her arms. After a time, he told her he could feel tingling in the toes on his left, and soon after, they both laughed and cried as they watched the blanket over both feet move up and down.

Isabell now had every reason to be confident that Alexander would gradually get better and hopefully be able to walk again in the future. But she knew she had to be careful and selective about how she invoked the services of the brooch. These were dangerous times as evidenced by the actions of the crowd of men against Flora.

Alexander and Isabell vowed to keep silent about their knowledge of the brooch, lest someone accuse her of witchcraft. If he indeed got better to the point of being able to walk again, they wouldn't have to explain it since no one would be able to explain it either. All they needed to do was keep quiet and not disclose it to anyone, not even Myrna.

The Witch of Brentwood

*****

Amelia was a proud woman, especially before she married Clement. One of the concoctions she used to make was a form of aromatic perfume she called sweet water. Isabell remembered this very well, as they used to prepare it together ever since she was a young girl. They would gather roses, lavender, and sometimes juniper, mix those plants in boiling water along with a few orange peels, let it boil for a while, and then let the water settle back to room temperature. Amelia would then splash this sweet water behind her ears and at times put some in her bath water. It was used as perfume mostly worn on Sundays for church or for special occasions. Amelia even let her daughter splash some on since it didn't have such a strong aroma as some of the loose women wore.

With her mother now deceased, Isabell had taken upon herself to go into her mother's room without Clement knowing, to take possession of some of her belongings before he got rid of them in one of his drunken fits of fury. Her bottle of sweet water was one of those items taken, which Isabell hid in her room.

On the same night that Alexander was able to wiggle his toes and before Clement came home from work, Isabell was in her room making herself beautiful. She let her hair show its natural curves by letting it hang to her shoulders. She wore the nicest dress she owned and didn't bother to fasten the top buttons, letting the cleavage of her breasts show a little below her brooch. She pinched her cheeks like her mother had taught her to add color to her face. And finally, she splashed some of her mother's sweet water to add fragrance to her beauty; some on her neck and even more where the top of her breasts was exposed.

She was a little nervous about what she'd planned but she now had great confidence in her ability to heal and hurt, as Flora had told her. She had to move quickly now since she could hear Clement's horse arriving. She looked at herself once more in the mirror and was beyond pleased with the contrast of how she looked now compared to the previous few days when she tried her hardest to not be attractive to Clement and prevent his advances. Now she was ready to look beautiful for him. After one last look at herself, she got up from her chair and walked to her bedroom door to open it. Then she quickly went back to sit in front of the mirror, closed her eyes, and clutched her brooch.

She heard Clement enter and opened her eyes. The sun had set so the dim light of one lantern in her room and the fireplace in the kitchen was all that illuminated the two rooms. Myrna was with Alexander in his room where they were talking ever quietly between themselves.

Isabell stood up and looked at Clement without saying a word. He looked back at her and saw her as beautiful as he'd ever seen her and became lustful in an instant. He also saw the brooch around her neck and became furious at her deviance. Was she trying to mock him, he thought? But his fury was mixed with a feeling of lust, which provoked him even more.

He walked slowly into her room and shut the door. She smiled at him. As he approached her, he could smell the same fragrance as when he'd first lusted after Amelia. She gasped a little when he grabbed her roughly by the shoulders, which made him want her even more. Feeling no resistance from her, he lowered his hands to touch her breasts. He had no intention of ripping the

The Witch of Brentwood

brooch from her neck this time, as it made her that much more beautiful. There would be time for that later. He kissed her passionately on the lips. Next, he moved his lips to her neck and then lowered them to kiss her brooch and then lower still to the top of her breasts.

Suddenly, he stopped. He held her shoulders at arm's length and looked at her in disbelief. Seeing this, she began to smile. She saw the pain in his face and then her smile turned into a laugh; a laugh that scared him, for it was a vengeful laugh.

He felt a pain in the pit of his stomach, which turned into unbearable nausea and difficulty swallowing.

"What's the matter?" she asked, still laughing. He couldn't answer at the moment from the nausea but also because he was confused by what was happening. *Why this pain? Why is she laughing as though she's the cause of it?* "Tell me, Clement, do you feel ill? Do you like the smell of my potion that you kissed and invited into your body?" she laughed again. "It was the essence of all those you've killed. But hear this; I am a witch as well as those you killed, and you shall become too sick to kill *me*.

Upon hearing this, Clement made an attempt to reach his room so he could lie down but never made it. He fell to the floor clutching his stomach as Isabell clutched her brooch. Her laughter soon became just a smile as she looked at him defenseless and knew he would become more defenseless still as he struggled with an illness that would torture him until his demise.

What Clement felt were the symptoms of progressive adenocarcinoma; cancer of the stomach lining. Isabell didn't know this specifically but what she wished for was a disease that he would have a small chance of surviving even with the greatest of care.

After a while of Clement lying on the floor in a semiconscious state, Isabell buttoned up her collar and ran into Alexander's room to get Myrna for help. She wasted no time in running to her father.

"What happened?" Myrna asked, bending over her father and listening for his heartbeat.

"I don't know. He came in from work and collapsed." Isabell answered.

"Father, are you alright?" Myrna asked him.

Coming to his senses but still feeling pain, he pointed at Isabell and answered, "Beware the witch."

Myrna looked at Isabell in wonder.

"This must be a delusion." Isabell said to Myrna, "You must get him to bed right away. Tomorrow we should talk to the doctor."

Myrna agreed. Never had she ever seen her father in such a state of delusion and pain. She was able to get him back on his feet and helped him to bed, where he lay in pain; a pain that would last a long time before he died, as Isabell promised him.

The Witch of Brentwood

*****

For eight months Clement lay in pain and agony. There was nothing the doctor could do but make him comfortable with opium and other such drugs. Myrna cared for him as she had with Alexander; washing him and making sure he was fed to the best of her ability, as he had no appetite and had dwindled down to weighing a mere ninety pounds. His face was drawn, and his hair had turned completely gray. His groans of pain were frequent and everyone, including his own daughter, thought he would be better off dead and couldn't wait for the day when it would happen, for his own good.

Everyone of Clement's business acquaintances, clergy, and court officials who visited him could see how delusional he was throughout his long battle with cancer. His constant claim that Isabell was a witch had become normal to them and some even went along with the 'delusion' and pretended to be his confidants. Some went as far as to play along and vowed to hang the witch just to appease him, for they knew his final days were near.

Also, all outsiders who came to visit were in full acceptance of Myrna being pregnant and her promise to be Alexander's wife. The secrets were revealed some months prior when Alexander started to recover from his accident and the clergy and doctor were invited to investigate. That's when they decided that the truth must be known. If it meant being excommunicated from the church, they were willing to accept it. As it happened, their future marriage was approved by the church because Amelia was no longer alive, and they were no longer considered brother and sister. As for the fornication out of wedlock, they were suspended from going to church for three months and nine days, after which they were allowed to return and start anew. The truth of the matter was that the pastors were so amazed by God's mysterious work through Alexander's recovery that they didn't dare go against His will for Alexander and Myrna.

As for Isabell, she visited Clement only to make sure the progression of the disease was on track. Myrna asked her not to go in his room often because her appearance gave him a terrible fright, but sometimes she would bring him food just to check on his progress, knowing full well the sight of food turned his stomach.

Although her father's dying was terrible, Myrna still had much to be happy and thankful for. She was in her ninth month of pregnancy and was scheduled to give birth soon. Her baby was now the main priority in her life, not her father. And she had renewed hope for Alexander who was doing very well on his own. His condition had gotten progressively better from the moment he could wiggle his toes. He was now able to walk on his own, albeit with the help of a makeshift cane he had made from a branch of a backyard tree. But his condition seemed to get better with each passing day. He even had a conversation with Mr. Berryman about returning to work at some point; a discussion Alexander was long anticipating. He also couldn't wait to begin working with his friend Derris again.

Then, came the day. Myrna was in labor and would soon give birth to a son or a daughter with the help of a midwife. *What a surprise to find out which it will be.* It was also Clement's wish to live to see his grandchild before he died.

It wasn't an easy birth, since Myrna was rather small, and her baby was heavy; notwithstanding the fact it was her first delivery. She pushed in pain as Alexander waited in another room. Isabell held her hands and assisted in making sure her legs were secured. There was also a tense moment when the umbilical cord was wrapped around the baby's neck and the midwife had to hurry the baby along, so it didn't suffocate. But finally, the baby girl was out of the womb and immediately started to cry. At that moment, the midwife had to assure Myrna and Isabell that the bluish color on the baby would soon disappear and turn to a normal pinkish look.

It was not uncommon for babies to not survive their birth. The reasons were unknown at the time but three centuries later, it would become widely accepted that a mother's good nutrition and well-being would become a major contributor to the baby's health. Myrna's baby, however, was healthy and strong. Alexander would later say that his prayers had been answered to not only get well but to also have a healthy baby.

Myrna held her baby for the first time after the necessary procedures were taken care of. Alexander came into the room and was overjoyed at seeing his baby girl for the first time, saying that he thought she had many of his facial features.

"Have you decided what her name shall be?" asked the midwife.

Alexander and Myrna looked at each other in agreement and then Alexander replied, "Amelia."

Isabell smiled and said, "That's a beautiful name for such a beautiful baby."

After a while of holding and nursing her baby, Myrna thought it was time for her father to see the newborn. She asked the midwife to bring her to see him because Alexander still had difficulty walking and Isabell frightened her father too much. The midwife agreed and gently picked up the baby from Myrna.

Upon entering Clement's room, the dying man appeared to be sleeping. However, there was a smell in the room; a new smell. She went over to him and placed her index and middle fingers on the side of his neck below the ear. There, she felt nothing. Where there was once a pulse, was nothing. She looked at his chest to see if it would rise and fall from breathing, and still there was nothing. Clement was dead. It was sad indeed to Myrna that he died without seeing his granddaughter who would never know him, save for the horrible stories she would hear from her aunt Isabell.

Clement would have suffered longer were it not for Isabell not wanting him to see the new baby. After months of pain, bloody diarrhea, and vomiting, Clement was no longer suffering but he suffered for a good long time.

There was also something strange that happened to Isabell after the passing of Clement. She no longer had nightmares about the hanging woman who so often disturbed her sleep. Gone were the dreams of people attacking her for being a witch, which she always denied. Gone were the sleepless nights. The only thing that disturbed her sleep from that moment on was the sweet cry of baby Amelia calling for her mother to feed and clean her. Isabell welcomed such disturbance. It reminded her of the innocence she used to know and that the terrors of her life had disappeared.

The Witch of Brentwood

*****

It wasn't long after Clement's death in 1693 that things began to change. The days were longer as the summer sun shone through, baby Amelia was starting to sit up on her own, and Alexander was almost fully healed of his injury from the gunshot accident. In fact, he was now in negotiations again with Mr. Berryman about returning to work; with the light-hearted understanding that he would take every possible precaution to not shoot himself again. But the most impacting change of all was that Myrna became Mrs. Whitlock and Isabell became Mrs. Blackmoore. In fact, they decided to get married at the same time in a double wedding.

It wasn't a big wedding, to be sure, since the women had kept to themselves ever since they arrived in Brentwood. It was better to have as little friends as possible or no friends at all. Myrna feared being accused of being in a romantic relationship with her brother, Alexander, while Isabell feared accusations of being a witch from being seen with Flora and that God awful birthmark on her neck. She somewhat regretted visiting the old cunning woman during the daylight when anyone could see, but she admitted to herself that those visits were crucial. It was through Flora that the brooch had been returned to her, after all.

One other important change was the news that was circulating about the witch trials of Salem coming to an end in May of that year. But there were still some who were too frightened to put it behind them. Some were well aware of witches who had escaped Salem; women who would have eventually been accused had they stayed. After all, witches were witches whether they were accused or not. It was rumored that even Brentwood had become a sanctuary town for some of them. Both Isabell and Myrna were well aware of what a mob of people were capable of doing when in the wrong frame of mind. So, they kept a low profile for a long time.

But both women were happy with their lives finally. Alexander, Myrna, and the baby lived in the cabin they inherited from Clement and Alexander's mother. Derris and Isabell decided on a little place not far from where Derris and his sisters lived.

The secret of the brooch was still kept from Myrna. Alexander was not one to keep secrets from anyone much less his wife, but at least for now, it was best for Myrna not to know how he recovered from his accident and how her father died. Isabell had never told Alexander of her spell on Clement but he knew all too well that she had something or perhaps everything to do with it. Her fury was too great to control her powers over Clement and make sure he suffered greatly before he died.

Isabell also kept the brooch a secret from Derris until their wedding night when she absent-mindedly forgot to remove it from around her neck before getting ready for bed. He had seen that brooch before, remembering it from the first time they made love in the thicket. He looked at it for a while until she realized it was around her neck. She instinctively put her hand over it.

"Is that the brooch you'd lost?" he asked.

"The brooch?"

"Yes, the one you're covering." She looked away and didn't respond. "May I see it?"

She pulled her hand away and said, "It's a different one."

"It looks very much the same as the other."

"Yes, I was very fortunate to find something similar."

"It isn't the same one?"

"How could it be, silly? Anyway, let's forget about that, Mr. Blackmoore." she said with a smile too inviting for him to ignore.

"Very well, Mrs. Blackmoore." he replied in kind.

And that was the end of that. They never brought the subject up again.

She was determined that the brooch and the mysticism that came with it would remain a secret between Alexander and her for as long as possible to avoid further pain and suffering. For God knows, there had been too much pain and suffering throughout their lives until now. It was time to let go of the past and start living for the present.

Réal Carpentier

Chapter 15
2 Years Later

The tumultuous days of Salem witch hunts had been over for a few years but the ramifications were still in the air. Although the trials and executions were in the past, there was still a strong belief in the metaphysical evils that lurked about. How else could recoveries from terminal conditions occur, as well as the sudden burning of a human with no apparent fuel or form of ignition? Also, Clement's accusations from his death bed of Isabell being a witch and responsible for his terminal condition, were the fuel of more rumors, specifically about Isabell.

The rumors were not all bad, however. Isabell had come to be known as the new cunning woman to replace the old Flora. Certain people who were brave enough, visited her to heal what ailed them, making sure to visit her discreetly after sunset. And she *was* able to heal them in whole or in part. But there were still others who advised staying away from the Brentwood witch at all cost, to be sure. Once in a while, an accident or other negative occurrence would happen and ultimate suspicions arose about Isabell's involvement, whether direct or indirect. Rumors always travel quickly in a small town. Such was the case when a forest fire had started in the outskirts of Brentwood and burned two and a half acres before it was brought under control. This unfortunate incident was soon followed by the disappearance of a young boy who was later found dead in a nearby river.

Isabell paid no mind to these rumblings around town. The dangers of being tried as a witch no longer existed and she didn't really care about what people thought of her. Derris was more self-conscious about what people thought even though Isabell tried to convince him that it didn't matter in the least.

She finally told Derris the truth about the brooch and her ability. She waited two years before doing so, fearing his reaction and the possibility of his leaving her. She assured him she had nothing to do with the fires and other incidents around town. The hardest part about telling him the truth was how she got the brooch back from his childhood sweetheart. But he was a noble and loyal man. He promised her he would always be by her side. He didn't understand how such a supernatural thing as a brooch with mystical powers could occur, but he accepted it and after all the time of being married to her, the phenomenon became a natural way of life for him as it had for her.

They were happy living in Brentwood and never would have any intention of moving to another town or other colony. Derris had become a fine gunsmith along with his good friend Alexander, who was now fully recovered from his accident; so much so that he didn't even walk with a limp anymore. But the mere thought of leaving their town would mean no longer working for Mr. Berryman in a career Derris loved. In fact, Mr. Berryman spoke many times of soon retiring and leaving the business to Derris and Alexander as co-owners.

Isabell and Myrna became close friends and organized many family dinners a year; even on days that were not holidays or special occasions. However, Myrna was never told of the brooch and its powers through Isabell. This was a strict order from Alexander, as he was sure Myrna would not be able to accept such strange happenings. But if she did, it would create too much doubt as to whether Isabell had anything to do with her father's torturous few months before his death. All in all, the two couples were living well, and happy.

There was still one more thing Isabell had to do before moving on to living in the present and letting go of the past. She still owned the acorn from the oak tree on which the hanging woman was killed. For some reason, she couldn't part with it until now. It was in her trinket box all these years alongside her brooch when she didn't wear the jewel around her neck. But it was now time to dispose of it and she wanted it as far away from her and her family as possible.

It was around that time that Alexander and Myrna decided to take a small vacation and visit other areas of the Colony of New Hampshire. Alexander had been in bed for too long not able to move or be active as he once was. Now that he was fully recovered, he wanted to move and explore other places for no other reason than to feel the freedom of being able to go where he wished. So, Isabell and Derris paid them a visit with a favor to ask and to also see baby Amelia who was getting so big. Once alone with Alexander, Isabell gave him the acorn and made her request.

"Do you know what this is?" she asked.

"It's an acorn."

"Yes it is, and it's a very special acorn." she said. "I'd like you to take it with you."

"How is it special?"

"It's from the tree of the hanging woman."

"You took an acorn from that tree? Why would you do such a thing?"

"In my mind, it was the best way for the poor woman to be remembered. Also, I wanted a piece of the home we left in Salem."

"Why do you want me to take it with me?"

"I wish you to dispose of it; far away. The further the better. I'm ready to move on without thinking of the past. This acorn is now nothing but a reminder of what was. We have a different life now."

"Throwing it in the river would not suffice?" he asked.

"No. I need to be as far from it as possible; in a different town at the very least."

"Very well, then." he said as he took the acorn from her. "I shall make sure of it. You needn't worry."

"Thank you, Alexander. I love you."

"And I love you as well," he replied.

Then they rejoined Derris and Myrna and sat down to have their dinner. It was the last time Isabell saw that acorn and never gave it a second thought.

*****

Alexander and Myrna left early one morning for the vacation across the Colony of New Hampshire. They visited many towns and found various areas for lodging. The mountains were majestic, and the air was cool. It was the most they both had traveled in their lives and vowed to take another trip the following year if his work schedule allowed it. They were also hopeful to convince Derris and Isabell to come along with them as well.

On their way back home, they stopped at an area called Manchester where the population was considerably vaster than Brentwood and other little towns they'd visited. This appealed to Alexander since there were so many people about and so much to see. They stayed there overnight and then made their way back home. But before leaving, Alexander remembered the promise he made to Isabell about ridding her of the acorn from Salem and thought Manchester was as good a place as any. It was certainly far enough away from home.

They got back in the wagon and started on their way. Finding the right spot where there was an abundance of trees, Alexander reached in his pocket, grabbed the acorn, and threw it towards the woodland. He heard it hit one of the trees and fall to the ground. Myrna asked him about what he threw, and he simply answered, "It was part of the past, and now it's gone."

Myrna knew better than to inquire further. As far as she was concerned, it was insignificant.

They continued on their way and arrived home several hours later.

Isabell never dared visit Salem again, but she often visited the area where Flora lived. She was no longer afraid of the cemetery that was near the old cabin where the buried bodies of the many souls were laid to rest, and it was now a special place for her as well. For you see, before the group of men had cleared the area of Flora's burned cabin, Isabell had taken one of Flora's bones and buried it in the nearby cemetery, if for no other reason than to visit her old friend again. She remembered how frightened she was when her mother would take her to visit her grandmother where her body lay. But that was then.

There were many changes in Isabell in those days and days to come. It was all due to that wonderful magical brooch that gave her new life. But regardless of the fact that her night terrors were gone, and she now lived a happy life, she would never forget the past.

She couldn't. It happened. And it would haunt her forever.

The Witch of Brentwood

Epilogue

An acorn is just an acorn. A brooch is just a brooch. It sounds like the most mundane wisdom from the least learned person. But the reader now knows that that isn't true. The fact is that it was a very special brooch indeed, but so was the acorn. And one would not expect to grow an oak from an acorn that had fallen from its branch years ago. But expectations are sometimes naive.

When the acorn Alexander threw fell to the ground, it was already split from hitting a tree. A few hours later, rain began. The muddy ground swallowed the oak seed almost immediately and it began to sprout the necessary buds needed for life. This process allowed for shoots to grow and grow and grow for centuries.

Approximately 300 years later, the massive oak was bigger than the trees surrounding it. New Hampshire was now a state and Manchester, a big city within it. The population had grown considerably and living close by was a young boy named Barry Kay.

Barry would one day climb that tree and fall from it, causing brain damage that would allow him to read other people's minds, and soon evolve into being able to control their minds as well.

One would think it was a freak accident; that the phenomenon was not caused by a mystical acorn that fell off of a tree where a witch was hanged and was stored in the same trinket box with a most magical brooch that belonged to the witch of Brentwood.

One would think it was a freak accident.

But you and I know better.

#####

The Witch of Brentwood

Réal Carpentier

The following is an excerpt from Sarah Goldman

It was a Tuesday evening in January. There I was, entering the halls of the University of New York where I taught psychology. It was a pleasant day for the winter season, and this was the first day of the spring semester. The sky was overcast as any normal winter sky, but still fairly mild. A light jacket would suffice. I made my way to the classroom in a hurried fashion because, God knows, I have a propensity to be a little late at times, and I was. I peered through the window of my classroom door as I approached it and could see there were students already in place at their desks wondering what kind of professor would put them through the torture of a graduate school education. I finally reached the door and entered.

I looked their way and nodded, and they returned the sentiment as I walked to my desk. It was a class made up mainly of young women, with a few young men here and there. I wondered if those young men were there because they knew psychology attracts young women; a possibility which was and is most probable. There were still a few seats unoccupied, but like me, some are always a little late. I apologized for having them wait for me but made sure to warn them against complacency; class, after all, starts promptly at 6:00PM. I then proceeded to get my papers in order, take a quick attendance, and handed the syllabus out to the class.

"Are there any questions on the syllabus?" I asked. There were none, as the syllabus contained all the necessary information everyone at this grade level was used to. "Please note my contact info, as well as the assignments due, and grading for those assignments." I saw in their faces the normal anxiety a student gets when realizing all the work that had yet to be completed by the deadlines. "I'll be distributing the details of reports, their formats, and other pertinent information at our next session. Please have the listed textbook in your possession by then." If I didn't know better, I'd say they were already apprehensive about the course. So, I began.

"Welcome to Mind and Society; course number 502. If you are in the wrong class, please see your advisors now. I don't want any disruptions during class." No one moved, so I continued, "As you can see in your syllabi, Mind and Society covers a variety of topics, including social cognition and behavior, emotions, development, personality, and psychopathology. All these topics will be covered separately or together. Moreover, lectures will go into depth about topics I think are important, or interesting, or both."

I looked around and found no reaction; normal first day of class, I thought. I began a little review.

"All of you have had psychology courses in the recent past. Who can give me some names associated with the founding fathers of psychology?"

A young lady's hand went up after a spell.

"Yes, Miss…?"

"Leah Ferguson, sir." She replied.

"Go, Leah."

"Well, I think one of the names was Wundt?"

"Wilhelm Wundt, was the name; very good." I said. "Anyone else?"

Another brave soul raised her hand.

"Yes?"

"John Watson?" she asked.

"Are you asking, or telling me?"

She gave a little smile and answered, "Telling."

"Correct, Miss...?

"Kayra Huda." She replied with a thick Middle Eastern accent.

"Very good, Kayra. Anyone else?"

Everyone stared blankly at me as though they thought it would be a very long course. So, I had no choice but to bolster their fear lest they started thinking this was going to be a glorified quiz show. I began my lecture.

"Some of the names that come to mind are William James, Sigmund Freud, Carl Rogers, and many others who contributed to the evolution of psychology. But I'd like you to consider where the term psychology originated." I'm of the opinion that a good foundation of knowledge is critical to a good education. "The term psychology finds its origin in Germany by a theologian named Philip Melanchthon. It was probably coined in the mid sixteenth century as psychologia; the word logia, meaning 'the study of', and the word psykhe, meaning 'breath, spirit, or soul'. And so, the 'study of the soul' came to fruition, and soon after, 'the study of the mind', which is the real definition of psychology, was recorded in 1748."

They were all taking notes, I was happy to see. I knew from being a student myself for many years, when you hear a date, you had better write it down. As I was about to continue, a young lady walked in the door to totally disrupt my momentum. Yes, I was annoyed.

"May I help you?" I asked.

"Sorry I'm late." she said, "I just had my schedule changed. I need this course to satisfy my degree audit. I won't graduate without it."

"Are you telling me that you belong in this class, young lady?"

"Yes." she replied, "I didn't want to miss a minute of your lecture. Oh, I'm sorry. Here's my schedule." She handed me her schedule, while fumbling and almost dropping her books. "I just had it changed." she said.

I took her schedule without moving my eyes from hers to let her know I was displeased by her interruptions. She had long brown hair flowing passed her shoulders. Her body was slim and shapely, and she was dressed in modest attire. Her brown eyes were big and bright; one might have thought she had a frightened look, since they were opened wide enough to expose much of the white around her iris. She wasn't wearing much makeup at all, as she seemed to be naturally pretty with her fair skin and facial features having almost perfect shape. These are the things I first noticed about her. Her other attributes I would notice later.

The Witch of Brentwood

Réal Carpentier

The following is an excerpt from Barry's Brain

She came at him with a frying pan still hot from the stove, as he tried his best to protect his head from the impact. The impact was right on target, due to his intoxication impairing his reactive abilities greatly. It made a ringing sound that reverberated across the kitchen. It was a sound anyone in close proximity might have heard except for the two involved because they were much too busy screaming obscenities at each other. Barry had run into his room to hide with ears covered in an attempt to muffle whatever sound he could. The neighboring tenants were yelling in the hallway for them to stop making such a ruckus, but it was none of their lazy-ass business, as Leeza was so fond of saying. Turk tried hard to restrain her, but the blow to his head was too much to bear. He stumbled back and bumped into the table, set for three. Some of the utensils fell on the floor and the pork chops slid off the plates like someone dealing from a deck of cards.

"Ya fuckin' bish, looka wha ya did!" Turk shouted loud enough to be heard throughout the tenement house.

His head was bleeding from the top, and the pain from the burn was beginning to get worse. He couldn't tell where the blood was coming from, but he knew he was hurt.

"Good, ya bastard! Now get the fuck outta my house!" Leeza shouted back.

Turk Carbueno stumbled out of the apartment hurriedly to not get hit again. On his way out, he passed the tenants who cursed him for making so much noise, and the ones who just smirked at his injuries. He gave them all the finger on his way out.

You couldn't tell at the time of their little quarrel, but he was a strong hairy man with a deep low voice. He didn't have much to offer by way of being able to provide, but then again, neither did Leeza. However, for the time being, she was willing to put up with him and let him live with her and Barry. At least he was there to shovel in the winter and do some menial yard work in the summer if he got yelled at enough. His disability checks didn't hurt either. What a waste of precious space, she would say about him. She admitted she liked his dark brown eyes with lashes women would die for, but he was a loser with every meaning of the word.

"Barry, where are ya? Get out here, he's gone!" Leeza shouted in the direction of his room, as she lit a cigarette.

Barry heard her, but he didn't have to. He knew the coast was clear because there was no longer any sound of breaking things or people bouncing off the walls. He cautiously came out to check on his mom.

Barry Kay was a thirteen-year-old, who had troubles of his own. He knew his head was too big for his body, as everyone remarked. He also had a deformed ear, which was usually the target of ridicule from his classmates. It wasn't too bad if you looked quickly but upon closer inspection, one could tell it was larger than the other and stuck out from the side of his head almost like the handle of a teacup. All the kids called him Brick, which soon evolved into Brick the Prick. He wasn't sure where the name came from but thought maybe it was from his oversized head. Although, he liked to think they came up with the name Brick from an abbreviation of Barry Kay. It didn't much matter, though because Brick was meant derogatorily and that was bad enough without knowing its origin or its originator.

"Are you okay, mom?" Barry asked.

"Yeah, I'm okay, but that bastard got hurt bad." she replied with a scowl on her face. "Now, go and finish up your dinner 'fore it gets too cold, while I try 'n clean up this here shit."

Leeza Kay tried to be a good mom, which was the reason she moved to Manchester, NH in the first place. She hoped the cost of living would be better than her previous residence. She had Barry of her own free will, after all, and she was determined to protect him and take care of him the best she could; an ability she lacked from the time of his birth. She was a good-looking woman when she took care of herself, which didn't always happen. When she took the time to color the gray strip in her hair, she looked younger than thirty-six, and was able to attract the guys she served drinks to at the local bar. She was proud of the fact those guys could get lucky with her sometimes. It made her feel like a prize; like she was important; like she was someone else besides Leeza the Pleasah, as they sometimes called her. She took the nickname with a grain of salt, though, and sometimes even considered it endearingly sexy. She hardly made enough to support her son, but Turk collected his disability and that helped a bit. Barry had asked about his dad as he grew, but Leeza could only give him general white lies, since she wasn't sure which guy it was. She had met all three in Vegas one week while on vacation a few years back. She wasn't proud of the fact she got pregnant there, but at least it was a week she'd never forget.

"Was he alright when he left?" Barry asked his mom.

"Why you askin'?"

"I hope he's hurt real bad." he said without remorse.

"He'll live." she replied. "I'm sick and tired of hearin' 'em call me bitch and shit like that."